Jocelyn Miller

Tanglewood Plantation II
Adventure in the Everglades

A Novel

Jocelyn Miller

Cover Graphic: Original Oil
By
Jamie Tate

ISBN-13:978-0988621404
ISBN-10: 0988621401

Thanks to my husband, Bernie, for his boundless support and creative ideas.

Many thanks to my editors, Carolyn and Sally, and to my first reader, Joan. Your input is most appreciated.

Thanks to Jamie Tate for a beautiful cover.

Jocelyn Miller

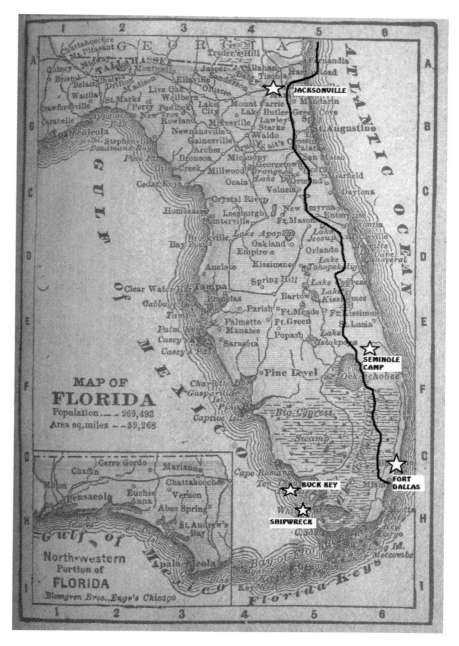

Jocelyn Miller

Genealogical line of Taylor Yank Woodfield

Jocelyn Miller

In the beginning...

Tanglewood Plantation
Book I

Summer Woodfield doesn't have an inkling of what adventures await her when she inherits the family estate, a dilapidated antebellum rice plantation in Georgia. Not only is she confronted by ghostly apparitions upon her arrival, but is whisked back in time to the American Civil War. Confused and terrified, she experiences the war not as the mistress of the manor, but as a slave on her own plantation!

Join Summer in Tanglewood Plantation, Book I, as she experiences the war from the darker side of history, rekindles a 150 year old love affair, and unravels the mysteries of her family tree....

* * *

Books by Jocelyn Miller

*Broken Chords

**Tanglewood Plantation

Tanglewood Plantation II
Adventure in the Everglades

Available in paperback and Kindle at **www.amazon.com**

*Top 100 Best Seller Amazon Kindle!
**A #1 Best Seller on Amazon Kindle!

Jocelyn Miller

He who has a thousand friends has not a friend to spare,
And he who has one enemy will meet him everywhere.

Ali ibn-abi-Talib
(602AD - 661 AD)

Jocelyn Miller

1

No sound. Don' make no sound! Cherry slid her body between the pine floor and the makeshift cot in the back room of the kitchen. She tugged her skirt close to her body, should any tell-tale patch of fabric give away her hiding place. She could barely breathe; the splintered bottom of the cot boards pressed against her breasts restricting her lungs. She gasped, and then forced herself to control her breathing. Should the Yankees find her, she couldn't live; she couldn't suffer at their hands again. Already she was bruised—both body and mind. She trembled with the memory...they were evil men, *dos Yankees.* Evaline told her they were there to help— that they had helped to set them free— but if this was freedom, she didn't want any part of it....

* * *

Summer Woodfield was dithered. Wasn't it enough to deal with the memory of her great-great-great-grandmother Evaline's gruesome death? Wasn't it enough that she remained in her dilapidated, haunted ancestral home as the will instructed? Indeed, she wondered the fate of her ancestors—the ones she had left behind during the great Yankee invasion, the burning of the fountain—but when did it end? *When would the ancestors stop haunting her?* It was her understanding that Evaline, though gruesomely killed by the alligator, was finally with her beloved Robert in death. At least that is how Summer perceived the last message written in the time-worn journal. But now, Cherry? Cherry, illuminated in her ghostly form, beckoned from the attic.

"She apparently needs help, or she wouldn't have shown herself to me."

Guy was not at all receptive to this new revival of the dead, and there was pressure enough with their relationship. She had accepted his marriage proposal and yet she had pushed the wedding off time and time again.

"Here we go again," he replied, none too happily. "The time-travel darn near killed you last time."

"What am I to do? I *know* her. I *love* her; she's my cousin. Do you think for a moment that this will be the first and only time she appears?"

"We could hope?"

She fully understood the dangers of time-travel. It *had* nearly killed her last time, but these were her people. There was no mistaking the glowing figure at the top of the attic stairs, it was Cherry, and Cherry beckoned for a reason. *Cherry needs me!* Of course Guy would say that he needed her, too, so what was she to do?

Later that day she found Guy in the rose garden, the garden that secretly held the graves of the three unfortunate Yankee soldiers and Guy's ancestor, Mick Mason, the prior overseer of Magnolia Plantation. Summer leaned on a fencepost and observed as he weeded and hoed. "Mick is pretty lucky to have you to care for his grave, considering what a rotten..."

"Okay, Summer. I hear you. I understand completely how rotten he was, but he *is* my ancestor and someone has to look over his final resting place." He gave her *that look,* the look that represented both aggravation and wonder that she could possibly know what happened to the man in 1863. Guy took special care over Mason's grave, caring and cultivating, pruning, and fertilizing. It was a spectacular garden, and he was proud. The Yankee soldiers, too, tucked away in their corner, were blessed with a display of brilliant peach and red roses.

"See how you care for them—the dead ones? Cherry deserves the same."

Jocelyn Miller

Again he gave her 'the look', only this time with total aggravation.

Summer stood back and straightened herself. "Just like he is *your* responsibility, Cherry is *mine*. I have to help her."

* * *

"Summer, girl, you just don't get it. My folks don't talk about, or want to talk about, the old slave days. It's an embarrassment; and I guess whatever stories there were, were lost along the way. The only story that survives is the story of Evaline and her mysterious disappearance which you managed to resolve for us—*in your strange way.* "

Summer and Jesse sat on the big porch overlooking the entrance road. At last, fall had come again replacing the hot, humid summer air with a refreshing dryness. The old slave cabins beyond the gate were repaired over the past year and now a standing memorial to days long gone.

"But where did Cherry go after the burning of the fountain? Why haven't you ever heard of her? How will I find her? I can tell you this; the darn thumbprint doesn't work anymore. I tried it. Nothing. Zippo."

"Maybe it wouldn't work, since Evaline no longer exists in that time period? Ha! I'd like to have seen you trying to fly off into yesteryear with that darn fingerprint business!"

"Guy thought it was pretty silly, too, but if Cherry is calling me, there has to be a way to get to her."

They sat in silence while the late afternoon sky displayed its colorful descent into darkness.

"What about Percy? You never heard of him, either, but somebody somewhere must know something."

"Hm. Percy...wait a minute!" Jesse exclaimed.

"What?" Summer nearly jumped off the rocker. "Do you know something? Tell me you know something!"

"I'm not sure, but we do have a cousin—he's pretty old now—who lives down in Savannah somewhere. I don't recall his name. I'll ask mom or granny. I don't know just how this guy is related. Nobody ever said, come to think of it, and I've never met him." Jesse stood. "I'll look into it and let you know. In the meantime, I'm outta here. It's getting dark. Thanks for the tea."

Jocelyn Miller

"Don't forget to call later with the news. You know I'm waiting with bated breath."

"Oh, yes, I know, *super-hero to the dead ones*, that's you, always willing to help a ghost in need."

"I would think you'd show more enthusiasm, considering that we're pretty sure Cherry is you great-great-great-grandmother."

"I *am* enthusiastic. I just don't have your ability to travel hither and yon as a body-snatcher in a different time period, and I feel at a loss. There are apparently some folks in the past I should know of, and don't. It's frustrating. That's the curse of slave descendants, dead end trails."

"Okay, chill. Don't stress yourself. We're on the trail of that dead-end trail. Find out what you can about the cousin: name, where he lives, etc. I'll be waiting."

* * *

Indeed, Summer *had* tried the thumbprint approach as her portal to the past. Guy looked on; arms crossed over his chest, as she pressed her thumb to the thumbprint Robert Mason had marked on the antiquated love-letter to Evaline in 1863. She had removed the letter from its protective plastic sheeting thinking that touching the thumbprint directly would speed her journey. But, instead of opening her eyes in the 19th century, she stood foolishly in the kitchen, letter in hand.

"Don't laugh," she warned.

Guy shook his head. "You've had the vision of Cherry only once. Maybe she won't return and you can give up this obsession."

"It's *not* an obsession. Boy, they're right when they say you don't know a person until you've lived with them."

"What's that supposed to mean?"

"I could use a little compassion, that's all. I was *there*, Guy, you weren't. I know these people; I love these people. I can't expect you to understand, but I would appreciate a little support." Summer slipped the letter back into its protective sleeve. "I'll find a way," she muttered, and left him standing in the kitchen.

* * *

Jocelyn Miller

"River Crest Nursing Home, here we come!" Summer was ecstatic as she slid into the passenger seat of Jesse's Prius. Jesse had tracked the cousin down and they now headed to Savannah, hoping to gain information as to Cherry's life after the war.

"Don't get your hopes up, Summer the guy is 96 years old. Apparently, his familial relationship is hearsay. Nobody in my family has ever met him, and he may not even know his own name at this point."

"What *is* his name?"

"Taylor."

"Taylor what?"

"I was saving that for a surprise. Taylor Yank *Woodfield*."

"What? Are you kidding? He's a Woodfield?"

"Nope, I'm not kidding; and yep, he's a Woodfield."

An hour later the women stood in the parking lot of the River Crest nursing facility gaping at the building before them. The manicured landscape framed a lovely and modern two-story structure set against a background of sculpted lawns and flower beds. Spanish moss-laced live oaks edged a bluff overlooking the Savannah River.

"Beautiful! Guy would love this."

"What did this guy do for a living? This place must cost a buck or two."

"We're about to find out."

They entered the building to a pleasant and well-lit lobby ornately furnished, neat and tidy, every object thoughtfully placed: a vase of flowers here, an artificial plant there, a tree, a sculpture, a fountain trickling aqua-colored water over artificial rocks into a pool below. Pastel historical river scenes decked the walls, while cheery print valances perched prettily over picture-windows.

"Taylor Woodfield? Hmm...." The receptionist's voice trailed off as she reviewed the computer screen before her.

"Oh, he'll be in the dining room. Down the hall to the left; you can't miss it."

"How will we recognize him?" Jesse asked.

"Ask any attendant when you get there, and they'll direct you."

The dining room was as impeccably furnished as the entrance. Linen napkins in fall shades stood peaked at attention at cloth-covered tables. The clang of silverware and tinkling of glass welcomed them.

Jocelyn Miller

Despite the oppressive vision of elderly and infirm diners, the atmosphere was pleasant.

"Smells pretty good in here," Jesse whispered. "Maybe Taylor will invite us to lunch."

"Excuse me," Summer said to a young woman in nursing uniform. "Could you please point out Mr. Taylor Woodfield?"

"Sure. See that gent over there sitting alone, the one in the blue cardigan? That's Mr. Woodfield."

"Are you sure that's him?" Jess asked.

"Sure as I'm standin' here," the attendant said. "Hope you're thick-skinned," she added as she walked off pushing a cart.

"Are you thinking what I'm thinking?" Jesse asked.

"Most likely," Summer whispered.

"That man's as white as…as white as my teeth!" Jesse grinned like the Cheshire cat.

"I thought you said he was your cousin?"

"That's what I thought. He looks more like *your* cousin."

"Well heck, Jesse, *we're* cousins, too. I guess that blows that theory out the window."

"If we need to be thick-skinned as that lady suggested, I guess the old guy can still talk. Let's see for ourselves."

They approached the table as Taylor Woodfield fought with the lettuce and a tomato slice slipping out of his sandwich.

"Mr. Woodfield?" Summer asked, a few decibels above normal.

"No need to shout, young lady. I'm not deaf yet!" was his retort.

Summer cleared her throat. "So sorry, Mr. Woodfield. My name is Summer Woodfield—Woodfield, like yours."

"So what?"

Slightly surprised by his tart answer, she continued. "This is my cousin, Jesse Williams."

Taylor Woodfield looked from Summer to Jesse and broke out in laughter. "How the hell did that happen? Guess there's a story in there."

Same as it happened to you, buddy, she wanted to say, but put on a smile. "I'm glad you asked that, sir. May we sit?"

"Why not?" he said, wiping his mouth with his napkin. "A little spicy diversion might be good for this old man."

He was old, all right; wrinkles sank into deep crevices on his face. His sparse white hair lay thin as spider-webbing over his spotted

Jocelyn Miller

scalp; his teeth, yellowed and browned. His body was slight; dark veins stood out beneath the flesh of his hands and his voice crackled deeply when he spoke. He was feeble, the fact told by the wheelchair in which he sat. Surprisingly, his blue eyes—oddly bright for someone of his apparent age—still shone vividly and intelligently in the overhead fluorescent lighting.

The threesome sat a moment in silence. Summer didn't quite know how to approach the man; he wasn't what she expected. She didn't know exactly *what* she expected, but it certainly was not the frail yet crusty white man sitting before her!

"Well?" he asked. "Am I supposed to guess?"

"I'm sorry, sir. Let me begin this way. You see, you and Jesse, my cousin here, are supposedly related, and...."

The old man smirked. "I don't think so."

"Jesse's family," she continued, "believes that you are a cousi...."

"Young lady," he interrupted, slamming a bony fist on the table. "I am not related to any niggers!"

Summer cringed. "That was uncalled for, sir!" she struggled to keep her temper in check.

"I beg your pardon!" Jesse cut in. "Just what century do you live in?"

"What's uncalled for is you bringing that woman in here and telling me she's my cousin!" he yelled. Heads turned in their direction.

"Is something wrong, Taylor?" A young man in the River Crest uniform appeared, his hands resting on the handles of Taylor's wheelchair.

"I don't know who these women are, but they are insulting me. Take me out of here, Jack. Better yet, get them out of here!"

"But, Mr. Woodfield, if you would only wait a moment! We just have a few questions...."

"There is no relationship between me and that woman!" Taylor jabbed a finger in Jesse's direction.

Jack, the intern, pulled the chair away from the table. "I'm afraid you ladies will have to leave. You're upsetting Mr. Woodfield."

Summer was frantic. She had botched the only chance— the only clue— in tracking down Cherry!

Jocelyn Miller

"Wait!" she yelled, following the attendant and Taylor down the hall. "Mr. Woodfield, we're trying to find a link to Cherry. Do you know that name? She…."

The chair stopped all of a sudden and Jack turned Mr. Woodfield around to face her, his startling bright eyes pierced hers.

"You want to know about Cherry? Go to the Everglades, but don't you ever come here again making accusations…don't you ever come here again," he warned, shaking a long skeletal finger at her. Jack turned the chair and proceeded down the hall.

The Everglades? It didn't make sense.

Jesse was beside her now. "Well thank you, Miss Summer Woodfield, for dragging me on yet another of your most enlightening adventures. I just love to be embarrassed and insulted in public."

"I'm so sorry, Jesse. Who knew what a bigoted idiot he'd turn out to be? He's supposed to be your cousin. I just assumed he'd be black. In fact, I was praying he'd still have a head on his shoulders so we could talk to him and ask questions. He has a head and then some. Ha! I didn't bargain for this!"

"I'll tell my mama to take Mr. Woodfield off the family tree; I don't want to be related to that old, white geezer."

2

Muddy boots. Cherry smelled the Savannah River on them as she lay entombed beneath the cot. She squeezed her eyes shut until tears came. Her heart beat like a drum as from her vantage point, the boots came too near for comfort. She desperately tried to control her breathing; *no sound...don' make no sound!*

"Tom, the damn troops have pulled out. We'll git in a heap o' trouble for bein' deserters. I ain't gonna get shot for no darky wench."

"Well git, then, Hank. Go! I ain't goin' back. I'm done with the fightin'. I made it this far alive and I ain't a'goin' back to no bloodshed."

The boots shuffled on the pine floor causing dust to drift up Cherry's nostrils. She struggled to squelch a sneeze.

"What am I gonna say when Corporal asks where the hell you are?"

"Yer gonna say nuthin', boy, that's what. Yer gonna say you don't know beans 'bout Tommy C. Quinn or his whereabouts."

A scuffle; then more dust threatening a sneeze.

"Christ, let me go, Tom!"

"If you say one word, boy, I'll know it, and I'll be a'comin' after ya."

Jocelyn Miller

Cherry surmised Tommy C. Quinn had given Hank a mighty hard shove, as a thud resonated in the small room and then a body hit the floor.

"Christ, you're a mean one, Tommy Quinn!"

The voice was practically in her ear, and by natural reflex, she turned her head toward it. In horror, she stared eye to eye with the soldier.

"She's under the bed!" he yelled, scuffling to rise from the floor.

The world exploded, whirled and twisted; a deafening sound erupted as she was dragged from beneath the cot. Her safety, her life, threatened as she was brutally dragged from beneath the cot. She shrieked, kicked, screamed, but a large and rough hand slammed against her lips. He held her tight, her back against his barrel chest.

"Why, Cherry, you bad girl. Watcha hidin' from me for?"

"I'm gone, Tom. I ain't having no part of this again. I'm catching up with the troops. Don't worry, I don't know your name. I don't know where you're gone to. Good riddance, far as I'm concerned."

Cherry trembled uncontrollably as Hank departed, leaving her in the grips of her captor. Tom Quinn turned her to him, promising to slap her unconscious if she made a sound. It was the first she had seen him in daylight. She was stunned by the bright blue of his eyes and horrified by the leer therein.

"Cherry girl, you're comin' with me," he said, locking her in the vise of his powerful grip.

"No!" she cried. "I ain't! I'ain't goin' nowhere! If you gotta do me, mister, do me here. I ain't goin' nowheres!" Surely to leave Magnolia would be death!

"Listen good, girl. We're goin' south, you and me. Gets lonesome on the trail and I got a likin' for ya."

"But...," she sobbed. "Don' take me, mister! This is my home. I don' know no south...my boy...my mama...Evaline...." Tears ran like a broken dam.

"Shut up," he said, and pulled her to the kitchen door. Day was fading, but it did not hide the crackling flames from the burning furniture in the fountain. They shot high above the big house, while billowing black smoke filled the air with the scent of burnt wood, acrid, ominous, dark and deadly.

Jocelyn Miller

"What happened? Where's dat smoke comin' from? Where's my boy, my mama? Where's Evaline?" A greater fear shot through her body. *Where's da people?*

Tommy C. Quinn dragged her across the great yard toward the river. She hurt; she was bruised; and she was broken. She shook with terror, looking over her shoulder at the big-house, bright against the backdrop of black smoke. *Where's da people? Where's my Percy? My mama?* Tears continued to fall in a cascade down her bruised cheeks. "Evaline!" she screamed as she took a last glimpse of her home and the only world she had ever known. Night would soon fall, taking with it, Cherry of Magnolia Plantation.

Jocelyn Miller

3

"Everglades...hm." Just what do you suppose he meant by "Everglades?"

Guy peered over the top of the morning paper. "Maybe Cherry ended up in Florida?"

"Gosh, that's strange, isn't it? How would she get from Georgia to the Everglades? Why would she leave everyone she knew? She did mention, once, after the Emancipation, that she would head to Savannah and work in a big house, wear fancy clothes, but...the Everglades?"

"You're full of mysteries, Summer. Maybe that's why I love you so much."

"And you're sweet and patient, Guy. I know it's a lot to put up with, me and my dead ancestors. Please, just bear with me on this."

* * *

That night, the vision returned but was far different than the last time. She woke to fiercely rattling doors. Her first thought was the wind. Guy snored softly beside her as she rose and crossed the floor in her bare feet to the great doors that led onto the portico from her bedroom. The drapes were closed against the night, shielding her from what was

Jocelyn Miller

beyond; a chill ran up her spine. She stood a moment debating whether to spread apart the drapes or not. Her neck hairs spiked like quills. She jumped when the doors rattled again. "It's the wind, idiot," she whispered, and stepped forward again. In one swift movement, she spread the drapes apart.

Cherry! She stood on the other side of the doors, transparent— yet not—a luminous vision against the dark night. Cherry frantically shook the doors, looking from side to side, terrified of unseen danger. Then, she stared at Summer—stared *through* her— without recognition..

"Cherry! What's wrong? Wait, I'll let you in!" There was no response, and try as she might, Summer could not get the doors open. Cherry continued to search frantically from side to side and behind, into the darkness. She appeared to be in great danger and terribly frightened. Then Summer saw the reason for Cherry's fear, and her hair stood on end. Gooseflesh rippled her flesh in waves of horror. Behind Cherry came a figure out of the darkness, a tall and burly figure of a man, his face misshapen, bashed in on one side, bloody and raw. An eyeball dangled against a bloody cheek, His hair was matted with blood. Even in the darkness of night she could see the horrid vision. She fumbled with the locks on the doors while Cherry, on the other end, looked behind to see the figure approaching and screamed—a silent scream that sent terror through Summer, her hands shaking violently in her desperate attempt to open the doors.

Again, Summer was helpless. Cherry looked *through* her, her dark eyes wide in horror, her mouth open in the silent scream.

"What's going on?" Guy asked, causing her to jump at the voice. "What are you doing?"

"I'm letting Cherry in!" she shrieked. "She's scared! I can't get the door open. Help me, hurry!"

Guy was beside her in an instant. "Look, Summer, look out there. *No one is there.* You're dreaming."

Indeed, Cherry and the man had vanished. Had it been a dream? *No!* "I'm sure she was there, Guy. It was too real!"

"Come back to bed. It's 3 a.m. for God's sake."

* * *

Jocelyn Miller

"I know she was there, Jesse. I just know it." Summer held the cell phone close to her ear. She stood on the upstairs portico where she searched in vain for a clue left behind from the previous night's ghostly encounter. "I know Guy is perturbed with me, but what am I to do? Ignore Cherry? I can't!" She paused. "Okay, I'll tell you what I'm going to do; I'm going back to River Crest. Are you coming with me?"

Jesse opted out of River Crest, having been insulted enough in the one trip she ventured there with Summer.

* * *

It was lunch time again when Summer drove up to the pristine nursing home grounds. She told Guy she was shopping in Savannah. Well, she *was* shopping in a way; she was shopping for clues, for information that would help Cherry in whatever dilemma she was in.

"I've come to see Mr. Woodfield. I know where he is," she said flippantly to the receptionist as she breezed past the counter and made her way down the hall to the dining room before anyone stopped her. Apparently the receptionist knew nothing of the previous visit. Summer had visions of white-suited attendants throwing her out the front door on her behind. Taylor Yank Woodfield's last words still rung in her ears: *"...don't you ever come here making accusations. Don't you ever come here again."*

She could justify this visit. For one, she hadn't brought Jesse with her to ruffle Taylor's feathers; and two, she had not come to resolve the connection between Taylor and Jesse.

"Let's wipe the slate clean, Mr. Woodfield." Summer stood beside his wheelchair as he brought a spoonful of tomato soup to his lips. He looked her up and down, the bright eyes narrowing in recognition.

"You again!" Down went the spoon, completely submerged into the soup bowl.

"Wait! Before you call Jack again, just give me a chance, would you? I'm not here to harass you, honestly! Please, Mr. Woodfield. This is so important to me and I have no one else to ask."

Taylor Woodfield scrutinized her through narrow slits and then released his eyes, showing again the bright blue so mesmerizing in the ancient face. "Okay, but you connect me with that cousin of yours again, and you're outta here. I got pull, you know. I can make it so you can't

Jocelyn Miller

even put one car tire in the driveway without getting arrested. Got that, young lady?"

"Yes sir, I do." She said, demurely. "I promise to not offend you."

"Sit," he ordered, and she promptly sat.

"I live in an antebellum plantation named 'Magnolia'. It used to be called 'Tanglewood Plantation' for many decades before I inherited it. I'm in the process of restoring it to its original condition and name."

"I've heard of it," Taylor said, retrieving his spoon from the soup bowl. "Bring me another soup spoon, Liz!" he yelled across the room to a waitress.

He's heard of it? This holds promise! "There was a slave who lived there once, during the Civil War days, and her name was Cherry." Summer searched his face for any reaction, but there was none. Liz brought the soup spoon and he continued with lunch. "Go on, he said."

"It's very important to me that I find out what happened to Cherry. I don't know what you meant by *'go to the Everglades.'* I'm hoping you will fill me in so that I may continue my search."

"Miss Woodfield, I can't imagine why in the world you'd be searching for an old slave woman who's long gone, buried and forgotten."

"I can't really explain without you thinking I'm...I'm crazy."

"Hell, I already figured you were nuts, coming in here and accusing me the way you did."

"Let's forget the visit the other day, okay? I'm only interested in finding out what happened to Cherry, and you apparently know something."

Taylor Woodfield slurped soup from his spoon.

"Do you know something about Cherry?" Summer asked, hoping their meeting wasn't over already.

"Just hold your horses, I'm thinking, girl."

"Okay."

Summer glanced around the room and spotted Jack, the attendant staring at her. *Most likely waiting for a signal to throw me out,* she thought, then averted her eyes so as not to inadvertently draw him to her.

"I remember my old grand-pappy Yank, mentioning a Cherry person. You see, my family comes from Southern Florida—the Everglades—so I don't know, and don't want to know, how you and I

Jocelyn Miller

ended up with the same surname; but I can tell you that there was a Cherry woman connected with the family, but don't know the connection."

Summer nearly cried. This was something she could go on, a real clue! Were Yank's Cherry and her Cherry the same person?

"That's all I know, young lady."

"That is more than I expected, sir, and I can't thank you enough. Wait…what year was your grandfather born?"

"I don't know for sure. I think somewhere around the time of the war, the War Between the States."

Summer floated on a cloud of elation as she walked through the door at Magnolia.

"What are you so happy about?" Guy asked. You must'a bought out the stores, but where are the packages?"

"In here, my love," she said, tapping her temple. "Right in here."

Jocelyn Miller

4

"**S**top your fussin', girl. Ain't the end of the world, you know." Cherry glanced in the direction of her captor as he fed small dry branches into the fire. She was cold, having been torn from Magnolia without a chance to grab a shawl—or any piece of clothing, for that matter. Her tears hadn't stopped falling since yesterday, and even she was surprised at the river of water she held behind her eyes. "I wanna go home, mister."

"Forget home. Your home is with me now, until I tire of you, and that may happen soon if you don't stop your bawlin'."

"My home is Magnolia." she whispered under her breath. "I'se cold, mistah."

"Come and sit by the fire then, or I'll come over there and warm you up, if you know what I mean."

Immediately, she stood up off the log where she had chosen to sit as far removed from Quinn as possible. The night was black, no moon. Not only was she cold, but scared out of her mind. *What's happened to my peoples? What was all dat smoke?* Thoughts of home, Percy, Mama, Evaline and the rest attached like leeches to her thoughts. *I wants to go home!*

She settled on the dirt across from him while the fire crackled and hissed between them. He wasn't bad looking—for a white man. His

Jocelyn Miller

eyes were blue as the sky; she had never seen such a color in a person's eyes. His hair was dark brown and stuck out from beneath his cap in wisps, *like chicken feathers*, she thought.

She eyed him through the flame and smoke; tall and barrel chested, a dark stubble of bristly beard sprouted on his cheeks and chin. It scratched her face when he had her...*had her*...she fought back tears lest he yell at her again. What had she done to deserve this fate? Was she to spend the rest of her life pinned beneath this horrid man...this disgusting enemy? His uniform was dirty and torn, and he smelled. *She* smelled—she knew it. She could smell herself; she was unclean from *him. This ain't freedom, Evaline! This ain't how you told me it would be!* Oh God in Heaven, if Evaline were only here to help! Evaline was so brave when she dealt with the soldiers; this never would have happened had Evaline been there, in the kitchen, when Quinn stole her away.

He plunked himself down in the dirt on the other side of the fire and stretched himself out, resting on an elbow. "Ain't this cozy," he said.

"How come you's goin' south if you's a Yankee?"

"That's the point, gal. I ain't gonna be no Yankee soon as I can find me another set of clothes. They're gonna be lookin' for me up north. We're goin' south, you n' me, Cherry girl."

"Where is dis place?" She had no clue. How could she? She had never been past the gates of Magnolia, not even to Savannah, though she had heard plenty about the bustling city either from her master and family when they spoke at mealtimes while she served their meals, and sometimes from passing slaves who had been to Savannah with their masters.

"I ain't sure, girl. We're gonna stick close to the river for a while; see if we can get us a little boat somewhere. Can't pass through Savannah and take a chance on meetin' up with my troops."

"I ain't never been on a boat." She shivered as the warmth of the fire diminished from the settling flames.

"We'll get you some warm clothes, too," he said. "Come on over here, gal, and I'll warm you up. Don't make me come and get you."

* * *

Her sleep was restless sleep. It was to be expected considering her circumstance, but an eerie strangeness crept into her dreams. A slender white woman began to appear, a woman with cropped hair the color of flax, eyes the color of the sky. Her clothes were not at all the clothes a woman should wear, but long pants and a shirt—a shirt without sleeves and a scooped neck that exposed the swell of her breasts. A door separated them—a door that could not be opened. The woman reached out for her, mouthed her name, pounded on the glass, but always, the door remained shut. Fear rose high and electrifying as Cherry tried desperately to open the door—the door to safety and the woman with the flaxen hair.

She woke, terrified, shaking, and not knowing where she was until the sound of Quinn's snores and hot, putrid breath delivered her firmly back into her misfortune.

Jocelyn Miller

5

Rattle…rattle…rattle.

Again, Summer woke to the shaking of the portico doors. She glanced at the digital display of the clock; 3:00 a.m.. Guy snored lightly beside her. She tiptoed across the floor in her bare feet to the drapes. Her hands shook uncontrollably as she spread them apart knowing full well what she would find on the other side— Cherry, and the grotesque man!

Cherry shook the doors until Summer thought the glass would break. She was alone, but not for long, for behind her out of the darkness came the burly man. From his damaged face only one eye was visible and his look—the look he gave Cherry as he approached from the darkness—caused Summer to rattle the doors herself, in an attempt to open them and bring Cherry to safety.

"Cherry!" she screamed. "Run!"

"Not this again!" Guy groaned, as if on cue.

"Hurry, Guy! Open the doors!"

Guy rose from the bed and crossed the floor. "I don't see her," he said in a sleep-crackled voice.

"She's there! *Right there!*"

But the vision was gone.

Jocelyn Miller

* * *

"Are you nuts?" Guy asked the next morning. They sat in the dining room with toast and coffee that grew as cold as the tension between them. The paintings of the ancestors looked on as if absorbed in their conversation.

"I have to go, Guy. I have to. Please understand. I can't let this continue. I'll never get any sleep, and neither will you."

"You can't go there alone, I won't let you. And just how am I supposed to take time off? I have multitudes of properties to care for, including this one."

"I'll be fine; I'll call you every thirty minutes. Well, not every thirty minutes, but every morning, noon and night."

"Jesus, Summer. I love you but we can't keep goin on like this. I'm starting to worry about you."

"I'm not nuts. This is really happening. I'm flying to Naples, renting a car and meeting a woman there from the historical society. It's all arranged, and all very harmless."

"Far be it from me, the lowly fiancé, to prevent his love from…from what? Ghost hunting? What do we call this?"

"*Saving Cherry! That's* what we call it."

As her flight took off for Florida, Summer reflected on her first flight to Savannah. It was as if a millennium had passed since she stepped off the plane into her new life. She could never have imagined what adventure lay before her at that time. Her travels to the past had been an eyeopener, a new understanding of what her heritage meant and why she had to cherish it, and why she had to answer the call of her ancestors. Evaline had wanted her to know what had happened to her— why she had disappeared—and now, Cherry. Cherry needed help and for whatever reason Summer had been beckoned, she would heed the call.

* * *

"So, how can I help you, Miss Woodfield?"

Mrs. Latimer, the historian, listened intently while Summer explained that she was searching for information on a freed slave whose last whereabouts, in 1864, were known to be the Everglades."

Jocelyn Miller

"Oh my," Mrs. Latimer said, after Summer divulged all she could without going into the actual and unbelievable details of time-travel and hauntings. "This is a difficult task you've chosen! As you know, freed slaves are not easy to find. At least in the 1850 census schedules, names were finally recorded instead of just sex, age and color. Perhaps we can take a look at...you said 1864? We can look at the 1870 census and see if she is listed. Where do you suppose she would be at that time?"

"I have no clue, Mrs. Latimer. The Everglades, that's all I know."

"Well...do you know what surname she would go by?"

Silence. Surname? *Does Cherry have a surname?* "I really hate to be so ignorant but I never heard her...uh...heard anyone mention a surname."

"It was pretty common for a slave to take the surname of their master. Do you know what that would be?"

"I'll take a gander that it's the same as mine, 'Woodfield'."

"It's a start, providing your Cherry was in Collier County in 1870.

Summer sat opposite Mrs. Latimer, the desk and computer between them. She watched as Mrs. Latimer adjusted her head to peer through her Ben Franklin style glasses. "I'll do an alphabetical search for Woodfield."

Summer crossed her fingers.

"Mmmm. Mmmm." Mrs. Latimer hummed as she squinted through her narrow lenses, clicking the computer mouse as she went along.

Ages passed.

"Not in Collier County, Ms. Woodfield. But here, let's take a look at Monroe County, down by the Keys."

Another eternity passed as Summer contemplated what she would do were there no results. How could she go home empty-handed? It would only fuel Guy's opinion that she should leave it alone. She couldn't; Cherry needed her.

"Oh! Here is a Woodfield."

Summer's heart skipped a beat. She jumped to her feet.

"Let's see. It was written by a very sloppy census taker." She peered over her glasses at Summer. "It's hard to make out, but I'd say the

Jocelyn Miller

first name is…Yahn…no, Yank? Why don't you come around and take a look?"

Summer flew to Mrs. Latimer's side. Indeed, the writing was very scratchy and faint, but there it was! "How do I read this?" she asked, as she had never seen a census before."

"Read straight across the line. Here is the head of household, uh…" Mrs. Latimer leaned into the monitor. "Buck Henry, it looks like. Buck Henry, colored, and a child named Yank Woodfield, age six years, white. White?" Confusion edged the woman's voice. "That's odd, isn't it? A white child living with a black man in that day and age? Oh well, that's the Everglades for you. It's a mixed-up bunch down there; Seminoles, black Seminoles; Crackers, Cubans; it's a hodgepodge.

"Where were they living?" Summer asked, still peering over Mrs. Latimer's shoulder.

"The town is listed as… hmmm."

Mrs. Latimer sure hummed a lot.

"It just says 'Island homestead."

"Great. Now what? Aren't there something like ten thousand islands out there?"

"Yes, well…not quite. That's a bit exaggerated. Collier and Monroe Counties both have jurisdiction over the Ten Thousand Islands National Park, and I'm assuming that's what 'the islands' means in this case. Key West is the county seat of Monroe County, and that's a distance. Why don't we see what we can find in the 1880 census?"

Jocelyn Miller

6

The skiff was old and battered, almost 16 feet in length with a deep draft. The bow deck held a small mast pole. A set of long oars with attached locks, lay across several seats, a rope and canvas on the floor. Cherry didn't at all like the idea of traveling by water and especially the Savannah River in such a small and unsafe looking mode of transportation. Visions of Juba and his gruesome death by alligator played over and over in her mind. Surely they would tip over in that thing! Stepping into the skiff did not relieve her anxiety in the least; it was a frightening experience. The craft moved, quivered, and listed from side to side as she fought to keep her balance. She held onto the sides of the boat to steady herself as she made her way to the stern end.

"Sit down, girl. Ain't got all night. There's a war goin' on out there, and we aim to miss it."

He pushed the skiff off the dock and, once settled, the boat stopped rocking. He put the long oars into the locks and set off. Cherry had no idea where they were, and apparently neither did Tom Quinn.

"I guess you ain't gonna be any help figuring out how to by-pass Savannah."

Jocelyn Miller

"No sir. I ain't never been der." She shivered. It was cold and dark. Quinn had taken a few clothes and two tattered blankets from a nearby deserted farm, along with the fishing skiff that had been tied to a rickety dock. The threadbare sweater he gave her was better than nothing, and though she pulled it tight around her body, it could not deflect the sharp air that bit through the weave all the same. She wrapped one of the blankets around her shivering shoulders. Quinn had changed into a plaid shirt that stretched across his barrel chest and strained the buttons. He was disappointed that he couldn't find a pair of pants to fit, fearful that the faded blues would give away his Union status.

He muttered curses to the air as he attempted to master the oars. At times the skiff turned and twisted, sometimes circling haphazardly as the current carried them along. Once rowing was mastered, he rowed the skiff close to shore. Darkness enveloped them as they rode the river, blind to any dangers of boulders, fallen trees, sandbars, snags, branches, or any form of river debris. Once, he rowed too close to the shore and a branch slapped Cherry in the face; she screamed in alarm.

"Shut up, girl!" he said. "You give us away and I'm throwing you to the gators!"

It was warning enough to keep her still as a mouse. They rode the river until the rising sun began its ascent, at which time Quinn rowed as close to a small bank as the skiff would allow before hitting bottom. He stepped out into the water to drag it the rest of the way. "We'll camp here, and get some sleep."

The brush was thick as pea soup. Cherry recognized much of the flora, though the proper names she didn't know; wax myrtle, juniper, and glasswort. Sable palms stood tall above the lower shrubs. She was hungry. At home—*home!*—they were sometimes allowed to cut down a Sable palm, eating the inside of the tree[1]; swamp cabbage, they called it. Yes, she was hungry.

"What's we gonna eat, mistah?"

"What we can catch."

With the skiff secured, Quinn surveyed the surroundings. All Cherry could see was vegetation and water.

---

[1] Sable palm is the tree used for 'hearts of palm' and in the South sometimes referred to as 'swamp cabbage'.

Jocelyn Miller

"Closer we get to Savannah, the closer we get to Union troops. Sherman's gotta be there already. By land or by sea, this is tricky business. I don't know how long this river goes a 'fore it hits the sea, but sooner or later, we're headed into a Union stronghold in Savannah."

Cherry tried to make sense of his jabber, but all she knew was that she was cold, hungry, terrified, and she wanted to go home! Maybe if they came across some *good* Yankees, they would help her. That thought briefly took her mind off her growling stomach, but in actuality she hadn't met up with a good Yankee yet; all they had done was to hurt and humiliate her.

Tom carefully dug into a pocket and pulled out a fishhook attached to a string. "That ole' farmer must'a known we were comin'! I need some bait, girl; give me a hand."

They walked along the narrow bank, he in front, she in back, perusing the shallow shore for baitfish. "Der!" she said, pointing to a darting school of small and slender fish visible in the green, shallow bank. How they were supposed to catch the tiny minnows, she hadn't a clue.

Quinn took off a well-worn boot. "Shit," he said. "Guess I ain't got a choice." He crouched on his haunches and gently placed the boot on its side in the water. "Okay," he whispered. "Shoo 'em over here."

Cherry spotted a dried palm frond nearby. With that in hand, she brushed the water behind the fish with the frond, sending the minnows darting frantically in the direction of the boot.

"Good girl. Now, let's see what we got." Quinn lifted his boot out of the water and stared into its deep well. "Hot damn, girl, there's a couple in there!" He handed her the soggy boot. "You got small hands, see if you can fish one of them outta there. Don't lose 'em," he warned.

Cherry tipped the boot toward the heel end and squinted into the abyss. How she wished she were home, warm in the kitchen with her mama, Lucy, Evaline and little Percy; not here in this strange place with Tom Quinn, trying to catch a tiny fish out of a boot full of water! She couldn't see much once she stuck her hand into the boot. She turned the boot toward the rising sun. Two minnows darted madly in the heel of his boot. She looked at Quinn and he raised his eyebrows.

"Go on, now. You wanna eat, don't ya?"

"At home we done noodlin' for catfish."

"Well we ain't home, girl. Get me some bait!"

Jocelyn Miller

She thrust her hand into the boot well and clamped it shut. Nothing. Again she tried. Nothing. Then, without pause, she strained the water out of the boot, leaving the two minnows flopping on the inside.

"Smart-ass darky you are!" Tom said, grabbing the boot from her. Go on back to camp and make us a fire. No green wood; don't want no more smoke than we have to."

Another cold night passed. Cherry huddled by the now diminishing campfire, Quinn directly across on his back, a steady rhythm of snores expelled from his throat.

She couldn't sleep; she was still hungry and had to pee but was afraid to move an inch from camp. Quinn had managed to catch one small catfish which they split after he gutted and roasted it over the fire. It wasn't nearly enough to sustain them; but hunger had been her companion for quite a while, due to the Yankees stealing their food at Magnolia and leaving them to starve.

The night had its own rhythm, seeming to correspond with Quinn's snores; at every pause of a snore a grand crescendo arose from the mysterious critters within the thicket. At last, she could hold it no longer and stood from her cold bed. A partial moon gave light enough for her to find her way into a minimal pocket of space between the outlying brush. She squatted and prayed there was not a snake to bite her bare behind. *I could run.* It was a fleeting thought, as visions of flight through the thick shrub in the darkness of night perhaps held more dangers than this perilous journey with her captor.

On her return, she threw the few remaining twigs into the fire and settled on her bed of brush beneath the worn, stolen blanket. Cold, hunger, fear; *dis is all I has.* She drifted away on the small pittance of warmth from the dying embers; drifted into unconsciousness, where a dream took hold and carried her away from the circumstance of cold, hunger and fear, carried her away from Tom Quinn, and into a blessedly peaceful place where she walked, unafraid, through the Gullah island forest. The stress of the journey was exchanged for a sudden sense of relief. Even a crackle of branches in her dream did not alarm her and when the strange flaxen haired woman stepped out onto the path, Cherry ran to her, was circled in the woman's arms and was safe at long last.

Jocelyn Miller

7

Summer drove the rental car eastward along the Tamiami trail. On the right was a vast savannah, flat, grassy, sometimes covered with shallow pools of water upon which multitudes of various birds fed. To the left, beyond a guard rail, a canal ran parallel to the road. Across the canal cord grasses grew in thick, tall tufts, creating a wall of endless vegetation that looked, to Summer, quite impenetrable.

It was a deceiving impression, though, as there were many spots where the patches of grass cleared, leaving her to shudder at the size of the alligators sunning themselves along the bank. The memory of Bruno still rang clear in her mind. *Poor Evaline. Such a gruesome way to go.* She tried in vain to erase the memory from her mind—tried not to think of the terror and pain Evaline felt as the alligator's razor teeth tore through flesh, deep into her thigh. The strength of the terrible beast was overpowering. How she had struggled to hold tight to the muddy bank, her nails thick in the deep sludge, trying desperately to keep from going under. In vain she struggled against the cold water, against the death that awaited. The water…tasting of muddy particles, of algae, of waste—of death. It filled her lungs and forever muted her screams.

Summer pulled off the road and put the gear in park mode. She broke out in a cold sweat with the memory and had been so deep in thought that she must have slowed to a crawl, as a trail of cars had showed in her rearview mirror. The other drivers passed, instinctively turning their heads to see the driver of the parked car. She tried to still her heart. It wasn't a good thing for her to remember Evaline's death. She avoided the Savannah River at all costs; she knew how it felt beneath the water's surface. She had lived and died as Evaline, and knew what it was like in that dark and foreign place of monsters. "Thank God for Guy," she said aloud. He, alone, had comforted and saved her. It wasn't an easy task, and here she was pushing him to the limit again.

She opened the car door and stepped out. Across the road was another clearing, and there they were, the gators. Three large adults sunned themselves alongside the bank on the other side of the canal. It was as hard a task as she could remember, crossing the street to face her fears. If it hadn't been for a truck coming at a good pace, she may never have crossed over, but having to move or die she found herself standing directly across the canal from the gators.

"I know you," she said to the threesome. "I know all of you, and you're an evil bunch of useless creatures; *murderers.*" The gators hadn't moved, but remained trancelike on the bank. She couldn't tell if their eyes were open or closed, but she knew how fast they could move should they choose to do so. "You don't fool me, sitting there like statues. I know what you have on your minds—dinner! Well it won't be me today, I can guarantee you that."

"Excuse me, miss, are you all right?"

Summer jumped at the voice and turned to find an officer in a patrol car slowed to a halt, three cars slowed to a stop behind him.

"Oh, uh…yes, yes I'm fine. I was just checking out the wildlife."

"Okay—if you're sure. Don't want a call about a pretty young lady falling in the canal on the Tamiami Trail—death by alligator." He laughed. She couldn't.

"You won't read about it, I can assure you of that. Thanks for your concern."

The officer waved and drove off. *I must look like a nutcase standing here talking to alligators.* "I *am* a nutcase," she said, and crossed the street to the rental car and continued down the highway, averting her eyes from the breaks in the bushes along the way.

She followed the Tamiami trail to Route 29 and turned right, headed to Everglades City. The 1880 census that Mrs. Lattimere had

Jocelyn Miller

looked up in her computer at the historical society, showed that Henry Buck and Yank Woodfield were in Everglades City, but Cherry Woodfield was again not listed. Was this Yank Woodfield connected to the old man in the nursing home? Were they somehow connected to Cherry?

The flora was rich and lush alongside the road to Everglades City. Anhinga birds filled the trees, some with their wings spread out to dry like laundry in the warm sun. At last she approached Everglades City, a very small city with big businesses; airboat tours, kayaking, boating, a hotel or two, seafood restaurants, and a post office. The city was flat and minus the thick vegetation she had witnessed on the drive in. The lack of it made any building of stature stand predominantly in view. Mrs. Lattimire had told her that the historical Rod & Gun Club[2] was the place to stay to experience the 'old' Florida, so she made a reservation prior to arriving. Mrs. Latimire also told her that Everglades City, before its shortlived boom in the 1920's, had also been a trading post in 1864, the exact year that Evaline was killed by the alligator! If Cherry had somehow made her way to the Everglades, perhaps she had been here, where Summer stood now in the 21st century. She parked her rental car and removed her suitcase from the trunk; she was glad to have a home base. It was a pleasing sight, where she stood now, suitcase resting on the ground beside her. The Rod & Gun Club rambled on before her, across sprawling green lawns. It nestled amidst tropical flowering shrubs and trees, its white paint stark against a blue sky dappled with tall palms. A balmy breeze rustled her hair, kissed her cheeks, and she closed her eyes as if to absorb the moment, to engrave to memory the breeze, the sky, the palms, the scent of flowers and this moment of calm.

Stepping through the doorway of the hotel was indeed a step back in time. Rich, dark, glossy Pecky Cypress paneling presented a perfect backdrop for an array of wildlife artifacts that greeted her; a stretched alligator hide, a taxidermy swamp bear, bobcat, spider-lobster, various paintings and vintage photos. An antiquated and obviously once prestigious billiards table still held its charm, lit by one of many vintage chandeliers that stretched over it, and the rest in a neat row across the entire lobby. The rich, carved furniture spoke of the elegance of the birth

---

[2] The Rod and Gun Club is a historical hotel in Everglades City, Florida

Jocelyn Miller

of the Rod and Gun Club in the 1920s. It was a living museum of history, boasting many famous guests from presidents to wealthy sportsmen and land barons.

Its old fashioned ambience was comforting, and the stress of her journey rolled away as she feasted on the look and feel of her surroundings. Even the registration desk was a step back in time, a continuation of the glossy dark paneling that embraced her, swallowed her whole and locked her into its time-forgotten hold. A vintage cash register sat upon the small counter, as well as a large alligator head, its jaws opened to reveal its rows of sharpened and deadly teeth. *I can't escape them,* she thought, signing her name to the credit card slip while the alligator head loomed in her peripheral vision. Her room, on the second (and top) floor looked over the Barron River and seemed a busy thoroughfare for boats of all nature.

After checking in, unpacking, lunch on the wide veranda looking onto the picturesque river, and calling Guy, she walked the paved walkway that ran along a stretch of the river, steps away from the lodge. The river fed into the Everglades National Park and the Ten Thousand Islands, her destination. Boats continued to pass, to and fro, reminding her that she would have to find herself a guide and travel the islands. She had to get a grip on what Cherry's life involved living here, in this strange and exotic land. If she followed her instincts perhaps, somehow, she could find the portal to Cherry and help guide her home to Magnolia.

8

Traveling by night, sleeping by day, hidden in brush and coves, dirt, sand and mud, Cherry was exhausted, cold, wet, dirty, and tired to the bone. Her fear turned to extreme anger, and she began to fight back at Mr. Tom Quinn. She despised him. True, he took care of her the best he could under the circumstance. She even depended on him as she had to, for he was her sole protector. However, his anger was vented on her when things went wrong. If fish didn't bite and they spent a horrid, cold and hungry night, she took the blame. If Yankee troops were near causing them to fight against the current, hanging on for dear life to branches to keep the skiff from traveling into view, *she* paid, *She* was the brunt of his anger. It was *all her fault*, or so he made it seem; but it was also she who was pinned beneath him without consent, gratifying his lust, letting him forget the stress of their journey, while she, on the other hand, suffered it all without relief.

The longer the time they spent together fighting for their lives and safety, the more she felt acquainted with him and the more she felt compelled to talk back. He didn't like it one bit, as was apparent by the slap she received across her cheeks on those occasions in which he caused her blood to boil.

Jocelyn Miller

"I ain't your slave," she said, when he commanded that she, exhausted to her core, travel into the brush for firewood while he sat on his haunches resting from the night's travel.

"Long as I keep your sorry ass alive, you are my slave," he answered.

"Don't feel like 'alive' to me," she muttered, at which time he rose from his comfort to grip her arm in his fist.

"Just keep smart-assin' and see where it gets you."

There was no recourse for her but to do as he bid, though the small measure of gratification she felt from her resistance gave her strength and self-satisfaction, even with a few bruises to show for it.

They were nearing Savannah, or so he said. In the distance dim lights were visible. She had always wanted to go to Savannah, to work in a fancy big house and wear nice clothes, a hooped skirt, a bonnet. It saddened her to think that this was all she would ever see of the city, and that she came in rags.

"This ain't gonna be easy, girl, gettin' past here. Near as I recall, we're almost to the mouth of the river, headin' into the sea. Gotta pass the forts first. Don't recall exactly where they all are, 'cept Fort Pulaski[3]. Ain't gonna be easy," he repeated.

Ocean? Forts? She didn't know anything about forts except that there was nothing but suffering involved in anything that had to do with the war. All she knew of the ocean was that it was vast, endless, deep, and full of monsters.

"Don't think we can pass Fort Pulaski until tomorrow night."

Stars shone brilliantly overhead. Quinn sculled the skiff as it drifted along on the outgoing tide, staying as close to the opposite shore as he could; the further from Savannah, the better. The current became stronger as they rounded a bend in the river.

"Holy..... vessel ahead!" Quinn gasped. He frantically rowed to the river bank. "Grab a branch!" he whispered. Cherry stood, gaining her balance and grabbed at the branches that slapped against her figure in the darkness. Quinn also grabbed and held. There they stood in the skiff, struggling against the tide and flow of the river.

"Damn!" he said.

---

[3] Fort Pulaski National Monument, Cockspur Island, Georgia. A Confederate stronghold taken over by Yankee troops in 1862.

Jocelyn Miller

"I can't hold!" Try as she might, the branch slipped through her fingers, surely cutting into her flesh. She let go, and the stern pivoted to the front with Tom Quinn now behind her, still holding.

"Damn, girl!"

"I can't hold!" she said, tears forming in her eyes. She was frantic at this new chaotic episode. Quinn let go of the branch and fought against the drift of the skiff trying to right the bow to the front again. He paddled frantically while Cherry sat, her bleeding hands gripping the cold, damp side of the craft and praying they would not capsize or crash into the vessel ahead.

It loomed like a black giant against the night sky. Even without its sails, it dwarfed the fugitives in the dark of the river. As Tom gained control of the skiff, they again hugged the shoreline. Cherry was confused, not knowing whether it was good if they were caught, or just another horrible event in a short life that seemed doomed from the beginning.

"Shut up," Tom hissed. "Don't say a word."

She didn't. She sat stone still, except for the tremors from a fear that was her constant companion. Tom stopped rowing as the skiff settled into a path of drift seaward. The Atlantic pulled them steadily toward its hungry mouth. In silence they drifted past the schooner, she, looking at Quinn, he, looking upward at his enemy. They were so close to the vessel she thought for sure they would bounce against it and be found. She longed for a deep breath to satisfy her lungs but was fearful that such a breath might seem loud as cannon fire in the quiet of the night.

The vessel faded into the background, as did the city of Savannah. Tom took the oars again. "It's behind us, girl!"

But not for long. Ahead, shadowed against the night, were more vessels, some anchored in the deeper water, some moored along the shoreline on the south side of the river.

"This ain't good, girl."

"Ain't nothin' good when you's in it," she said, knowing he was too busy to slap her.

They passed along a stretch of land, a long island that appeared to run down the center between the north and south banks. Tom Quinn steered the skiff to the left of the island. It was dark, as if not at all inhabited, leaving as the only danger the ships that were anchored or moored. In the distance ahead, the horizon showed its first hint of

Jocelyn Miller

sunrise. Cherry saw the northern and southern shores clearly outlined black against the dawning sky. A light appeared toward the mouth of the river.

"I'm thinking that's Fort Pulaski ahead." Tom said. "Maybe we can pass it before daylight, with a little luck."

The outgoing tide had become much stronger. Waves lapped against the sides of the skiff rocking the craft and causing Cherry alarm. She noticed Quinn having trouble controlling the skiff while a frigid westerly wind picked up behind hastening their pace. Cherry was wet, cold and terrified as Quinn maneuvered the small craft around another large vessel, then another.

"Halt!" A voice yelled from above.

"Can't!" Tom answered. "Tide's taking me out!"

"Who goes?"

"Fisherman!" he yelled, and left the vessel behind. "Hope they don't shoot." He said loudly, over the sounds of waves and wind.

Jocelyn Miller

9

IT didn't take long for Summer to hire a guide to aid her in her search. The most difficult part was explaining what she was looking for, when she didn't even know herself. She couldn't say that she was looking for Cherry, a young black woman who had disappeared 150 years before; that wasn't who she was looking for directly since, of course, Cherry was long gone. She was searching for clues...for an idea of *how* Cherry lived on 'the islands' and what could possibly have happened to her.

As she and 'Captain Jack', as he had asked to be called, set out on his skiff, a rusting contraption moored to a floating dock by Captain Jack's home along the Barron River, she had the fleeting thought that perhaps this was not the safest thing to do. After all, she had no references for Captain Jack. He was curt, but likable enough. Perhaps 40 years old, muscular, tanned. Sun bleached hair tumbled down his browned forehead and fringed the tops of his ears. She picked up her cell phone and quickly punched #1, Guys number on her quick-dial list. He didn't answer, but she left a message on his cell phone, just in case things weren't on the up and up with Captain Jack.

"Hello love," she said into the tiny phone speaker, loudly enough for her guide to hear. "I'm heading out on a skiff with Captain Jack of

Jocelyn Miller

Everglades City. It's 9:00   a.m. and I'll call you when we return this afternoon. Love you. Bye bye."

"Always good to leave a flight plan," Captain Jack said. "Is that your husband?" he asked.

"Yes," she lied. *What business is it of his?*

As the skiff left the canal into the waters of the glades, Summer settled into her front row seat hoping not to be splashed. The morning was on the cool side and she pulled her lightweight jacket around her. Wisely, she had opted for a pair of jeans as opposed to shorts. The wind created a wind-tunnel coiffure of her hair as Captain Jack cranked up the speed once they exited the river. Soon they were weaving through mangrove islands that did not at all look like they were inhabitable and not at all how she pictured the Everglades..

"Nobody could live on these islands!" she yelled, throwing her voice back to the Captain.

"No, but there are a few habitable islands out there. There used to be plantations on them," he yelled against the wind.

The word 'plantation' brought to mind the stately Magnolia Plantation of her heritage. She couldn't imagine what a 'plantation' would look like out here, surrounded by water and mangrove islands.

"I'd like to stop at one," she yelled over the roar of the motor.

"Sure thing!" Captain Jack yelled and swerved the skiff in a different direction.

She was relieved to be out of the wind when they pulled up to a small dock. This island had solid ground and was not composed of the gnarled and matted mangrove roots. Her face felt windburned as Captain Jack helped her off the boat where she was immediately attacked by a swarm of hungry mosquitos.

"Hold still and close your eyes," he instructed as he sprayed her with insect repellent. She coughed as a mist of spray made its way down the back of her throat.

"Good grief," she said. "Could you give me a little more warning when you're going to blast me with chemicals?"

He smiled.

"Are you kidding me?" She asked, looking around the small clearing. *Cherry lived on one of these islands? Why?* The vegetation grew thickly the further away from the dock. "People really lived here?"

Jocelyn Miller

"Come here," the captain said. "There are footings of a house over this way."

…Said the spider to the fly. Now, far away from civilization with a strange man, in the middle of the Everglades with absolutely no protection, she wanted to kick herself for partaking on this adventure to discover what? How absurd to think that in this geographical spot of mangrove mazes she was going to find a clue to Cherry's whereabouts in 1864.

"Come on." Captain Jack waved her forward. "I promise, I'm not gonna bite," he said, as if zoning in on her fears. "I do these tours all the time, for Pete's sake."

Summer shook herself loose from her lurid thoughts of rape and murder. He was becoming a little more humanized and familiar, and at least he recognized the fact that she had her trepidations; and, as a good captain and man, he was seriously trying to make her comfortable in his own way.

"Sorry," she said, under her breath, and moved forward.

"Here," he said, tapping the top of a four foot gray wall. "It's made of shell, if you look closely. This is the foundation of a house. It's raised for protection from flooding. The folks who lived here grew sugar cane."

"Unbelievable."

"In fact," he continued, "a lot of molasses came from this little homestead, and was transported to the Keys and then to who knows where else. I'll bet somewhere back there in the brush there was a still for the making of rum."

"It must have been a lonely existence."

"Some folks came here to hide away from society, or maybe they were running from the law. Maybe it suited them just fine."

And Cherry? What was she doing here? Was she here?

"Spray me again with that stuff and I'll wander around a bit, if you don't mind."

"Well, there isn't too much to see here, except what we're looking at. There's another little island a ways from here, and you can walk around there if you like. There are a few artifacts, like broken-down rusty motors, footings, and a collapsed cabin."

Again they boarded the skiff and wove through several mangrove islands for what seemed forever before docking at another

Jocelyn Miller

small island. Captain Jack sprayed her with insect repellent, and she wandered off while he stayed near the boat to smoke a cigarette.

She followed a narrow trail, though it was not well-worn, and at one point had to climb over a fallen tree that had blocked the pathway. The brush began to thicken and the path narrowed to a nearly indecipherable trail. Digging into her jean pocket she pulled out a crumpled tissue; she had to pee! She checked her surroundings for snakes (and Captain Jack,) before crouching in a cramped clearing within the brush. Immediately the mosquitos swarmed around her head, and she fought to keep her balance while fanning them away.

The still air within the low protection of growth amplified the sound of an approaching motorboat. Thoughts of poisonous snakes and insects vanished while a slight wave of relief diffused her nervous thoughts about Captain Jack; *Tourists!* They had not spotted another boat all morning. The motor stopped. She had definitely lost sight of the captain and the dock and had only just begun to investigate the island. *Should I return and see who has arrived?* Instead, she followed the narrowing curve of the vanishing trail further into the unknown. Voices drifted to her, distant men's voices, though she couldn't understand the words spoken.

Within a matter of minutes, the voices grew louder, so much so that her hackles rose; the red flag of instinct flared. She quietly backtracked toward the dock, creeping along the narrow trail with trepidation, for the closer she came to her destination, the louder the voices, and what was unintelligible before, was now perfectly clear.

"...well, I haven't got it, and you will just have to wait."

"We're tired of waiting on your ass. You're stockpiling and trying to screw us."

The more she heard, the more she fought to control her anxiety ...*this is not good!* She stopped when she was close enough to hide in the brush and view the strangers through the tall weeds. One was a skinny, tattooed white man with thin, straggly hair secured into a ponytail that ran down his back, and the other, a thick-set black man with heavy dreadlocks flowing over his shoulders. Both men wore jeans and t-shirts like Captain Jack.

"Listen, you shitheads, I'm *not* stockpiling. I can't give you any cash until I sell the stuff and that won't be for two days yet. You'll have to wait for the pickup. Now, get outta here. I have a tourist with me and she'll be coming back any minute."

"Bull shit. You're here waiting for someone."

"I told you, I *am* waiting—for my passenger."

Summer muffled a gasp as one of the two men, grabbed Captain Jack by the crew collar of his t-shirt.

"You're fucking screwing us," he yelled into the Captain's face.

Captain Jack, without hesitation, slipped both his fists up between the skinny man's grip and in one power-packed move, flung the man's arms off his shirt. "God dammit, Mel, get the hell out of here."

"Get him, Rashon!" Mel yelled, and in a flash, Rashon, the dreadlocked black man, was behind Captain Jack, holding him in a powerful grip.

"What the hell...." The Captain was interrupted by a swift slug to the diaphragm. If Rashon hadn't been holding him up, he would have fallen to the ground.

Summer was terrified!

There was no time for Captain Jack to catch his breath, as again, Mel, the skinny man, punched him in the diaphragm. The Captain cried out, or tried to, but Rashon hooked a large, muscled arm around his neck in a stranglehold.

What can I do? Summer felt like a cowardly witness, watching the horrifying scene before her and doing nothing to stop the captain's torture. On one hand, he seriously needed help; but on the other, she was sure she would put her life in danger if she made her presence known.

Captains Jack's face glowed red, locked in Rashon's iron grip.

"Where is it?" Mel demanded, but Captain Jack could give no reply. "Let him go before he passes out," he instructed, and the captain fell to the ground upon release.

Mel kicked him as he gasped for air. "God damn it!" He kicked him again. Rashon joined in, and they continued an endless stream of kicks until, Summer supposed, their legs tired.

"Fucking asshole," Mel said, and lit a cigarette. There was no chance of retaliation on the Captain's part as he lay in a groaning heap at their feet.

"I don't see any tourist, do you?" Mel asked, checking the surroundings.

Jocelyn Miller

Rashon glanced briefly in Summer's direction and she held her breath. "No way, man. He's lying through his teeth."

"Let's get out of here."

Oh, please, go! Go! Go!

Mel hopped onboard the small motorboat in which they had arrived, while Rashon untied the line from the dock.

Summer's moment of relief turned to sheer horror as Captain Jack, still lying in the dirt, pulled a small revolver from his jean pocket and aimed it at Mel.

"Oh, no!" she whispered. How did she get mixed up in this mess?

"Look out!" Rashon yelled. 'He pulled a gun!"

In a flash, Mel leaned over in the bow and came up with a large handgun. *Thud, thud, thud,* and the captain lay still.

It was all Summer could do to stifle a scream and keep herself from fainting. She thought guns made loud noises, but the dull thud, thud, thud of Mel's handgun was chilling.

"What if he weren't lyin' and there *is* someone else here?" Rashon asked, after they kicked the captain's body again, to make sure he was dead.

"You can go looking, if you want, man, but I'm getting outta here."

"What about him and the boat? We can't leave 'em here."

Summer didn't wait for the answer. She crept backward, quiet as a snake in the grass, before she turned and dashed down the ever-narrowing path. When she felt she was far from earshot, she ran, the branches of trees and thorns of brush cutting at her bare arms, as she had left her jacket in the skiff. She didn't realize she was crying until salty tears slipped between her lips. Soon, she was out of breath and fearful that in her terror and flight she had made sounds that would bring the murderers after her. She gasped for air, hands on knees, thanking her good sense for wearing long pants, as her legs would now be as bloody and sliced as her arms.

She stood straight again and checked her surroundings Nothing but trees, brush and mosquitos. *What now?* In the distance she heard the motorboat and listened until the sound weaned off into the distance. At that point, feeling safe, she leaned against a tree and sobbed.

10

The sea hit like a train. Cherry hung on for dear life as Tom Quinn tried his best to steady the skiff against the onslaught of swells, wind and sudden rain that pelted with stinging icy needles. The sky to the east was dark with black clouds but streaks of sunrise, red as blood, knifed through in jagged, horizontal slashes.

"Hold on, Cherry girl," he yelled against the howling wind. "We got us a gale here!"

Cherry shivered against the biting cold. Misery prevailed as icy tears flowed down her cheeks. She looked behind at Fort Pulaski's dim entry into daylight. Ahead, Tybee Island Light still glimmered through the wind and storm.

For hours they tossed upon the angry sea, Fort Pulaski out of view and the lighthouse behind them. The wind howled in their ears, and the rain battered their faces until they were numb. When it seemed they were locked into this hell for eternity, Quinn managed to steer the craft around a hook of land and into a shelter from the storm. He pulled the skiff halfway up the beach and tied it to a palm. Cherry sobbed as she climbed her way off the boat only to find herself flat on her back on the sand, having lost her balance, and having not regained her land legs.

Jocelyn Miller

Without a word, Quinn lifted her from the beach and carried her into the shrub. There, they huddled, wrapped in each other's arms, shaking from the cold but at last, off the deadly sea.

They slept; and when they woke, it was by the warmth of the sun. The wind had lessened considerably, and their shivering had stopped. The sun was directly overhead.

"We did it, Cherry girl!" He freed his arms from her and stood, turning in all directions. "Don't see a ship or nothin'!"

Cherry stood and shook her skirt; sand fell like an hourglass. "I's a mess." She felt her hair, and it was coarse and sticky from sea salt. Thirst and hunger gripped her. Quinn had filled his canteen with water at the farm where he stole the skiff, but it was nearly empty, even though it had been severely rationed.

"Now what we gonna do?" she asked. "We need food, and I'd surely like some water." She wanted to sit down and die. Anything would be better than where she was now, lost on an island somewhere with her abductor, tired, hungry, thirsty and on a journey to an unknown land.

They trudged inward, away from the shoreline in search of fresh water, through the grasses, the sea oats and wax myrtle, before reaching a forest of live oak, pine and cabbage palm. Spanish moss hung from the oaks in ghostly drifts and that, too, reminded her of home.

They continued through the gnarly lower growth of the forest and eventually, with much jubilation, they reached a fresh-water creek. "I'll bet there's fish in there!" Quinn said, and pulled the farmer's fishhook and line out of his pocket and searched for a branch to tie it to.

Cherry undressed after finding the spot most hidden by brush— enough to partially hide her naked body from Tom Quinn. She desperately wanted a bath and couldn't bear to think what a vision of nakedness would do to her captor. First and foremost, though, she needed to be clean. The water was cold— so icy!—nearly causing her to change her mind about the bath; but her filth overruled and she splashed and washed until satisfied. She also washed her clothing and red bandana, which left the dilemma of what to put on as it dried. She thought of the story of the man and woman in the Garden of Eden. The visiting preacher had told the story once when she was a child, and she never forgot it. She wished it was Juba with her, and not this bad white man who had stolen her away from all she knew and loved.

Jocelyn Miller

She had no choice but to throw on her wet underclothes, a muslin shimmy her mama had made. It was cold and clung to her body—which was now covered in goose-flesh—but it was better than giving Tom Quinn free reign to climb on her.

* * *

"Now tell me that ain't good, girl!" Tom said as he pried open a clam with his knife. She was so busy stuffing fish into her mouth, she could only answer with a muffled "mmmm." Her action spoke for itself.

Luck was with them. He caught not only a few small fish with his hook, but a cap full of small squirming shrimp as well when he waded offshore from the beach. Cherry was jubilant from clam digging, and was proud of her contribution.

She had skewered the shrimp onto a thin branch that Tom had sharpened. Starting the fire was a delicate operation because of the torrential rains that had fallen during the storm. Cherry was sent back to the forest to forage for dryer kindling. *I could run,* she thought, but, again, she didn't know where she was and if this were an island, how would she get off and where would she go? After she returned with the kindling, Tom was able to light the fire with the lifesaving flint striker he carried in a pocket.

The sun was low on the horizon, creating splashes of orange and pink against the low-lying clouds, as they sat devouring their feast. A beautiful sunset, but it only meant one thing: they would soon be traveling. The thought of leaving the warm fire and good food behind saddened her.

A small number of cooked shrimp and roasted clams were put aside for their coming journey, as well as the canteen full of fresh water.

"I hope dis is enough," Cherry said, packing the seafood into her red bandana. During the journey she had removed it and tied it securely around her neck, a vain effort for warmth. Now, it had become quite handy as a satchel. "Ain't enough water, I knows dat for certain," she said, nodding to the canteen tied securely to Quinn's belt.

"Got nothin' else to put it in, girl."

At dark, they pushed off from the bank of the island and continued to follow the land in a southerly direction.

Jocelyn Miller

"Ain't no storm tonight," she said, pulling the tattered blanket around her. "But I's cold and want a coat, mistah. You gots to find us come warm clothes."

"Ain't you the bossy one."

Why not? Long as wants me, he gots to keep me warm and keep my belly full.

11

"Enough!" she said, wiping her eyes. The one tissue she kept in her pocket had already been disposed of as toilet paper. "What now?" She desperately wanted her purse out of the boat and wondered if it was still there. Did she dare return? The humane thing to do was to return to the dock and check on Captain Jack; maybe, by some small grace, he was still alive. She would patch his wounds and they could make their way back to Everglades City; she was sure of it. She prayed her purse was there with her cell phone. Perhaps there was a cell signal and she could call for help? Hesitantly, she turned and headed back down the trail, a trail she had seen too much of lately. Surely the men had gone, but still, quietly, she retraced her steps until she came to the spot from which she had witnessed the shooting. Peeking through the tall grasses, she saw…nothing! Not only was her purse gone along with the skiff, but Captain Jack's body as well. Nothing remained!

She walked to the site of the horrible crime and stared stupidly at the dirt, wet with dark blood, where the Captain had lain. *Poor, poor man. If I hadn't hired him, he'd still be alive.*

Jocelyn Miller

Reality struck hard, as she stood staring at the dirt. She was stuck on an island—God only knew where in the Everglades—without food, water, shelter, any possibility for help, and a witness to murder, terrified that the perpetrators would return to hunt her down. Tears welled, and she stiffened her body against the assault of weakness. *I will survive! I survived slavery, I survived a Yankee invasion or two. I survived Mick Mason and Elizabeth Woodfield. I will survive this!* Surely another tour guide would show up sooner or later and rescue her; rescue was imminent…she hoped.

She sat on the dock for hours waiting and watching for a boat to stop, but it did not happen. As the afternoon wore on and twilight threatened, it became apparent that rescue would not happen today. Standing, she brushed the dust from her behind. *Now what? Should I sleep on the dock?* She was most fearful of alligators and wondered if this water was too salty for them. It didn't appear to be alligator territory, but what about crocodiles? What about snakes? Hunger was gnawing at her gut, as well as thirst. *What a mess this is…*

A sudden burst of thunder clapped overhead and she looked up to discover a premature darkness of the sky. "Damn!" she yelled. "Isn't it enough I'm stranded here?"

"*…footings and a collapsed structure…*" she remembered Captain Jack saying. *Where?* Perhaps she could find shelter for the night? Torn between waiting at the dock for a boat to pass or looking for shelter, the approaching darkness answered the question; shelter was definitely more important at this moment considering the ominous sky overhead. Back she went, through the thicket and trees, the narrow path narrowing by the footstep. *Surely a path leads to somewhere…* she hoped.

It was nearly dark when she stumbled across the collapsed dwelling that the Captain had mentioned. Its foundation, very like the foundation on the first island, was constructed of a rough material. She assumed it was of shell, but it was too dark to see. Not only had darkness fallen, but the cold had enveloped her and she shivered as the first drops of rain fell. It was very difficult to hold back the tears; she was terrified. She could not see what critters were to share her abode for the night, and she knew that Florida was full to the brim of poisonous snakes and stinging insects. The mosquitos had already discovered that the insect spray was long gone, and she was covered with bites and continually swatting the buzzing menace which was now unseen due to nightfall. In

Jocelyn Miller

the remaining glimmer of light, she saw that the ceiling of the structure had collapsed leaving a cave-like entrance. Gathering all her grit, she knelt and crawled into the triangular opening, and into the dark abyss. The grasses and weeds had grown over the flooring and provided a soft carpet upon which to crawl. She stopped as soon as she no longer felt the rain pelleting her shivering flesh. Huddled in the cave-house, she sat, drawing her knees to her chest and wrapped her arms around her legs in an attempt to keep warm. In a while, her eyes drooped from exhaustion and the trauma of the day. She lay, not caring what snakes or insects kept her company in the darkness. She wanted sleep, she wanted to forget, she wanted to be away from this horrid day, and so she drifted off in this fashion.

"*Evaline!*" The voice woke her from the depths of her dark exhaustion. Branches cracked. *Where am I?* The cold and damp brought to light her dire situation…*lost in the Everglades!*

* * *

"Evaline!"

It was a scream— and so close!

"Cherry!" Summer crawled quickly to the triangular opening of her hovel. The rain had passed over, as above shone brilliant stars seemingly close to the touch. And the moon! It was bright and cast a frosted glow to the surrounding. Another crackle of branches startled her, and she dared not go further than her head out of the opening.

Closer came the sounds of movement in the brush until the luminous form of Cherry appeared. "*Evaline!*" screamed the ghostly vision. "Help me!" Cherry was frantic, searching from side to side just as she had in the visit on the portico at Magnolia.

Summer crawled forward in an attempt to exit the hovel to rescue her, but another crack in the brush caused her to pause. There was nothing to separate her now from the reality of the haunting; there was no wood, no glass, no door and now from the brush appeared the man with the smashed face carrying a club! He too was luminous in the moonlight and both figures radiated in a blurred glow before her. She watched in horror as Cherry screamed and disappeared into the thicket, the horrible man chasing from behind.

Summer was ashamed. Frozen in terror when the man appeared, she couldn't move a muscle forward. It was a bone chilling scene causing her to quickly back into her hovel, which was, after all, much more appealing even in these dire circumstances than what she had just witnessed.

12

The barrier islands of Georgia had saved them from starvation, from Union ships which patrolled the coastline from Confederate blockade runners, and from the sea itself, which found no mercy in Tom Quinn's quest to reach the southern tip of Florida. The islands supplied them food and fresh water, shelter from storms and allowed them to rest from their nightly journey. At one point, upon shoving off from shore, they found a small barrel-type object floating amidst the swells. Behind it dragged a rope of ten feet or so. They quickly pulled it aboard and found that its bung hole was plugged. Tom shook the cask; there was liquid inside. He pulled the plug for a whiff.

"Rum!" He took a swig and held the cask out to her. "Have drink, girl. Maybe it will improve your disposition."

Cherry found the cask heavy, so lowered her face for a whiff. "I ain't never had no liquor," she said.

"Well, ain't it about time?"

"It's too heavy."

"I'll help ya." He stood and the skiff rocked with the weight of him.

Jocelyn Miller

"I jes drink da water, mistah," she said, but he held the bung hole to her lips.

"Drink!" he commanded, and she did, finding small comfort in the burning sensation as the liquid spilled down her throat, as well as down her chin. However, when it hit her belly she felt a rush of strange warmth, a rush that was not unpleasant. It was her one and only sip, as there was a night of sailing ahead of them. The skiff rocked precariously with the small swells and splashes of the sea against their craft as they continued their way to the strange land.

The rest of the journey that night not only included the task of keeping close to the shore, fighting the waves, the wind, the cold, but also included Tom Quinn getting progressively drunker as the night wore on. By dawn he was singing songs Cherry had never heard, and eyeing her in the way she dreaded. When dawn showed pink on the horizon, she helped to get the skiff ashore; it was that, or who knew where they would end up, for Tom Quinn was unsteady on his feet and fell out of the skiff into the shallow water. She was thigh-high in the cold, slapping waves as she pushed the craft up onto the sand as far as she could with what strength she could muster after this frightening night at sea with her drunken captor.

Quinn staggered ashore and grabbed the rope that was tied to the bow of the skiff. She was glad he had a smidgeon of sensibility left, as she was terrified as to what would happen should he pass out. She watched as he stumbled in the breaking dawn; rope in hand searching for a place for which to tie it securely. A thick bodied tree which had washed ashore, showed itself in the early morning light. He gripped its jutting roots and tried to move it, but it remained stationary. "Good," he said, winding the rope around its base.

She hated the sticky salt water, for now her wet skirt and shimmy clung to her legs, which were covered in gooseflesh from the wind as she stepped onto the sandy beach. She hated him, too, watching as he staggered and collapsed aside a low shrub leaving her to fend for herself.

I could run, she thought, as she often did, but where would she run to? Instead, she climbed back aboard the skiff and lifted the cask from the floor. It was heavy, and she struggled, but managed to lift it over the bow and roll it onto the beach. Onshore, she unplugged the bung hole and tilted the cask, pouring the remaining rum into the sea.

Jocelyn Miller

"He ain't gonna be happy 'bout dis," she said, cringing at the thought of his reaction when he realized what she had done.

From there, she used all her strength, which was dwindling quickly from her exhaustion of the long night, and hefted the cask onto her head, as she had done a hundred times or more with the heavy laundry baskets at Magnolia. *Magnolia!* Oh, how she missed her people! She prayed they were safe, but could have no idea since all she saw was smoke coming from the front of the great house as Quinn stole her away. How was her baby, Percy? Mama? Lucy? Evaline? How was old Pompeii? Tears formed as she disappeared into the brush, holding the cask to her head as she walked. It was heavy; it was uncomfortable. She needed a pillow to put between her head and the cask but there was nothing.

She had learned the way of the islands on this journey: the way the sand led to the brush, the brush to the thick and taller bushes and trees, and then the forest. It was always a challenge to get into the forest as it was thick with vines and thorns. She tried not to think of the snakes and critters that were surely there, hiding, waiting for a victim. She hummed to keep herself company. With luck, she found a small stream. There, she unplugged the cask and put it sideways into the running water and filled the keg. She would leave it there when it was full, alongside the stream, plugged and waiting for Quinn to retrieve it.

Now she was very hungry; she would have to fend for herself for several hours ahead. When she returned to the beach, Quinn lay in the sand, face up, snoring. She gingerly reached into his pocket and pulled out the hook and line. *I ain't starving, you fool brute.*

She took one of his boots off and gave no thought to the consequence; it was already soaked from his fall into the water. From there, she crept along the shallow water looking for baitfish. Managing to trap a few in the boot, she pulled a branch from the brush and tied the rig to it. She walked back to the stream, as it was deep enough to hold fish, or so she hoped. There, she strained the water from the boot and hooked one of the flopping minnows to the hook. A spot close to the cask of water appeared to have a deeper pool, so tossed her hook into the water and waited. She had never, ever fished in this fashion, but she had watched Quinn often enough. She jiggled the branch a bit, waiting…waiting…waiting. A nibble! She waited a moment more, and when the tug became stronger she yanked the branch upward and back

Jocelyn Miller

and knew by the weight on the other end that she had a fish! The branch curved as she held tight. *Don't break! Don't break*, she prayed.

When Tom Quinn woke from his drunken slumber, Cherry had set up camp by digging a fire-pit, gathering kindling, removing the flint-starter from his pocket and starting a fire. The fish was cooked, his share waiting for him.

"Uh?" he groaned, rising up onto his elbows. "Where are we, girl?"

"Dunno," she answered. And she didn't know. How could she, a freed and uneducated slave of a sorrowful past, have any idea where they were?

Quinn hefted himself to a sitting position and looked at his surroundings. Sand fell from his now dry clothes, and he brushed what he could from his shirt sleeves. He spotted the fire. "You did good, girl."

"It was dat or starve," she said.

He suddenly gripped his head. "Guess I had too much rum, but a hair of the dog will help. Bring me the keg, girl."

"Ain't got it here," she answered.

"Well, where the hell is it? You didn't lose it, did you?"

"No sah, didn't lose it."

"Well, don't keep me waiting or I'll tan your hide."

"It's in dem woods, der. You gotta get it. I filled it wid water and it too heavy for me."

"You...? Did I drink it all?"

"Yes sah," She lied.

He groaned, and tried to stand, his body uncooperative. "Help me up, girl. I gotta relieve myself."

As he pulled himself up with support from her arms for leverage, she smelled the sea on him, the sea and urine.

"You stinks."

"Don't sass me," he said, but not in his usual gruff voice, as he must have felt quite sick after drinking the entire keg (or so he thought) of rum.

"You caught a fish?" he asked, spotting the remains on a palm frond near the fire where she had placed it after cooking.

"Yes sah."

He patted his pockets and realized that the hook and line were still there, as well as the flint starter.

Jocelyn Miller

"Good girl."

* * *

Much to their alarm, they ran out of barrier islands. Hugging close to the shoreline, they made their way south, stopping again at daylight to rest when an adequate spot presented itself.

Alas, after many nights of traveling, their lifesaving barrier islands far behind, they witnessed a growing brightness on the horizon.

"Der!" Cherry pointed. "What's dat?"

"I don't know girl, but we're gonna find out."

No matter how hard Tom Quinn paddled, the little skiff didn't seem to get any closer to the distant lights, but one thing was certain; the lights involved people—many people. Eventually, more and more ships came into view: dories, other skiffs, three-mast sailing vessels, and steamships. This was a seaport, and a big one! It was a futile effort to hide in such traffic, so Tom continued to paddle the boat southward toward the lights maneuvering through the parade of vessels. They were, after all, just one vessel amidst others and certainly wouldn't draw attention to themselves.

"Looks like a river, girl, and we're taking it. I've had enough of the sea."

Cherry had never seen so many ships in one place. Riverboats had stopped at Magnolia to load their rice for transport to Savannah or Atlanta. From there, she did not know where they went for she had no knowledge of geography. All she knew was that her people toiled in the paddies from dawn until dusk, and the rice—the product of their labor and sweat—was loaded onto boats and gone forever. Now, here she was on the sea, thus far having survived this treacherous journey with her captor and witnessing a vision of ships and craft of such magnitude that her mind could barely take it all in.

Quinn maneuvered the skiff around the bend of land and into the mouth of the river. The sun had risen in the east, and they were tired and hungry. The weather had grown warmer, and Cherry wondered how long had she been gone from home. *Percy.* She thought of him often, as was natural, and wondered what had happened to her people. *They think me dead.* She was sure of it.

Jocelyn Miller

Too tired to travel further down the river, Tom rowed the skiff to a thickly brushed area on the shore. They went about their own respective camp duties, and soon were settled around the campfire, fresh fish skewered onto a branch and roasting over the fire.

"I think this is Jacksonville in Florida," he said. "If I recall, this is the St. Johns River, and we can head inland now and get off the sea."

"We gotta get clothes," Cherry said.

"Clothes, food, supplies," he added.

The thought of a city brought hope to Cherry. Maybe she could escape Quinn and somehow find her way back to Magnolia? "We got money?"

"Ha! Ain't no money worth anything down here. I'll get us all we need without it."

Their habit before retiring was to select palm fronds and other vegetation to cover the ground before they lay to rest. Cherry inspected every inch of her bedding searching for insects of any nature that could cause hysteria. There were so many insects, even in the cooler weather, that sometimes she had to leave well enough alone and deal with nature's rule; she was part of the ecological food chain and she knew it, though not in those terms.

With the bedding chosen, gathered, inspected and placed the correct distance apart (her rule), they settled into sleep. There was a possibility, considering the amount of traffic on the river, that they could give up their nocturnal traveling, and move with the rest of the water traffic down the St. Johns, but first, they needed rest.

* * *

"Wake up!"

Cherry opened her eyes to the horror of a Yankee soldier standing over Tom Quinn, rifle ready. The sun was past midpoint in the sky indicating that they had slept awhile, but she was still groggy and trying to register with the present.

"Get up, buddy." The soldier kicked Tom Quinn's boot.

"Huh?" He lifted himself to his elbows and squinted at the figure before him. Realization that they had been discovered brought him to full attention.

Jocelyn Miller

"What are you folks doing here?" The soldier asked. He eyed Tom Quinn suspiciously. "You got Yankee pants on; why ain't you with your troops?"

Cherry stared wide-eyed wondering how Tom Quinn would respond to the question.

After a pause he said, "Cause you folks burned my farm, my clothes and all my belongin's along with everything else I owned. I took these off a dead soldier."

"Maybe you're a deserter. Maybe I should take you in." The soldier sported a stubble of beard, was of stocky proportions and looked to Cherry like he could certainly take on Tom Quinn should it be necessary.

"Maybe I ain't. And I ain't on your side anyway so why take me in?"

"Who's this woman?"

"Freed darkie from my old plantation."

"Where you going?"

"Away from the war."

Cherry was terrified Quinn was going to pull the knife he kept in his boot. He had remained seated, but Cherry watched as his hand rested on the boot cuff that held the knife.

The soldier scrutinized them both for several uncomfortable seconds. "Get goin' then," he said finally. Cherry stood immediately. "You can't sleep here," he continued. "We patrol this area."

"Yes sir," Quinn said, extremely out of character and much to Cherry's relief.

They watched as the soldier disappeared into the brush.

"Whew, that was a close one!" Tom said, rising from his bed of palm. "Pack up Cherry girl, we're going to Jacksonville."

Jocelyn Miller

13

S ummer woke to the buzz of mosquitos, and ached from head to toe. By the time she pried her eyes open, the events of the previous day and night flashed with alarming clarity. It hadn't been a nightmare; *it was real.* She had witnessed a murder and was stranded on an island in the middle of the Everglades; no food, no water, no escape, and to make matters worse, had been visited again by the horrible vision of Cherry and her assailant!

She felt her eyes, puffy balls of soreness. Her arms were ribbons of dried, bloody scratches. *Damn bugs. Thank God for the jeans.* She sat and perused the immediate surroundings of her hovel in the Everglades. She could just hear Guy yelling at her now...*Oh, Guy! The phone message!* She had called him yesterday and he would by now be frantic since she never made the second call on the return of her excursion! She sighed with relief, thinking that rescue was definitely imminent now, with Guy on her trail.

The sun had risen, melting away the chill of night. It was creepy in the hovel, of that there was no doubt. Thankful that no snakes or serious insect bites had befallen her during her sleep, she got on her hands and knees and prepared to exit her cave when a glint of metal caught her eye. To the left, sitting haphazardly in a corner on what must

Jocelyn Miller

have been at one time a beam or rafter, was a rather large object. Dare she crawl to it? Would a giant python be hiding in the corner darkness waiting to swallow her up? She had already been eaten by an alligator as Evaline, and was not eager to die as herself, swallowed by a snake. *I came all this way for clues,* she reminded herself and crawled across the grassy mat toward the object. She reached for it and screamed when a dark chunk of wood flew out at her, a loose piece from the crumbling structure. "Dummy", she said, regaining her composure.

The box was not as small as it looked. In fact, it was quite large and resembled a chest, like a smaller version of a pirate chest. The latch was corroded with time, and she wondered how long it had sat precariously on the beam. She pried the latch open, breaking a fingernail in the process. Despite her dismal circumstance, the thrill of an undiscovered treasure momentarily relieved her misery.

Peering into the cavity of the box, she saw what looked like a cloth. She closed the lid and pushed the box ahead while crawling awkwardly toward the entrance to the hovel. Once outside, stretching to her full height was an experience in pain after the cramped quarters of her cave. She opened the box again in the light of morning and her heart nearly stopped; inside was a bandana—a very faded bandana—that could *only* have belonged to Cherry! Where once it had been bright red, it was now a dismal dried-blood brown, but it was Cherry's for sure. Ruth had embroidered an outlined cherry on a corner of the bandana, and there it was, a cherry, a stem, and two leaves! Goosebumps rose on Summer's flesh. She had seen it hundreds of times on Cherry's head. *Always,* she wore the red bandana! Overwhelmed by her discovery, she sat on a nearby fallen tree; it was that, or faint. She had come all this way to find a clue, and here is was in her hands! Providence had guided her. She must be close!

Her joy in finding the treasure quickly turned to disbelief and then horror as the bandana began to shake in her hands. Soon, her arms shook beyond control. She could not let go! She ran a short distance, her arms shaking wildly, the bandana clenched tightly her fists. She banged her arms against a tree, hoping to release its grip, but to no avail, it remained tightly clenched as if it were a part of her own body. Terribly frightened, every hair on her body standing at attention, she screamed before collapsing into the brush.

Jocelyn Miller

14

Lo and behold, Jacksonville. It was a welcomed site to the travelers in the small skiff as they maneuvered their way through the many ships, boats, and other craft that congested the harbor. Cherry's excitement at viewing a city in daylight faded as they neared the dock. Jacksonville had suffered a severe impact from the war. It was a busy dock with ships loading and unloading their cargoes. Union soldiers stood about directing laborers, some of color, which made Cherry even more homesick for her family. Their voices carried unintelligibly across the water to the travelers, but what struck Cherry most were the charred, burnt and demolished buildings that stood as grave and dismal reminders of the truth of war.

"Ain't nothin' here," she said in astonishment.

"Ain't nothin' we can see, but somethin's there for the taking, I'm sure of it."

"What we gonna do now? We need food, water....clothes." Her hopes fell deeper with every glance at the ugly vision as they drifted past.

"Don't you worry, girl," He said, and continued rowing past the dock, past the burnt buildings, past a scattering of houses until they came to a stretch of land with a favorable docking point. Once ashore, he secured the boat to a tree and stood a moment eyeing Cherry in that particular way that made her skin crawl. "Git yourself cleaned up, girl, do somethin' with that hair. Make yourself pretty. We're goin' to town!"

Cleaned up? Her one skirt and blouse were a tattered disgrace! Never had she been such a filthy mess! In the slave days, Miss Elizabeth would have whipped her good for looking the way she did now, standing on the sunny bank at the edge of a demolished city.

"Do the best you can. We need you to look good."

Those words caused her concern. Why? *Why I need to look good?* She was afraid to ask, but knowing Tom Quinn the way she did, she was very suspicious.

Two hours later they were standing near the Jacksonville dock, the sun fading over the horizon. It was chilly, and she pulled her threadbare and filthy sweater around her body. The buttons that had once secured it in the front were long gone. She had smoothed her hair back and tied it with the worn bandana, the only clean article on her body as she had washed it in the river and it was still damp. Her clothes she could do nothing about as they were stained with dirt from her perilous journey, and torn in many places. The sweater, which once was of an indigo blue color, now had the appearance of a dismal and dirty gray rag. She was embarrassed at her appearance. The gray skeletal buildings that stood as their backdrop only enhanced the way she felt inside.

"You stand here," Quinn instructed, indicating the entrance to an alleyway. "If one of them soldiers comes over, you act real perky, you hear? You give him smiles and promises of a good time." He unpeeled the sweater with which she had covered her chest, and unbuttoned the two top buttons of her blouse, breaking one which had only been hanging on by a slender thread. She heard it fall but had no needle and thread to sew it back on.

"Git that sorry look off your face, ain't nothin' gonna happen to you. Long as Tom Quinn is here, ain't nothin' gonna happen." He put a hand on her breast. "I ain't sharin'."

Cherry was terrified! The realization that she was to be soldier bait was horrific enough without wondering what the rest of Tom Quinn's plan was.

"I'll be right back here," he said, pointing down the alley, which was fading quickly into darkness with the setting sun.

A few moments later, Quinn had disappeared and she stood alone, petrified in the cooling night. She leaned against the alley wall

Jocelyn Miller

pondering her sad life and watching the workers as they toiled at their labor. There were many boxes in the process of being loaded onto an impressive two-mast schooner. The dock was lit by a procession of several gaslights placed strategically to enable the men to work in the dark of night and allowed her to watch her surroundings.

Eventually, one of the soldiers who had been issuing orders noticed her. Although involved in the loading of the ship, he glanced in her direction several times and said something to a companion; they nodded in her direction.

When the ship finished loading, he and his companion made their way to where she stood. She shook as she watched them approach. Her life had been sheltered. Perhaps she had been a slave for most of it, but it had been sheltered just the same. She had a home, she had family, and now she was a stranger thrown blindly into the world, unprepared for most circumstances.

"Good evening, miss."

She remained leaning against the wall as it was support for her trembling body. "Evenin'," she said, barely audible.

One of the soldiers rested his hand against the wall by her head and leaned toward her. "What are you doing here? This is not a safe city, you know. It's dangerous for young ladies to be out alone."

The second soldier nervously looked about.

"Guess you're needing a little money, huh?"

"Uh, yes sah, I be needing money for food…"

"I know how you can make some fast money. Do you?"

"No sah."

"Sure you do," he said, putting the other hand on her breast, where only a short time ago Tom Quinn had placed his.

She cringed.

"Oh come on, this isn't your first time, girl."

"Hurry up, Ben," the other soldier said, and stood in front of Cherry to block her from view from the dock.

"I have lots of money to give you," he said. "Come with me." He grabbed her by the hand, leading her into the alley.

"No sah!" she said, resisting. Where was Quinn? She saw him enter the alley, but when was he going to save her from this man?

"Come, missy." Further they went into the alley until the soldier, Ben, stopped. He turned her to face the wall. "Bend over he said."

Jocelyn Miller

She did, her head resting against the brick of the building. He placed his hands on her hips, then lifted her skirt and shimmy, exposing her flesh to the cold air. She was trembling uncontrollably and could barely stand.

"Atta girl," he said.

She wanted to scream! Where was Tom Quinn?

No sooner had that thought entered her head when she felt a whoosh of air followed by a 'thump'. Feeling that the soldier was no longer there, she turned, quickly lowering her skirt to its rightful place. The soldier lay crumpled at her feet with Quinn pilfering through his pockets.

"Good girl!" he whispered, holding up paper money for her to see.

His joy was interrupted by the second soldier calling from the alley entranceway.

"Hurry up!" the soldier called.

"Shush!" Quinn held a finger to his lips.

"Ben!" the soldier called again. "We gotta report. Hurry it up!"

The sound of footsteps caused Quinn to step back into the darkness. "Stay there", he whispered to Cherry.

She watched the soldier approach and then his shock at seeing his companion lying on the ground.

"Wha'd you do to him, you tramp?"

"I...I..."

"I oughta break your neck," he said stepping toward her.

She stepped further back into the alley, but the soldier had her now, her arms gripped in his strong hands. "You're coming with me, hooker. If he's dead, you'll hang."

Hang? She nearly fainted.

Quinn sprung to action. A scuffle ensued and when it was over, the soldier lay dead and Tom Quinn was bleeding profusely from his right arm.

"Damn!" he said, covering his wound with his good hand. "He got me with that damned bayonet! Hurry! Go thru his pockets and take it all. Bring the rifle, too!"

Cherry did as he asked, but could see that Quinn was badly wounded, as blood oozed from between the fingers that covered his wound.

Jocelyn Miller

"Get their jackets," he said, and she did, with great difficulty, as it was not a pleasant task handling the dead men.

"Hurry. We gotta get outta here before anyone comes lookin' for 'em."

Gathering all that she had to carry, the items from the pockets of the soldiers, the rifle, and the jackets, they ran to the campsite. There would be no campfire or supper tonight. Cherry's belly howled for food, but Quinn's wound required care and they had little time. She had seen enough wounds while nursing the Yankee soldiers when they invaded Magnolia, but without the light of the fire she could not clearly see the wound and could only wash it with river water and wrap it in her precious bandana,

He was in pain—even in the dark of night she could see it on his face—and the pain was making him weak.

"We gotta get outta here, girl. I can't row. You gotta to do the rowing."

Cherry's stomach dropped to her knees. "Mistah, I ain't never rowed no boat!"

"You can catch fish and start a fire, so you can row the damn boat, too! Sooner or later, someone will be lookin' for us. Now get in, we're goin'."

As if things could not get worse! It was shear panic when they pushed off from shore. At first, she sat with the long handles of the oars gripped in her hands, not knowing exactly what to do with them. As they were caught in the current of the river, the skiff began to rotate, at which time Quinn, sitting opposite her, began to yell.

"Damn it, girl, row! Get us steady! We ain't goin' down this river ass backward!"

"Shush!" she yelled. "I's tryin', mistah!" Oh, to be home at Magnolia! This was surely the curse of her life! She struggled with the oars while the skiff rotated in a full circle as they drifted with the current.

Quinn stood a moment in an attempt to take over, the skiff wobbling back and forth with his weight and now traveling sideways down the waterway. "Damn," he muttered, and promptly plopped to the seat and passed out. Out of sheer desperation and much frantic maneuvering, Cherry was eventually able to steady the skiff. The flow of the river was in her favor, as it was not a strong current. She was proud; never had she been in such a predicament where her life depended

Jocelyn Miller

on her own cunning as much as this time on the river, and she handled it—they were on their way! Quinn's crumpled body laid half on and half off the seat. *Can't do nothin' 'bout dat. Serves him right,* she thought. The wound, the pain, the passing out, all were a good payback for stealing her away from all she knew and loved.

The longer she steered the skiff down the river, the more she wondered how Tom Quinn could have taken them so far, as her arms were at a breaking point from rowing, 30 minutes into their travels, not to mention the lack of sleep and empty stomach.

A ship's horn blew, haunting and low in the night. "Oh, look at dat!" she said out loud. Ahead, coming around a bend in the river, was a large side-wheeler, its two bold stacks pumping clouds of smoke while the side wheels churned the river around it, pushing it forward to its destination. She did not know the hour of the night as it was still dark but with a spray of moonlight, enough to illuminate the ship for her viewing. She veered closer to her own shore for fear of somehow drifting into the larger vessel as they passed. It was still quite a ways down the river from her, but inexperience made her cautious.

They had passed many ships on their journey, but this was the first sidewheeler; it was a diversion for her aching arms and growling belly. She looked forward to its passing. The skiff rocked a bit on the calm river, and the sounds of water lapping against the bow lulled her. She stopped rowing a moment to watch the vessel pass.

"Kaboom!" At that very moment a fierce explosion lit up the sky as brightly as she had seen once on Independence Day when Master Woodfield had purchased Chinese fireworks and set them off at Magnolia. She shrieked in absolute terror as pieces of the sidewheeler flew through the air, one hitting the side of their skiff sending it rocking madly in the river. She shrieked again as another explosion sent flames high into the night sky and more debris flew like cannon balls, a piece nicking her cheek. She ducked low in the skiff, her arms instinctively over her head.

"Mistah!" she yelled. Tom Quinn had finally come out of his swoon.

"Ach!" he groaned in pain. "What? Wha'd you do?"

"Mistah! Dat ship 'sploded and's on fire!"

Voices of alarm from the sinking, damaged vessel rang out in the night. The sidewheeler dipped forward, its bow already beneath the

Jocelyn Miller

river's surface. The alarmed voices grew louder and the glow from the fire lit the scene in which the drama played. Figures scurried about. A lifeboat was set into the water and immediately flooded with bodies. Men without the safety of the lifeboat jumped into the river to swim ashore.

The skiff was now directly across the river from the sinking ship, which now showed only the tip of the stern—just for a moment—and it was gone.

Cherry and Quinn both stared at the empty surface of the river where the ship had found its final destiny. They drifted past, silent, as a lifeboat made its way to the opposite shore. The skiff rocked side to side from the delayed wake of the sinking.

"Oh!" was all Cherry could mutter. She had experienced many things in her life; the whipping of slaves, of herself, the alligator death of her beloved Juba, the coming of Yankees, the rapes—so many for such a young creature— the destruction piece by piece of Magnolia, the starving, the death of life as she knew it; but she had never seen anything as large, loud or spectacular, *or quick*, as the sinking of the sidewheeler!

A sudden splash of water and a large, dark hand gripped the gunwale of the skiff. Cherry jumped, scared out of her wits as a head appeared from the river, followed by another large hand.

"Help! Help me!" A voice deep, a voice familiar, the voice of *her* people, rose from the water.

"Mistah!" she called to Quinn, forgetting that he was all but useless.

"We ain't pickin' up passengers," Quinn growled.

"Let me up!" the man called from the water.

"Let him up, Mistah! He'll drown!"

"No! No passengers! Swim to shore!"

"I'm comin' up, Mistah."

Quinn attempted to rise but was too weak, and fell backward. The man hefted his torso, resting it on the gunwale. A muscular leg was soon followed by another, and he stood a moment, his dripping frame stretching nearly to the heavens; a savior, as he appeared to Cherry.

Quinn raised his pain-filled eyes to the dark figure. "I said *swim,"* but any impact intended of the command was drowned in the weakness of his condition.

Jocelyn Miller

The stranger glanced at Cherry. "You got this little gal rowing this boat? I can row it for you, Mistah, get y'all to where you's goin' quicker."

"You got money?" Tom Quinn asked.

"Ain't no money good but Yankee money, and I gots a bit."

Cherry stared in awe, speechless, while the newcomer exchanged words with Tom Quinn. She couldn't take her eyes off him. For the first time since her abduction, she felt a relief wash over her, a relief that she wasn't alone, that perhaps her prayers had been answered; and that she would be saved from this terrible fate that God had bestowed upon her. *The man was her own kind!*

Jocelyn Miller

15

Where am I? Summer fought desperately to stay afloat in the cold, murky water. How long could she tread water before hypothermia set in, and how long could she stay afloat with wet, heavy jeans bogging her down? This was a terrifying predicament! The last thing she remembered was…was the bandana!

It was dark—wherever she was. It was a river, she was sure, as there was a distant shore on either side that she could just make out in the darkness. Fighting to control her increasing fear and panic, she chose the nearest land bank and began to swim. *What's under me?* Her self-control faded quickly with that thought. Dark water always made her fearful. *Alligators? Crocodiles?* "Where am I?" she screamed. She tread a complete circle again, as if to double-check her first impression of surrounding shores. *A river, yes, but where—why?* "Help!" she screamed, swallowing a mouthful of river water which caused her to cough and gasp for air while trying to stay afloat. The current pulled on her and she went with it, having no recourse. *This can't be the end!*

As she tread and bobbed along downriver, an object caught her eye between the rise and fall of the river swells. *A boat?* "Help!" she screamed again, careful to keep the river out of her mouth. "Help!" If there were anyone in the boat, they didn't take notice, as there was no

Jocelyn Miller

reply. The boat was coming toward her and she hoped it caught up to her soon, or surely she would drown in this strange, cold place. *That is not an option,* she told herself, and took off swimming in the boat's direction, an easy task considering they were on a collision course. She had to keep the blood circulating through her body—or perish.

* * *

"You hear dat?" Cherry asked the stranger, who was now rowing the skiff in her place. She sat sternmost, watching with wonder at how effortlessly the chore came to him. Tom Quinn was slumped on the floor behind her, passed out. She wanted to ask the stranger about his life. She knew nothing of other darkies except for the ones at Magnolia, but found herself shy in his presence—that is until now when she thought she heard a voice; someone was calling for help.

"I didn't hear nothin'," he replied. "What's your name, gal?"

"Cherry."

"Cherry," he repeated. "That's a pretty name, Cherry."

"What's yo' name?"

"Buck Henry. Work on the Maple Leaf[4] for the Yankees…or, I done work on the Maple Leaf but the Maple Leaf don't need no workers no more. Was a bunch of Johnny-reb prisoners on that ship. Don't know if they got off. Ain't my worry now."

At that moment, Cherry craned her head to look beyond Henry at the dark waterway ahead. "Der it is agin'. Sound like someone callin' fo' help."

Henry stopped rowing and listened. In the distance a faint voice rose above the splash of the waves against the skiff.

"Sure 'nough, gal, I hears it! You got good ears, Miss Cherry. Sounds like a woman out there, don't it?"

"There!" Cherry pointed. "Is dat somebody?"

Henry craned his neck and looked ahead.

"Help! I'm here! Stop!"

---

[4] The Maple Leaf sidewheeler hit a Confederate torpedo mine in the St. Johns River in Florida in April of 1864 while transporting Union supplies and Confederate prisoners.

Jocelyn Miller

"God Almighty!" he said rowing quickly against the current to the head bobbing on the water's surface, which was clearly visible now as the first sign of approaching dawn tinged the sky.

Within minutes, Henry had pulled the fledgling woman into the skiff where she sat drenched and shivering. The man towered over her, black against the lightening sky. "Whats you doin' in the water, gal? Weren't no women-folk on the Maple Leaf. Miss Cherry, you gots something to cover this lady with?"

* * *

Cherry! Summer could hardly believe her ears or eyes as Cherry struggled toward her in the cramped skiff. In the early morning light her face looked thin, but her body was covered by a Yankee jacket. What was she doing here in a boat with this man in the first place? And just where were they? All questions to be answered in due time but first, Summer struggled to keep from wrapping her arms around her old friend and telling her all would be well— or would it? 'Thanks," she said, as Cherry laid a ragged mess of blanket over her shivering body. They locked eyes. Cherry appeared momentarily startled, staring at the drenched passenger. Even after she made her way back to her seat, she continued to stare.

"My name is Summer Woodfield," Summer said through chattering teeth, and watched as Cherry flinched and cocked her head at the sound of the name.

"I'm Buck Henry, and this here is Cherry-girl. Cherry found me in the water, too, a while back. I didn't see no woman on the Maple Leaf."

"I—I don't know what the Maple Leaf is."

"Why, it's a big sidewheeler—or was. It exploded back there a 'ways and sank in no time a'tal."

"I was on a different ship," she said, and rolled with the lie. "Uh, I ran into some trouble with…with…some gamblers. Yes, I was working on a ship and these men chased me and…."

"Where's yo' clothes?" Cherry interrupted, still scrutinizing the half-drowned stranger.

Jocelyn Miller

"My clothes…uh…" she lifted the blanket to view her wet tee and cold jeans. "These *are* my clothes," she said, then realized that her clothes would look mighty strange to this pair.

"Dey only let you wear yo' underwear on dat ship?"

"…and that was the trouble," Summer continued. "I was in my underwear in my cabin when these men—these gamblers—broke into my cabin and accosted me. I got myself loose and ran onto the deck and just didn't stop running in time. Over I went, and here I am thanks to you folks."

"Hmph." Cherry crossed her arms over her chest and continued to stare. "I seen you somewheres before."

At that moment, a guttural groan hit Summer's ears. "What's that?"

Cherry turned on her seat to look behind onto the boat floor. "Ain't nothin' but Mr. Tom Quinn wakin' up."

"Who's Tom Quinn?"

"Cherry-girl been travelin' with Mr. Quinn. He gots a injury and can't row no more. I'se rowin' for him."

If the boat hadn't been so cramped, Summer would have gone to get a look at Tom Quinn herself. As it was, she couldn't get past Buck without a great hindrance to both of them, so she stayed put and tried to keep warm.

"You're traveling with this Mr. Tom Quinn?" she asked Cherry.

"Not dat I wants to. He stole me away from my peoples, from my home."

"Shut up," Quinn groaned from the bottom of the skiff. "She's lyin. She's one o' my colored."

"I ain't." Cherry said. "I ain't nobody's colored and I sure ain't *your* colored. He stole me!" Cherry began to cry.

"God damn it girl!" Quinn yelled and managed to lift a booted foot to shove her off the seat.

Buck stopped rowing and jumped to his feet. The skiff rocked with his weight, but he pulled Quinn up off the boat bottom by the collar of his shirt and shook him, the poor man hanging like a limp rag. "You do that again, Mistah, and I'll throw you overboard!"

Summer gasped as a beam of sunrise fell on the man's face; she recognized him! She had seen that face before at Magnolia, one of the Yankees who had tormented them!

Jocelyn Miller

Buck literally threw Tom Quinn back into his cubby on the floor where he landed with a hard thump, and groaned in pain. After helping the now-bawling Cherry back onto her seat, Henry again took up the oars. "Hesh now, Cherry-girl. That man ain't gonna bother you no more— not with Buck Henry around."

Summer longed to wrap her arms around her old friend—her cousin—and comfort her but contained the impulse. *Stolen from Magnolia?* She could only imagine the horrors Cherry must have suffered at the hands of Tom Quinn!

"How did Mr. Quinn get injured?" Summer asked, once Cherry's sobs settled to a few sniffles.

"Got sliced by a Yankee. He killed dem Yankees too, and him one of dem!"

"Shut up," Quinn groaned from the floor, but Cherry had composed herself and obviously wanted to tell her side of the story.

"He tol' me to make myself pretty so's he could make da Yankees back der in Jacksonville want me. Den we was gonna take money and things so's we wouldn't be hungry and cold no more. But one soldier stuck him wid da bayonet before Tom Quinn killed him. We run—we run like rabbits—so's nobody catch us, and him bleeding like a stuck pig. We got no food or nothin' 'portant, cep't da jackets. We just run like rabbits for da boat and here we is. I thank da Lord for Buck Henry cause…cause…." The tears reappeared as she tried to finish her tale. "Cause I don't have to put up wid dat bad white man no more…."

Quiet overcame the group as the sun rose over the horizon. It was as if everyone needed a moment to absorb the impact of Cherry's tale. All to be heard was the splash-splash of the oars as they hit the water. Summer looked at the sorry group; Cherry, red eyed and disheveled, her hair gone haywire without the signature red bandana to keep it under control; Henry Buck, his immense arm muscles flexing with the rowing; his jaw set tight as if angry in response to Cherry's tale. She could only see the top of Tom Quinn's head and wondered to what extent the injury was to his arm. Scoundrel or not, he was entitled to some form of medical care.

When they did speak again, it was of a place to moor the boat so they could rest. Cherry came into command and shared her knowledge of the importance of finding the right camp site; good coverage was required to hide them, or so Summer quickly learned.

Jocelyn Miller

"What are we hiding from?" Summer asked as she helped to push the skiff onto a section of muddy shore.

Cherry stopped to ponder this question. "I don' know." She said. "We was hiding from da Yankees, but now I don' know."

"Where are we?" Summer asked.

"We's on the St. Johns River in Florida," Henry said. I run this river all the time for the Yankees."

"Should you go back?"

Instead of answering, Buck turned to Cherry, who was perusing the surroundings on-shore. "Where was you going, girl?"

"Someplace called Florida where der's land," she said. "Dats what Tom Quinn don' shut up about."

He turned to Summer. "That's where we's goin' miss. You want me to put you off somewhere's alongside the river?"

"No, sir. I'm coming along with you," she replied. She had found Cherry, or Cherry had found her, and she was not letting go until she had Cherry safely back where she belonged—Magnolia.

Jocelyn Miller

16

W hat's a white gal like you doin' on this river?" Quinn asked as Summer tended to the deep gash on his arm.
"Same as you, I guess, heading south. And what right did you have to steal Miss Cherry away from her home?"

""Wha'd you care? she's just a nigger gal."

"She's a human being," Summer replied. "Not that you could possibly understand that concept."

"Don't sass me, gal. Bad as my arm is, I can still keep you in your place with one hand."

"Might I remind you, Mr. Nasty Quinn, kidnapper and abuser, that I am your nurse?"

"You got a mouth on you, gal."

Cherry was busy gathering brush to lay for beds while Summer tended to Tom Quinn's wounds, and Buck investigated the shore. All stomachs were empty and growled for food.

Cherry reappeared and reached into Quinn's pocket as he lay propped against a short palm. He was quick with his hand and imprisoned hers within his pocket. "What'r you doin'?"

"I needs da hook and line if you wants to eat."

Jocelyn Miller

After a moment, he relented and released her. "Bring it back," he said.

"I'se gonna give it to Buck Henry," she taunted, dangling the hook and line before his face. "You ain't da boss no more."

"You'll get what's comin' to you, gal, just wait!" he yelled, but Cherry had headed downriver and paid him no mind.

Summer was relieved the sun had risen, and discarded the tattered blanket from her shoulders. Examining Quinn's wound, which was quite severe, she removed Cherry's filthy bandana, tore a strip from the blanket and wrapped it around his arm. He winced in pain and she was quite sure the wound was infected judging by the angry red blotch that bordered the slice.

"So you killed a couple of soldiers?" she asked.

"They were Yankees, and this is war."

"You're a Yankee, too. You killed your own men."

"It's survival, gal. You wouldn't understand."

Oh no?

She left him sitting against the palm and followed the trail Cherry had left. She needed to gain Cherry's confidence instead of having the young woman stare at her suspiciously. *I look nothing like Evaline now*, so why *does she look at me the way she does?*

Summer was impressed when she found Cherry, knee deep in the river, hook and line attached to a sturdy branch, and looking very much like the serious fisherman.

"Looks like you have experience," she said.

"I does after traveling wid dat man. Never fished at Magnolia, jes watched the boys do it."

"Is that your home, Magnolia?"

Cherry's shoulders slumped. "Yes," she answered quietly. "Everybody der; my mama, my baby, my peoples. Dey don' know where I is."

"I'm sorry, Cherry. I will help you return, I promise."

Cherry looked her over. "I knows you. I seen you in my…when I'se sleepin'. I'se seen you b'fore."

Summer skin prickled. "What do you mean, you *'seen me'?*"

"I seen yo' face wid yo' hair cut like a man, yo'tight shirt, yo' long pants. Dem don' look like pantaloons."

Jocelyn Miller

"What am I doing when you see me in your...when you're sleeping?"

"You's just der—to help me, I think."

"I *will* help you. Your dreams are right."

"And how's you gonna help me get back to Mag...." At that moment Cherry's makeshift fishing pole snapped nearly in half. Cherry was quick and grabbed the broken end with the hook and line attached. "Sweet Jesus, it's a big one!" she yelled. "Help!"

Summer went quickly into the water, knee deep. "What do you want me to do?"

"Help me hold da stick!"

Both women stood in the water, their knuckles white from the tight grip on the remaining three feet of branch that held the line; their only link to food at this point, neither daring to let go.

"Walk backwards up onto the bank," Summer instructed, the veins of her neck standing red with the intensity of muscle it took the two of them to keep hold. Awkward as it was, they inched their way up the muddy river bank, pulling the fighting fish, still invisible to them, closer to shore. Backward they walked, holding tight to the broken branch, and searching the water's surface for any break, indicating an end to their struggle. At last a splash sparkled in the morning light. Then another; and finally a large, flopping fish was dragged onshore.

"Hold dis," Cherry ordered, leaving Summer with the broken branch. "Don' let go."

From her perspective, Summer saw that the catch was very large, perhaps two feet long. "You did good, Cherry!" she yelled, hearing her stomach growl in anticipation; hunger was showing its head. It had been quite a day and night: Captain Jack's murder, the drug runners, a night alone in the Everglades, the discovery of Cherry's red bandana and now this, her surprise portal back in time and rescue from the murky depths of the river, only to land in a boat with Cherry. God was good.

Not only was the fish large, but heavy as well. It took the two of them to carry the struggling creature back to camp where Buck prepared it for cooking. He had gathered firewood and already had a fire going in the pit he dug.

"You's a handy gal, Miz Cherry, catchin' a big'un like that," he said, winking.

Jocelyn Miller

Summer swore Cherry blushed as they sat around the fire tearing chunks of meat off the large roasted fish. Henry Buck took Tom Quinn his portion on a large leaf, where he was propped, leaning against the palm. Quinn didn't look well. His eyes were red and watery, glazed, even. She flinched at his swollen arm. "We need to find help for Mr. Quinn."

"He don' need help," Cherry muttered. "He da devil, dat man."

"He's still a person, Cherry, and he's helpless without us."

"I don' see no doctor here," she answered, glaring at Quinn who appeared to be now unconscious against the palm. Summer didn't know if he had passed out, was sleeping, or was dead. There was nothing else that could be done without medical help.

Jocelyn Miller

17

After the 10th day of Summer's river survival trek, Tom Quinn's condition had worsened considerably. His wound emitted a putrid odor that kept the others at bay. His days and nights were spent moaning in pain, semi-conscious. Cherry's bandana was repeatedly washed and used to cover Summer's nose when she tended to him. Cherry would not touch the hated man, and Buck's job was to get them safely to wherever it was they were headed, and Summer's self-proclaimed task was to care for Tom Quinn.

Soon after Summer joined the group, Buck attached the canvas to the mast which dramatically hastened the speed of their journey.

"Dumb white man couldn't think of dat." Cherry blurted around the campfire one night. "All dat time and he didn't know to put da sail on." She glared at Quinn, unconscious on his bed of branches.

The journey had been difficult, primitive, (in Summer's 21st century mind), food scarce, and had it not been for Buck's muscle and forethought, and Cherry's fishing abilities, Summer wondered how on earth she could have survived these 10 days. Without her care, Quinn would have been dead already, too. Perhaps tending to his wound was only holding his end at bay.

It was impossible to know how many miles they had covered over the last 10 days, but the land around them had changed. The

Jocelyn Miller

wooded forests were leveling out into stretches of marshlands, saw and cord grass growing tall and impeding their travel.

They now traveled in daylight, as the gunboats traveling the St. Johns River had long disappeared. For a day now, they had not seen a vessel of any kind, nor any structures onshore to indicate human life.

Impressive and helpful as the sail had been, it now had to be removed through the marshlands, and the wooden mast used to push the skiff through many areas of tangled grasses. At times they had to walk ankle deep in the diminishing river, dragging and pulling the skiff until there appeared water deep enough to float again.

After maneuvering the grasslands, they came to a canopy of cypress which provided shade and cooler air for the sunburnt and weary travelers.

"Der ain't no place to bank here," Cherry observed, looking in wonder at her surroundings. The cypress trees stood tall in the still waters. The sun filtered through the canopy of overgrowth, reflecting in bright flashes off the water's surface, and down the mangrove tunnels which forked off in different directions. All was still as they sat in wonder at this strange yet magical place. All was quiet as death until the shriek of a bird shook the group from their trance.

"What kind of place is this?" Henry asked, as a flash of white feathers flew overhead, down a tunnel created by the dense vegetation.

"Der ain't nowhere to dock!" Cherry was obviously alarmed.

"It's mangrove. Let's follow the bird, if we can find it," Summer said. The river seemed to have lost itself into many forks—forks disappearing into the mangrove—the water stagnant, unmoving. Which was the correct passage?

"Maybe the river ends here," Henry said, as if reading her mind.

"Dat bird went somewhere," Cherry said, gazing in the direction of its flight.

Henry rowed the skiff after the flight path of the bird, now long out of sight. The tunnel narrowed considerably as they moved along, but he persevered until the bird was seen ahead, branched in the mangrove; a dead end.

"Damn," Summer muttered. This adventure was becoming quite terrifying. *We're lost!*

Exhausted, mentally and physically, after traveling each of the tunnels only to find themselves facing impenetrable walls of mangrove,

Jocelyn Miller

they sat in their skiff, defeated, the daylight ebbing away as the sun receded downward toward its setting.

This time it was a shriek from Cherry that caused alarm.

"What?" Summer shrieked herself, in response.

"Look!" Cherry said, nearly crouching beside Quinn on the boat floor. "Look at dem spiders!"

Sure enough, as Summer studied a finely webbed overhead canopy, thousands of thin black legs came into focus; they were beneath a blanket of spiders!

"Oh my God, now what?" She didn't expect an answer; they were literally all *in the same boat*—confused, getting colder with the fading sun, hungry, tired, and increasingly scared.

A branch cracked. Their heads turned in the direction of the sound. Nothing. Then, another crack, another, and another; closer it came. Buck reached for the knife he had taken from Quinn under Cherry's direction, and tucked into his own boot. It was difficult to conceive what could possibly be making its way through the thick and tangled mangrove. They sat silently listening, still as statues, only eyeballs moving, searching the parameters for any movement. All was silent until Cherry let out a bone-chilling scream.

"Der!" she pointed. Summer followed her finger into the thicket, but could see nothing. Then, a flash; a flash of red, of yellow, a shock of color in motion. Buck was poised for battle.

"Maybe food…" he whispered, his knife ready.

"Istonko!"[5] The voice was male, and came from within the mangrove. "Istonko!" It came again.

"Who's there?" Henry commanded.

Another crackle of branch and a dark, wizened man stepped out into the open at the edge of the stagnant pool; a small man wearing a long tunic to his knees, and leather boots laced up with rawhide. A belt around his waist held many pouches and his headdress, a large turban adorned with white plumes, completed this astonishing picture. In his hands, he held a rifle.

"Istonko!" the man repeated, but the group was at a loss; it was a language strange to their ears.

---

[5] Miccosukee/Creek language of the Seminole meaning "Hello".

Jocelyn Miller

"Hello," said Henry, suspicion in his voice.

The strange man pointed to Henry's knife and indicated for him to put it down. He did, slipping it back into his boot. After all, a rifle spoke louder than the blade.

"I think he wants us to come," Summer said, as the man waved them toward him. He pointed and reached for the rope tied to the bow of the skiff.

"I ain't goin' wid him," Cherry said. "What is he? I ain't never seen nobody looks like him!"

"Ain't got a choice, Cherry-girl," Henry said.

Summer pointed to Tom Quinn, collapsed in a heap on the boat floor. "Sick man," she said, pointing, but the man ignored her.

"Sick man," Buck repeated.

The stranger glanced at Quinn, then Buck. "Come," he said.

"He speaks English!"

"Little," the wizened man replied.

Summer pulled Cherry toward the bow. "We're getting off. Hold my hand."

"I don' like dis, Miz Summah."

"I think he's here to help. We have to trust him." Summer reached for the man's hand, but he motioned her aside and pointed to Cherry.

"Okay, you go first, we're right behind you." Summer stepped aside for Cherry to exit the craft.

"I ain't goin' wid him!" Cherry argued, but Summer pushed her ahead and watched as Cherry accepted the stranger's hand and was pulled into a narrow trail in the thick mangrove. "Hurry up!" she pleaded, then disappeared beyond the stranger into the thick brush.

Again, the stranger motioned Summer aside and pointed to Buck.

"Her first," Buck ordered, pointing to Summer," but the man pointed at him to come, leaving Summer the only one on board aside from Tom Quinn crumpled on the floor. With Henry vanished into the opening in the mangrove, Summer held her hand out again, but the stranger turned his back.

"Ain't going without her," she heard Henry say.

"Bad," the man replied.

"She ain't bad, and I ain't going without her."

Jocelyn Miller

A few moments of silence and the man turned to her again, holding out his hand.

What is this about? Why doesn't he want me?

The first sensation she had as she slipped her hand into his was the roughness of his skin. The second sensation was riveting; an electrical charge, as if she had stuck her finger into a live socket, exploded throughout her body. He felt it too, she was certain, by the look in his eyes. His expression changed from distrust to shock, to a piercing stare as he pulled her ashore. The thought crossed her mind that, like the bandana in the box, they would not be able to separate their hands, so strong was the jolt.

He pulled her to bank, and to her relief, their connection severed. Her attention was now diverted to find a foothold on the slippery mangrove roots, which proved not difficult. As he stepped backward she was surprised to find earth at her feet, and more dark men in in similar costume waiting behind the stranger. At first her skin prickled in fear, as there was no sign of Henry or Cherry.

Remembering Quinn, she point toward the boat, her view blocked by the stranger. "The man in the boat," she said. "He's sick and needs help." Perhaps the stranger would understand her words.

"No white man," was the reply.

"No...? Oh so that's it, you don't like our color," she said, not knowing if the man understood or not.

"No white man. White man bad."

"We can't leave him here," she pleaded. Nasty as Quinn was, her conscience wouldn't allow it.

The man's eyes pierced hers, the intensity causing her to shift and fidget in place. The stranger was right, Tom Quinn truly was a bad man and this was a conundrum!

"Man make trouble," the stranger said, as if reading her mind.

Goosebumps prickled her skin as the stranger's stare intensified. As odd as it was, the sensation that he was forcing himself into her head became overpowering. Visions of Tom Quinn raising havoc played through her head like a movie. She saw him clear as day in a village, the man's village, club in hand, women screaming. *Oh my God, Cherry's assailant! Could it be?*

Summer shook herself loose from the vision, sure that this strange man held a power over her, that they had shared the vision, somehow; that they both knew what was to come. Still, she could not leave Quinn to rot in the skiff.

"I take care of man," she said, touching her hand to her chest. "Me. I take care of man."

It was an agreement between them, two people who shared the same vision. It was accepted, and the stranger indicated to two young men to retrieve Tom Quinn from the skiff.

"Come," the stranger said, and she followed behind with three other natives taking up the rear. Quinn was practically dragged by the two muscular, able-bodied natives, his head rolling on his chest, unconscious. They walked a short distance until they came upon a hut of sorts, a thatched roof of palm protecting a raised platform from rain and elements. There, the men laid Quinn. The plumed man crouched next to him and inspected his body, removing the soiled and tattered blanket scrap from his arm. The entire group of spectators stood beneath the thatched roof watching until the putrid smell of the wound reached their nostrils, at which time they simultaneously stepped backward.

The plumed man spoke his native tongue to the other men, and they dashed off into the trees while the refugees stood looking at one another.

"Where are we? What's gonna happen to us? I'se so scared!"

"Don't be scared, Cherry girl. I'm here and ain't nothin' gonna happen to you," Buck said, putting an arm around her.

What a predicament! Summer thought. Where the heck were they? Where were they going? What was Guy doing at this moment? Did he know yet that she was gone? Was she gone, or just gone over the edge? Most of all, how would they get out of here? How would she get Cherry home to Magnolia? How would she get home to Guy?

Jocelyn Miller

18

"Wha..., Quinn groaned.

The air hung heavy as a damp towel. A river of sweat ran down Summer's forehead, drenched her armpits and brought mosquitos like buzzards to road kill. Quinn was soaked to the bone yet shivered feverishly as he lay upon the hut floor. On arrival at the camp, she and Quinn were singled out and separated from Cherry and Buck, who were allowed to move freely about if they wished—which they did not—but sat stoically with their small group on the hut floor. Summer and Quinn, however, were forced to remain on display, though the women and children turned their heads away when passing; only the men came to stare and whisper to one another.

"Wha'd dey want?" Cherry whispered. "Why dey stare at you?" she asked.

Every once in a while a teenaged boy, accompanied by his cronies, came to spit and spew a few derogatory remarks—at least they sounded derogatory to the hapless hostages.

"Hatki Tayki!"[6] he yelled, his eyes angrily anchored on Summer. At his third or fourth pass, Cherry's tolerance level evaporated.

---

[6] Miccosukee language of the Seminole meaning "white woman."

"What's wrong wid him? I's hot and tired and don' like dat dumb boy yellin' at us." Cherry stood, much to Summer's surprise, and walked to the edge of the hut floor. "Git on outta here you dirty black boy!"

The boy grinned ear to ear.

"Well, that worked," Summer said and rolled her eyes. She already deduced that the natives did not particularly care for white folks, *but why?* Even if the women wouldn't look at her, she couldn't stop looking at *them* as they passed the open-air hut during their daily chores. Their skirts were full and long, made of calico or other prints, gathered at the waist, topped by a short, long-sleeved blouse which barely covered their breasts before ending to show an expanse of bare midriff. The nipples of old women, whose once full breasts were now sagged and flattened against their dark bodies, peeked out below their crop-tops. A gathered cape circled the neck entirely and ended just below shoulder length. Hair was fringed at the forehead and pulled back into a tight bun. Most amazing were the beaded necklaces which, strand after strand, circled the grown women's necks, some stacked all the way to the chin. Even the female children sported beaded necklaces, though not as many as the older women. It made Summer sweat even more, just thinking of the airless, steaming flesh beneath the layers of beads.

At long last, after several sweltering hours on the hut floor and countless verbal bashings by the local male native population, the old man returned. He pointed to Summer and motioned her to follow.

"You goin' wid him?" Cherry asked.

"Do I have a choice?"

"You go wid her, Buck."

He rose off the floor, but the old man motioned him to sit. "Guess you's goin' alone, Miss Summah."

"It's okay, Buck," and it was. Whatever electrifying event she and the old man had shared, she knew instinctively was not a danger to her well-being; they connected, somehow.

Summer followed the stranger to another open-air hut where he motioned her to sit on a thick chunk of log while he did the same across from her. He stared intensely; and she, not knowing what to say or do, or even if he would understand if she did speak, began to fidget.

"I know English," he said, finally breaking the silence. "I learn from white man who live with my people when I child."

"Why don't your people like me?" she asked.

Jocelyn Miller

"Because of war. White man make war."

She couldn't argue that.

"Women no look at white man. Bad. Child no look at white man."

"We're not here to make war."

"Why you come?"

Good question, impossible to answer.

"White man bad trouble".

"Mr. Quinn needs good medicine. Do you have medicine?"

"My mans bring medicine. You shaman. You fix. You go."

"Sha…? I'm not a shaman."

"You shaman. I see in eyes. You see in eyes. You see white man is bad, make trouble. You fix, you go."

"How do we go? We don't know the way."

"We take you Okeechobee. You go."

His eyes diverted past her shoulder, and she turned to see the two men who had been sent off earlier, returning with a pouch exposing vegetation which sprouted from its gathered leather opening.

"Come," he ordered, taking the pouch and moving to another hut, one with a primitive stove. The woman who had been preparing food in the hut, turned and left when she saw them coming. A fire was already blazing, over which was a pot of steaming water. The man opened the pouch and dumped the vegetation into the pot, then stirred with a carved wooden spoon.

"We make medicine," he said. "White man get better. You go."

"Yes, we go." Summer agreed. *We go, we go, we go where?* Other men of the camp had gathered around the hut, watching, or, more to the truth, watching Summer and whispering to one another. A younger man said something to the elder, to which he replied gruffly in their language. The young man did not take it politely and raised his voice, gesturing toward her.

Oh, oh, she thought. *This is about me.*

The other men laughed, and the younger man spewed a few nasty native words and left the group.

The elder continued stirring the pot, which now bubbled and spewed a shower of tiny hot droplets into the air.

"He want you. Say you be wife. Make you work hard," the elder said after a long silence.

Jocelyn Miller

"I certainly hope you said 'no'!

"I say no. You go."

"We go." *We go fast.* This was certainly not what she bargained for when she envisioned her search for Cherry. Certainly not to be the enslaved wife of a native!

Concentration returned to the pharmaceutical efforts of the shaman, as Summer began to think of the old wizened man. "What will we do with this…this medicine?" she asked, as the he drained the now green and steaming water into a small separate bowl.

"You see," the man said. For the wilted greenery, he retrieved a large wooden mortar and mashed the contents with a wooden pestle until it was a fine paste.

"Take," he instructed, handing Summer the bowl with the steaming water. "Come," he commanded; and she followed behind, he with the mortar and pestle and she with the steaming green water. Its vapor emitted a strong rotten plant odor, causing her to gag as she trudged along behind him.

Upon returning to the familiar hut with Cherry and Buck sitting on the floor a distance away from Tom Quinn, the shaman knelt beside the ill man and lifted his head.

"Give drink," he instructed.

Tom Quinn looked quite dead, and if he hadn't groaned as the Shaman lifted his head onto his lap, Summer would have thought he was ready for the graveyard.

Cherry and Buck now stood close to view the next process, which was to get the comatose man to drink the putrid green liquid from the bowl, and it was Summer's job to do so.

"I've been chosen to be the shaman's assistant," she informed her companions. She blew into the bowl to cool the contents before attempting the task.

"They want us out of here in a hurry," she said. As soon as Quinn is ready to leave, we have to go."

"Why can't we go back? Leave dat man here and go back?" Cherry asked.

"No!" the Shaman said. "No go back. We take Okeechobee. White man no stay."

"We have the boat. We could go back the way we came." Henry said.

Jocelyn Miller

"No boat," the Shaman said.

"Yes, we have boat," Summer replied.

"No boat. We take boat.

At that statement, Buck briskly stepped off the platform and took off in the direction from which they had arrived.

"Hmmph," the shaman said, and nodded, which Summer construed to mean '*hurry up*'. She proceeded with her attempt to get some of the green liquid down Quinn's throat. He coughed, though most of the concoction seemed to dribble down his chin and onto his filthy shirt. She held the bowl to his lips a second time with the same outcome; some down his throat, most down his shirt.

The Shaman was obviously not pleased with her nursing skills, and this time changed places with her. They traded places, she holding Quinn's head up while the shaman pinched the man's lips together and succeeded in pouring the rest of the liquid down Quinn's throat.

"Here he come." Cherry said, watching Buck return.

"Ain't there!" Henry said. "The boat ain't there!"

"No!" Cherry cried. "I jes wants to go home to my baby, my mama, Evaline...my peoples!"

"Where's our boat?" Summer demanded.

"Boat mine. I trade. This Seminole land. Boat mine."

The conversation was obviously closed, as the shaman, without any consideration of the lost boat, or the lost people, now unwrapped the tattered blanket bandage from Quinn's arm to expose the fetid, oozing wound.

Not only did Cherry weep in the background over the lost boat, but when the odor of the festering wound reached her nostrils, she gagged and coughed. Summer fought back nausea as the Shaman now scraped the green mush out of the mortar over the wound. He recovered it with the filthy blanket scrap bandage, and stood. "He sleep. Get better. You go," he said, and left.

19

"It's an unfortunate miracle," Summer said to herself as Tom Quinn disappeared into the brush to relieve himself. For ten days the small group had resided alongside the Seminole, waiting and watching as Quinn's wound miraculously healed itself, no doubt due to the mysterious concoction cooked up by the shaman. They were well fed, as the Seminole's gardens yielded much food: squash, corn and pumpkins, as well as the many fat pigs that wandered the campground.

"You go Okeechobee with the sun," the shaman informed them the previous night as they sat around their own private campfire. He had paid them a short visit with this blunt message and departed to join the men on the neighboring chickee hut. The tribe remained somewhat hostile to Quinn and Summer, but Cherry and Buck were invited many times to mingle with the natives.

Cherry objected in the beginning, but the lure of beads and fresh clothing enticed her. The women fussed over her, and the young men hovered like bees, which was, Summer noticed, much to Buck's disgust. Now, as she watched, Cherry appeared quite happy as the women dressed her in a brightly colored outfit in the same style as their own: long skirt, cropped top and neck cape. The attire well-adorned her trim figure, though the crop-top displayed a protruding rib or two due to so

Jocelyn Miller

many months of near starvation at Magnolia and her forced journey to Florida. The women of the camp also tamed her fuzzy hair into a neat bun, and adorned her neck with rows of beaded strands traded for by the young men of the tribe who wanted to win her favor.

"She looks like one of them savages now. It's her color," Quinn observed on his return from the brush. "They got their feathers ruffled with the Seminole wars. Don't like us white folks."

"So I understand," Summer said, watching Cherry twirl in her new outfit. "You look pretty!" she yelled across the expanse of yard. Cherry smiled a big toothy grin and waved.

Summer remembered how much Cherry longed for a fancy bonnet, hooped skirt and to live in Savannah after the Emancipation. *Far cry from that dream,* she thought.

"Don't encourage her to be like those savages," Quinn growled.

"Why not? She looks happy. What have you given her but abuse?"

"Shut up," he said. "That girl is mine."

"Buck probably has a thing or two to say about that."

"Buck, my ass. I took her, and she's mine. Ain't his."

Quinn had obviously recovered from the sorry state he had been in when they arrived at the camp, to a sorrier state of nastiness. It was difficult for Summer to digest, but here she sat in a Seminole camp in the swamps of Florida in the year 1864 studying Quinn's profile: grizzled beard, brows furrowed, face scowling as he watched Cherry twirl and laugh.

"Guess you've lost her then. Your charming manner couldn't keep her," she said, at which time she felt a painful slug to her arm. "Ouch!"

"You're a loud-mouthed Yankee bitch. Stop sassin' me."

Damn, that hurt. She moved a few feet away from him, out of reach in case he decided to punch her again. She had no protection here, as Buck had gone hunting with the native men. Shaman was too old to protect her, and, as a white woman, she was a despicable object to the tribe. That is, aside from the one young fellow who desired her as wife. She suddenly felt very alone and missed Guy...home...Jesse. Her arm throbbed from Quinn's punch and tears threatened just wondering how this situation would be resolved...*how will I get us home safely?*

Jocelyn Miller

As night fell, a great bustle of activity overtook the camp. Henry Buck and the hunters returned with a half-dozen wild turkeys and a huge alligator. All were skinned, de-feathered, sliced, diced, and any other form of utilization until all signs of meat disappeared with the women to their kitchens. This was obviously a celebration and Summer wondered if it were not in jubilation of their departure in the morning. *"He get well, you go,"* the shaman had said. Perhaps this was the big send-off?

As the fires blazed, bottles of whiskey were brought forth and shared amongst the men. One drunken native passed too close to their fire, where Quinn grabbed it from him and sent him on his way to sleep it off.

"You shouldn't do that," Buck said.

"Shut-up nigger. I don't take orders from you," he replied, swigged from the bottle and sat sullenly watching the group of Seminole men who sat talking and laughing around a fire in the next chickee hut. After a while he rose and headed toward the group.

"Oh, no," Cherry said, watching Quinn. "Dat man gonna be trouble if he drink dat bottle," she whispered to Summer.

"I don't like this one bit." Buck said.

The thought didn't set well with Summer, either, who had already suffered a punch from a *sober* Quinn.

"Stay away from him, Cherry. He's mad that you're dressing like one of them." She leaned closer, "...and mad that Buck has taken a liking to you," she whispered.

Cherry's eyebrows arched. "Him?" She eyed Henry across the fire. "He likin' me?" she whispered.

"Looks that way to me."

"Well he sure don' act like it."

"What you gals talkin' about?" Buck asked.

"Talkin' 'bout Quinn. He gonna be trouble tonight." Cherry replied.

"That man was born trouble," Buck replied, watching as Quinn stepped into the far chickee hut to hover in his drunken stupor over a group of Seminole men.

Dead silence. All chatter and laughter stopped from the Seminole group. The vision of Quinn, club in hand, and shrieking women, reasserted itself in Summer's mind. "Oh, oh," she said. Her heart skipped a beat with apprehension of what could come.

Jocelyn Miller

"What'sa matter, you rotten bunch of savages?" Quinn bellowed, and tilted his head backward for another gulp from the bottle. "Don't let ole' Quinn stop the party. Carry on." He wiped the spilt liquor from his chin.

Silence, as the stilled group kept their eyes on the intruder.

"Dammit! Carry on, I said!" He took another swig from the bottle, but apparently it was empty. He turned it upside down, shook it to no avail, and tossed it into the brush.

Buck stood. "This ain't good." He stepped off the chickee and walked toward Quinn. "Hey, Mr. Quinn, come on back. Best to leave these men alone."

Quinn either didn't hear him, or chose to ignore Henry's attempt to avoid altercation.

"Gimmee that bottle," Quinn said to the closest native. He swooped to grab the whiskey bottle from the man's hand but lost his balance and fell face first into the campfire.

The natives broke out in a roar of laughter as Quinn struggled in an attempt to rise, hollering like a banshee, while Buck raced to the chickee and pulled him from the fire.

"Damn savage threw me into the fire! I'll teach 'em a lesson or two!" He shook free from Henry's grasp and swaggered to the circle of men, forcing his face into the hapless native with the whiskey bottle. "Come on, you yellow-bellied-red-faced coward."

Henry Buck stepped backward off the chickee while Summer quickly hastened to his side. Both were helpless to interfere as Tom Quinn was beyond return to any semblance of order.

"Buck! Miz Summah! Git on back heah!" Cherry yelled from their chickee.

Tension was thick as the group of natives murmured and eyed one another. The words spoken were not understood by Summer or Buck, but before Summer came to any resolution of the situation, all hell broke loose. The natives, who to this moment had sat peacefully, exploded into a hollering-fist-flying-mob of angry men. Tom Quinn flew from the chickee like a cannon ball, landing unceremoniously on his behind and grunting incoherently as he struggled to raise himself off the ground. When finally on his feet, Buck grabbed him by the scuff of his shirt.

"Enough o' this, Mr. Quinn. You's gonna get us in a pile

Jocelyn Miller

o'trouble." He shoved the struggling Quinn toward their chickee.

Henry looked downright....*scary,* Summer thought, but with relief. Buck's anger made her feel safe and they definitely needed to feel safe at this moment.

Instead of heading to the chickee, Quinn staggered off into the brush.

"He bad man."

They turned to see the shaman behind them.

"You go with sun," He ordered.

"Yes," they answered simultaneously. Summer was sure that if they didn't, or at least Quinn didn't go, none of them would be on earth much longer; they had worn out their welcome.

Jocelyn Miller

20

"*Hatki Nakni...!*"
Summer couldn't make out the rest of words, but she knew instinctively that the decibel and tone of voice translated to nothing short of *trouble!* She sat straight up off her bedding on the floor of the chickee hut, as did Cherry.

"What? What goin' on out der?"

Henry too had woken and stood tall over them. "Quinn ain't here!" he shouted. It was obvious, even in the dark of the wee hours, that the big lump of Quinn was missing from his pallet on the floor.

More bloodcurdling screams shot Summer's neck hairs on end. "Oh, no! Something bad is happening!"

On cue, two young woman ran past the chickee. "Hatki Nakni!" they screamed and disappeared.

Soon enough, and much to the trio's horror, Quinn burst into sight, lumbering unsteadily, bottle in hand, and obviously still under the influence of the whiskey.

Jocelyn Miller

As he attempted to pass the chickee, Henry jumped off the platform, blocking his path.

"Wha'd you doin', Quinn?" he asked, poking Quinn in the chest as he spoke. "You done caused us enough grief. Git to bed."

"I'm gettin' me one of them little Indian wenches, so get outta my way."

"You ain't," Henry replied.

"And you ain't gettin' my Cherry girl, neither. Come'ere, girl," he ordered, spotting Cherry in the chickee.

"No sah, I ain't," she stepped behind Summer.

"You ain't touching her," Buck said.

"Damn you!" Quinn bunched a fist and slugged Henry hard on the chin. He stumbled backward, his fall broken by the platform of the chickee. Summer rushed to help him to his feet, but by this time the bottle of whiskey had dropped and was heard rolling across the floor. Dark or not, Quinn was fast. He leapt up onto the chickee, grabbed Cherry by the arm and dragged her into the brush.

"Oh, my God, get her!" Summer shrieked. "He's gone nuts!"

In the distance, the ground thump, thump, thumped; and before long a group of native men trampled through the dark of the chickee like a herd of wild horses and disappeared into the brush in Quinn's direction.

"They got rifles," Buck noted, and took off behind them, leaving Summer standing alone.

Immediately, a group of blanket-wrapped women appeared before her, barefoot on the dirt. Their appearance was changed from the neatness of their daily attire. Black hair hung thickly down their backs, and without the signature costume of cropped shirt and long skirt, they appeared to Summer as spirits of the night. She could barely make out their dark faces, but sensed their eyes hooked into her flesh, watching silently. She shook with the creepiness of it.

Jocelyn Miller

The spell was broken by the hoots and hollers of the men as they returned with a struggling Tom Quinn. The posse passed the chickee, leaving Buck and Cherry behind.

"Dat man is evil!" she cried, quite shaken from her ordeal and rubbing her arm where his grip had pressed indents into her flesh.

"You're okay now," Summer said, putting her arm around the trembling woman.

"I don't know what they's gonna to do to him." Buck watched the group disappear further into the darkness of the camp. They would find out soon enough.

After a very restless few hours of sleep, Summer, Henry, and Cherry were summoned to camp center, where Quinn was tied to a post. The sun had not yet peeked over the palms, but already the air was heavy and moist.

"It's about time," Quinn grumbled. "Tell them savages to let me go."

Despite his behavior, Summer felt an ounce of pity for the man. He was seriously disheveled, sweaty, dirty, and obviously uncomfortable standing stick straight with his entire body secured tightly to the pole—and probably had a massive hangover as well.

What on earth am I doing here? she asked herself. The situation was absurd. When she started out on this endeavor to find Cherry, never once did she think she would be on any grounds but Magnolia. At least she knew the people there, knew the layout of the land, but here— here she was a stranger and this was one heck of a predicament!

The shaman approached the group.

"Oh, oh" she sighed, not having a clue of what to say to him, or to Quinn.

The shaman looked directly at her. "He bad. You know. You go, bad man stay."

"No," Buck said. "We take bad man."

"No. He stay," The shaman replied, gruffly.

Jocelyn Miller

"We can't leave him here," Summer said to the shaman. "It's not right."

"Damn right you can't leave me here!" Quinn growled. "Get them damn savages to untie me!"

"Shut up. You're making it worse," she said. "You deserve to be left here. You brought this on yourself—and us."

The shaman was quiet, his old eyes staring at Quinn. "He fight," he finally said and then yelled in his language to men standing close by. They quickly approached Quinn with knives.

"Oh no!" Summer screamed, terrified of what could happen next. "Don't kill him!"

"No kill," the shaman said. "He fight."

The rest of the tribe understood exactly what to do, as men formed a large circle around the pole. Quinn was cut free, but his attempts to leave the circle were quickly curtailed as the circle was tight as a drum with bodies. Summer and Cherry could only peek between the shoulders of the natives to see what was happening. Buck, so well accepted in the tribe at this point, broke into the line and took a place in the ring.

"What's happening?" Summer asked, standing behind him. 'I can barely see."

"They gave him a club, and another man have a club. They gonna fight."

Summer's heart jumped at his words. "A club?" *The vision! Cherry at the portico doors, Quinn coming for her with a club!*

A great uproar from the crowd brought her back to the moment. She and Cherry bobbed their heads like pecking hens, trying to find a peephole in the circle of men. When she did find a viewpoint, she had to take turns with Cherry, alternating every moment or two.

Quinn's opponent was smaller than he but, unlike Quinn, was more muscle than bulk. He was lithe and moved quickly, darting and dancing around Quinn, striking the air with his club, twirling, circling, *taunting*. Quinn, meanwhile, did circles in place, keeping an eye on the man's club, gripping his own in what appeared to Summer to be a baseball stance at home plate. Quinn grunted and lunged several times, but missed the target.

Jocelyn Miller

Cherry hung tightly to Summer as they both pressed their heads together in order to view the spectacle simultaneously through a narrow space between Henry's arm and the native next to him. They flinched with each swing of the club, and when Quinn took a strike to the arm, he let out a yell of pain, and the women hung tighter to each other in alarm. Quinn's left arm now hung limp at his side as he continued his stand against the offending native.

The native, perhaps too sure of himself, circled closer to Quinn. Quinn swung the bat, the impact hitting the man square in the abdomen. He flew backwards, landing in the dirt. Quinn laughed. The native lay a moment in the dust at which time Quinn took advantage and ran full steam toward Buck.

"Let me by," he yelled. The natives on either side of Buck stood fast as Quinn barreled into Buck, breaking the line. Buck, too, fell to the ground as Quinn trampled him in flight.

Quinn, spotting Cherry, grabbed her by the arm. "Time to leave, girl." he yelled. She screamed, her feet flying, slipping as they ran further from the broken circle. The natives wasted no time in running after them, a noisy mass of testosterone in pursuit with Summer and Buck following behind.

This is insane! Summer thought as her feet pounded the ground. *Wake up! Wake up! I'm in over my head!*

* * *

Oh the memory—*the sound!* Summer shuddered covering her eyes with her hands, her elbows resting on her knees as she sat against a palm. She cried; it was impossible not to.

When the natives caught up to Quinn, he pushed Cherry into the brush and turned to face them. His left arm, most likely broken, hung pathetically at his side.

"Come on 'n get me, you dirty scourge of the earth," he growled. "I ain't afraid of you…come and get me."

They did. His prior opponent stepped forward, having not given up the game, the test, the fight to the finish. Summer was the last to arrive at the scene, as Buck's strides were much longer than hers. She stood panting, catching her breath; the natives were spread out like brown trees before her in the lush jungle. The flapping of wings was

Jocelyn Miller

heard overhead, and then all was still. All was still until Tom Quinn swung the bat with his one good arm—and missed. The bat flew out of his hands, landing a distance away in the brush with a soft 'whoosh.' His eyes registered total surprise—shock—as he stood facing his foe, his barrel chest heaving under the exertion, and the stress and fear of the moment.

Then…*the sound.* She couldn't shake the sound of his skull cracking as the opponent swung his bat, caving in Quinn's head with the one fatal blow. Cherry screamed from the brush as Quinn came crashing down next to her, *next to her for the last time on earth,* blood pumping from his severe wound, one eye dangling, looking downward, as if spotting where to land. No, it would never be forgotten; Cherry, screaming in the background, and the sudden burst of bright stars in a dark sky as Summer crumpled to the ground unconscious.

Jocelyn Miller

21

"Sun come up here, sun go down there. Follow path." Shaman pointed southward.

"Wha'd he say?" Cherry asked, sweat dripping from her chin. She looked pretty in her new attire, despite the high humidity.

"He wants us to head south; I think there's a path." *Oh for a compass!* Summer was darn nervous about setting out on this venture.

Buck was busy gathering whatever he could in the way of weaponry. He had nothing to barter with and Summer hoped that with his good graces with the tribe, they would at least give him a rifle.

The tribe was sending them on their way. Buck buried Tom Quinn the night before, close to where he lay in death, which had not been an easy task without a shovel. The grave was shallow, covered with palm leaves and whatever else they could scavenge. Now they had to move on.

The shaman indicated that Cherry and Buck were welcome to stay with the tribe. He even made an exception for Summer, and she supposed her acceptance was due to the 'visionary powers' she and the shaman shared. *We sure do*, she thought, shuddering at the memory of Tom Quinn and his battered face. That was one vision she'd like to erase from memory.

Jocelyn Miller

"We can't go back without the boat," Summer surmised as they sat around their chickee hut campfire the night of Tom Quinn's death. Decisions had to be made. None of them wanted to stay with the tribe, and they politely declined the offer. The shaman indicated there was a white settlement further south, and they decided to shoot for it.

As the women prepared to leave, Buck returned with a rifle, much to Summer's relief. "Not much ammo," he said. "Can't waste it."

"Hopefully there's nothing we'll have to shoot—except food...maybe...." Remembering her brief stint at skinning squirrels at Magnolia, she squelched a gag. "Good thing Cherry is with us," she added. "She's good at preparing meat."

"Now how you know dat, Miz Summah?" Cherry placed her hands on her hips and viewed Summer with great curiosity.

Oops. "I...I just suppose you are, considering where you came from." She quickly busied herself with the items that were her responsibility to carry: a cooking pot given by the women of the tribe, a carved ladle, two gourds filled with water, all to be wrapped satchel-like in the thin blanket that came with them on the skiff.

"Don' you know nothin' 'bout preparing meat?"

"Not really. I'm a city girl."

"Where you from, anyways?"

"Chica..." she stopped. Would Cherry remember? "Chicago," she finished.

"Dat sound like somthin' Evaline say one time, dat she from dat Chicago place."

"Who's Evaline?"

"Evaline, she my friend. I miss her. She'd know what to do here in dis...." She looked off into the brush. "...dis scary place."

For the next four hours the trio stayed on course by following a footpath well worn by the Seminoles. Hungry mosquitos relentlessly buzzed around their heads, and exposed flesh was raised with white and itchy bumps.

"Gonna get malaria if dis keep up." Cherry said. "Lot's of times my peoples get malaria from da 'skeeters in da rice paddies back home. Wish I was der now, and not here. Wish I could see my mama, my baby Percy. He missin' me!" Cherry's voice broke into sobs, causing the group to stop and rest while she composed herself.

Jocelyn Miller

Buck put a strong arm around her. "It's okay, girl. Buck here gonna take care of you ladies. You's gonna get home. You will."

"Yes you will, Cherry. Let's just keep going until we can find a boat to take you home. I'll bet there are big boats down there on the ocean that can take us all back to where we came from. *Well, not quite all of us.....* It sounded good, anyway. Just how this was going to play out, she couldn't fathom. From her time-travel experience at Magnolia, all she could do then was roll with the punches and let the mysteries of the experience work itself out. It was the same as now, she had no control; she had to keep on going, putting one foot in front of the other until she woke up with Guy next to her at Magnolia in the 21st century, and Cherry was home again.

* * *

Three hot, bug-infested, frightening nights later the weary group reached a great body of water, the Okeechobee. The Seminole path had blessedly led them right to it. Without delay, Summer and Cherry removed their satchels and ran into the water until they were up to their waists. Soon Buck followed and, like kids, they splashed and played, cooling their heated bodies in the coolness and reveling that they had come such a distance in the oppressive heat without collapsing.

"You're so good at this," Summer said later that night while watching Cherry prepare her bed. Summer followed suit, gathering dried grasses and piling them up enough to cushion her body against the hard ground. She covered her pile with the worn blanket, as Cherry had covered hers with two Yankee jackets, the very ones taken from the soldiers Tom Quinn had murdered in Jacksonville.

Quinn's hook and line were still in Cherry's possession, as well as the flint starter. Buck built a campfire while the women fished. Cherry's satchel had contained squash and half a dozen flatbreads, now all dwindling, that the Indian women had given them. With a few small fish, they were able to compile a meal, meager as it was.

Summer looked out over the great expanse of water and wondered what it looked like in the 21st century. It was a lovely sight at sunset; the colors of the setting sun reflected in the shallow water of its bank. Birds fed at the water's edge, some as large as a toddler. *Unspoiled*

Jocelyn Miller

and beautiful. She would have to visit the lake in present time and hoped she would not be disappointed.

Morning came and so did the sweltering heat. The fire was out and the mosquitos took it as an invitation to dine on the intruders.

"There's gotta be something here growing that will keep the damn bugs away!" Summer said. *Think…what did the Seminoles use at camp? Grass—some kind of grass.* "We need to find that tall grass that the Indians rubbed over themselves. Remember? They gave us some, too."

She and Cherry investigated the vegetation alongside of the bank. Most was scruffy, close to the ground, but as they walked they came across a patch of very tall grasses[7].

"Is dis it?" Cherry asked.

"It won't hurt to try."

They broke many blades off close to the root and carried them back to Buck. He had disposed of the campfire and was waiting for the women.

"Here," Summer said, handing him a fist-full of grass blades. "Crumple this up and wipe it on your body. I don't know if this is the right stuff, but we won't know until we try."

"Seems to be working," Summer said later, as they marched along the river bank, headed south—or so they hoped.

"Wish I knew where we was headed." Buck said, as if reading her thoughts.

Summer envisioned the state of Florida as they plodded alongside the lake. She placed Okeechobee, the big circle of blue on the map. South of that were the Keys. Southwest of Miami were the Everglades. In the Everglades sat Everglades City, where this crazy journey began. She thought of Captain Jack and wondered if he were missed at home. How much time had passed, she hadn't a clue, as time had no meaning in this circumstance. The journey would have to take its course; as much as she felt every part of it, she had to keep in mind that she was an observer on this journey, and this was Cherry's life. These events happened so very long ago and Summer was here to bring Cherry home. Somehow, she would get Cherry home to Magnolia.

---

[7] Citronella

Jocelyn Miller

22

"Shhh!" Buck ordered.

They crouched in the tall grass, their bodies now accustomed to the pricks and slices from the grasses and other unforgiving vegetation of the swamp. Two weeks of battling the creatures and elements in the humid steamy air had dulled their senses to the stink of their own bodies and the pain of the slices, scrapes and bruises. Stomachs ached from lack of and want of good food, and now, at this moment, they were hopeful in appeasing their hunger with a single small swamp deer that stood apprehensively still amidst the Cypress knees. Peeking through the slender blades, they held their breath as sweat rolled freely down their shiny faces. Buck raised the rifle slowly, quietly, but before he could pull the trigger another shot echoed through the cypress, and the small deer fell.

"No!" Cherry screamed. "It's ours!" she yelled, while scrambling through the grass to the fallen animal.

"Cherry, come back," Summer yelled, highly concerned over who, or what, would come from the brush to claim their kill.

"It was ours," Cherry cried, her hands resting possessively on the warm carcass.

Jocelyn Miller

"Ain't yours." A voice rose from the Cypress, and then its owner, a thin scraggly bearded filthy picture of a man, sauntered from the swampy wilderness. "Ain't yours, darky. It's won fair and square."

Summer and Buck rushed to Cherry's side, lest the filthy beast of a man cause harm. "Where do you come from? Is there a town nearby?" Summer asked the stranger.

"Ha! A town?" he grinned, black spaces in his mouth where teeth had once been. "Fort Dallas, if you can call that a town. Where you headed?"

"We want to get to the ocean. We need a boat to take us home."

Buck pulled Cherry from the fallen deer. "We needs food," he said.

The stranger looked Summer up and down. "What you doin' here with these darkies?"

"It's a long story, mister. Can you help us? We need food, a place to sleep and a boat to home."

The stranger eyed Buck and his rifle suspiciously. The strapping black man towered well over his wizened frame and presented a daunting figure with the rifle gripped in his muscular hands.

"You, boy, help me carry this deer and you can all eat."

Fort Dallas! Our prayers are answered! Summer thought as she and Cherry took up the rear on the procession to the fort. Of course she had never heard of Fort Dallas,[8] but it sounded like an oasis in the desert, a civilization from which they could hire a boat and head for home.

At the first sight of the fort, her heart leapt with joy, for here were several buildings which surely represented a civilized community. Oh, the disappointment to find that the buildings were occupied not by an army but by several grizzled men, some wearing the remnants of uniforms; faded blue, filthy grey. *Deserters!* Cherry clung close, as the stares of the disheveled group of men was surely reminiscent of her bout with the lusty soldiers of the invading Union army at Magnolia.

"I don' like dis, Miz Summah. I don' like da way dese men lookin' at us."

---

[8] Fort Dallas was built along the Miami River during the Seminole wars to house the U.S. army. The city of Miami sprouted from this area. During the Civil War years, it fell to ruin and was a gathering spot for deserters, vagrants and criminals.

Jocelyn Miller

"Just stay close, Cherry."

"Don't you gals worry," Buck assured them over his shoulder. "Ain't nothin' gonna happen with Buck here."

"Hey, Johnny, where'd you find an Injun Princess?" one of the men yelled. Cherry's Seminole attire, though tattered through its swamp journey, still flatteringly adorned her lovely shape as they followed their grizzled leader past the smaller buildings to the largest one. Buck and the stranger set down the carcass of the deer while the group of scraggly men gathered around them. A large man in faded greys broke through the gathering.

"What's with nigger boy and the women?" he asked, ignoring the trio.

"Found 'em in the woods. They was lookin' to shoot this deer, but I beat 'em to it."

"All we want is some food, a place to sleep and a boat to take us back home," Summer interjected. She fought to curb an uneasiness growing inside. The men were shifty looking and there were too many of them for poor Buck to battle if it came to that, despite his vow of protection. Her own clothes were a point of curiosity for the men; jeans ragged and torn, a filthy tank-top, certainly too revealing for this time period. She self-consciously crossed her arms over her chest to hide her breasts from the stares. She and Cherry were totally at the camp's mercy.

The man turned to her. "You ain't gettin' a boat here. Guess you don't know there's a war goin' on. Ain't no passenger boats pickin' up white women and darkies."

"We can eat and sleep then, and move on. This man promised us a share of the meat."

The man gave the hunter a look of disapproval.

"I did," he admitted. "This darky helped carry it here."

They built their own campfire that evening after perusing the grounds together. Buck was adamant that the women stick close to him and it did not take any arm twisting to convince them, as the filthy, disheveled men continued to stare lewdly.

The setting of Fort Dallas was lovely, nestled on the banks of a palm lined river that led, Summer assumed, to the Atlantic. When Buck remarked on a skiff tied to a post, she looked with longing at its empty interior. How she wished they could jump in and sail away from this

Jocelyn Miller

place— back to familiar territory—back to Magnolia! She shuddered; danger hovered here, of that she was sure.

Later, they consumed the meat with great relish around their campfire. Soon, they were offered pineapples and bananas from a few of the grizzled men who taunted the fruit before them.

"Comes with a price," they were informed. After a few more lewd barters and taunts from the gruff inhabitants of Fort Dallas, Buck stood to his full height, which well towered over the rowdy bunch.

"Git away. We ain't interested."

"Ain't talkin' to you, darky."

"I'se talkin' to you, mister. These women don't want your pineapples and bananas."

"Oh, but I got a big banana for them girls!" One man said, thrusting his pelvis forward. His cronies laughed, but Buck was not amused. He grabbed the man by the shirt and lifted him off the ground, staring eyeball to eyeball.

"We ain't interested!" he growled, and tossed the man to the dirt. The other men backed away, while the lewd gesticulator found his footing and rose from the ground.

"Who you shovin', darky?"

"You wanna fight, mister? Come on, I take y'all on." Buck removed his shirt, tossing it in Cherry's direction. "Come on," he repeated, his muscular and immense chest glistening in the campfire light. The spectators backed off, leaving the opponent alone to face his foe.

Realizing that it was a one-on-one fight, the man backed off. "A skinny white bitch and nigger gal ain't worth it," he said, and the group dispersed.

The women exhaled in relief. Trust in her fellow man in this time zone did not run high in Summer's veins and the uneasy feeling of impending danger clung to her like moss to a stone.

"We should make our beds close together," Buck said.

A small shanty at the edge of the larger buildings was to be their home for the night. They had left the Seminole camp with supplies, but as they had traveled further into the swamplands, they were forced to lessen their burdens and now they had with them only the hook and line, rifle, flint striker, water gourds, tattered blanket and the two jackets from the dead soldiers in Jacksonville. Cherry wisely refused to depart with the jackets, as they were the only comfort from the hard ground at night.

Sometime in the wee hours Summer woke to Buck's voice. "Wake up....something's happening out there."

"Wha...?"

Buck put a hand over her mouth. "Shhh."

The whites of his eyes shone in the darkness as he looked toward the door.

"What is it?" Cherry whispered.

"Don't know. Wait here."

Buck crept on all fours to a window, the women following behind. The moon illuminated the fort grounds before them.

"Der!" Cherry exclaimed. No sooner had she spoken when a great roar erupted from a band of Seminoles who exploded onto the grounds like a hoard of ants.

"Oh, my God!" Summer could hardly believe her eyes, but there they were, scattering bodies bathed in silver moonlight, swarming the fort.

"Let's go!" Buck ordered.

The women grabbed the blanket and coats and followed Buck as he crept out the door and around the back of the cabin. As they were on the very end of the settlement, they did not seem to be in the direct line of attack.

"To the boat!" he said. "Hurry!"

The rowdy group of deserters, asleep in the various buildings, were now awake. A great uproar of yells and screams filled the night, spurring the escaping trio onward to the river bank at high speed. Summer's heart pounded furiously in her chest at each scream of death or victory. The horrifying sounds grew louder as the battle waged on. They reached the skiff, scrambling to board the craft which rocked dramatically in the shallow water. A sudden shriek from Cherry drowned the uproar of battle.

"It's him!" she cried. "It's him!" She shrieked, pointing toward the fort.

Summer turned white with horror, for there behind them, illuminated in icy moonlight, came Tom Quinn, his face horrifically disfigured, the club grasped in the fist of his good hand, one eyeball

Jocelyn Miller

dangling against his cheek and the other staring chillingly and intently on Cherry!

"Hurry!" Cherry screamed repeatedly, while Buck found an oar and pushed the craft away from the bank.

"He's coming!" Summer yelled, grabbing the other oar and paddling furiously.

Tom Quinn trod forward, his good eye locked on Cherry. Even in the night, the vision was clear, punctuated by the glow of the moon. The closer he came the more transparent he became and the glow stronger. When the water came to his ankles he stopped, the club waving dramatically against the night. His horrid mouth opened, and they heard, even at their distance, a roar as gravelly and deep as hell itself. "I'll get you, Cherry girl!"

Jocelyn Miller

23

*T*his is not real...this is not real...I can't get hurt.   No matter how hard Summer tried to convince herself that she was merely an observer in another time zone, the more uncertainty she felt. *Heck, it sure feels real!* The vision of Tom Quinn on the banks of the river, sent a continuous wave of shudders up and down her spine.

"What was dat?" Cherry asked between sobs. She was visibly shaken. "He dead! How can he be talking to me?" Her sobs continued as Buck rowed furiously away from Fort Dallas.

"What you talkin' bout, girl? Who dead?"

"Tom Quinn! He dead and der he is sayin' my name!"

"Ain't no Tom Quinn there. Them was those Indians."

"Tell him, Miz Summah. Tell him we seen Tom Quinn!"

"I did, Buck, I saw him, too." She hated to admit it, but he *was* real, *a real ghost—a real ghost out for vengeance.*

"Oh Lordy, I ain't never gonna be safe from dat man!"

"He dead, Cherry gal. Ain't no worries with Buck around."

Summer hoped that was true.

Once safely away from the river bank, she gave up her oar and left the work to Buck. She was perplexed over the ghost of Tom Quinn.

Jocelyn Miller

Of course she had seen him back at Magnolia in the 21st century, in the wee hours of night chasing Cherry with the club, and then again while stranded on the mangrove island; but, did this mean that poor Cherry was haunted by Tom Quinn even before her own death?

At dawn the wind, which had begun as a light warm breeze, began to pick up. Buck kept the landscape in view as he rowed, but as the wind became stronger it blew them further and further away from shore.

"Bad storm coming," he said. The skiff rocked furiously in the oncoming swells, which had not been present previously, bringing to light the realization that they were now in the Atlantic.

"We gonna die! I can't swim!" Cherry screamed, as the craft rode a swell that teased to deliver them into the sea.

"Oh, my God!" Summer shut her eyes as another giant swell approached.

"Don't see no land!" Buck yelled above the clamor of thunder, which boomed deafeningly overhead. Lightning cracked around them, and all three passengers held on for dear life as swell after swell pulled them further out to sea. Torrential rains broke through the heavy overcast and came in hard pounding, stinging needles. Wet and shivering, unable to communicate over the fury of the sea and sky, they looked at one another with large saucer eyes, as if to count their number after each rise and fall of the cresting swells.

At last their luck ran out. A swell of grand magnitude raised them high on its crest and overturned the skiff on its decline.

Coughing and gagging, Summer rose to the surface of the turbulent waters, treading frantically. "Cherry! Buck!" she screamed again and again until she finally saw between the rough and tumble of oncoming swells, a head of dark hair in the distance bobbing on the surface, and then another. *They're safe!* She rode the next swell and paddled frantically to reach the others. But, naught stood still on the heaving sea; as she swam toward them, they moved further away.

"Wait!" she screamed, knowing full well they could not hear her or stop their motion. "Wait for me!" She caught a glimpse of the overturned skiff and realized it was that which kept the others afloat.

I'm not really here, she reminded herself, but after swallowing enough seawater and thinking she was a goner for sure, a miracle occurred. The storm, which had come on with such fast fury, dissipated.

Jocelyn Miller

The wind calmed, the sea flattened, the clouds broke to reveal a blue sky and bright sun, as if nothing drastic had transpired. All was back to normal—except their predicament.

"Miz Summah!" Cherry called, a black head bobbing in the gray sea. "Come on—hurry!"

Alas, she was able to reach the capsized skiff. Panting, exhausted, she held on for dear life. "This is not good, Buck," she said.

"What we gonna do?" Cherry asked through chattering teeth.

"We's gonna hold on, girl, and hope the sea take us back to land."

Hours, which seemed like days, passed in a rolling, salty grey blur of time in which the sun beat down mercilessly upon the trio.

"We're drifting further away from land," Summer noted, none too happily.

"I'se so scared," Cherry moaned. "What we gonna do, Buck?"

"Wish I knew," he answered, looking wistfully at the far distant stretch of land which now appeared again on the horizon. "I just don't know."

They drifted in silence for a while, the lap of waves lulling them to the point of continuously calling to each other for fear one would fall asleep and drift away. The sun was intense and by mid-day their faces and arms were red and blistered, but, as burnt as they were, the thought of drifting on the sea in the dark of night was more frightening than Summer could fathom, without going stark raving mad with fear.

Cherry cried softly against the side of the boat. "We can't hold on here forever— and I'se so thirsty."

"Don't drink the water!" Summer warned. She recalled this bit of lifesaving news from old movies or stories she had read. She tried to remember any other tips on sea survival, and came up empty. It occurred to her that all she had learned in her 31 of life had not prepared her for the misadventures that had befallen her since she inherited Tanglewood Plantation.

"¡Hola! ¡Hola!"

"Huh?" Summer was certain she had heard a voice over the lapping of waves against the skiff.

"¡Hola!"

"Hey!" Buck yelled, waving frantically. "There's a boat—we's saved!"

Jocelyn Miller

"Where? Where?" Cherry shrieked and waved so wildly, she slipped away from the skiff. Buck caught her by the red bandana knotted around a wad of black hair and pulled her back to the boat.

"*Iespera! ¡Venimos!⁹*"

Summer focused on a two-masted sloop approaching quickly. "Look!" she yelled.

"We's saved, we's saved! Thank you, Jesus!" Cherry sobbed with joy.

As the sloop approached, Summer counted nine men standing broadside. The man shouting orders was apparently the captain.

"*¡rápidamente, hombres! ¡antes de que ellos se ahoguen!*"¹⁰ The men on deck scurried at the orders and soon the sloop was near them and dropping a rope ladder into the water. Summer's tears mixed with the salt of the sea; she had never been so relieved in her life.

* * *

"What dey talkin'?" Cherry whispered. The group huddled on the deck of the ship wrapped in blankets, while around them men scurried about, back to the business of sailing.

"They're speaking Spanish." Summer said and stood, walking starboard to watch the tiny skiff drift off alone into the distance. It had saved them from drowning and she quietly thanked it as it disappeared against the grey mass of the Atlantic. Now they owed their lives to this Spanish speaking group of sailors for pulling them from a slow and sure death. Of course Buck and Cherry, in reality, were already dead, but what about her? Would she—could she?—have actually perished in 1864? As always, time travel was a boggling topic with so many unanswered questions.

---

⁹ "Hold on! We are coming!"

¹⁰"Hurry, men! Before they drown!"

24

"**I**t is good we find you, yes?"

"Oh, you speak English."

"May I introduce myself?" The Captain had crept up behind her as she said farewell to the lonely skiff that had saved their lives.

"Capitan Alejandro Verón Gutierrez Ruiz, at your service, señorita. Welcome to our ship, El DiabloVolante—The Flying Devil."

"Yes, it is very good that you found us. We would have died out there."

"It was bad storm, yes?" Even for us. And what is your name, *señorita?"*

"Summer Woodfield."

"Summer....*Verano..., que linda,*" he said, in approval. It is a nice name."

"Where is this boat headed?" she asked, noticing for the first time what a fine and handsome man the captain was. He was not tall, but of a decent stature, standing perhaps one head taller than her 5'6" frame. She assumed the darkness of his skin was due to not only his Spanish heritage, but to years at sea. Though not terribly young, there was not a hint of grey hair in his thick and shiny black hair. His lips parted in a smile that displayed two rows of white teeth—or so they looked against his skin and stubble of beard. A sudden vision of romping with this man naked in the Captain's quarters below clouded her thoughts for a moment. She shook them off, surprised and ashamed that the thought should even enter her mind!

"Where are you headed?" she repeated, hoping that the captain did not share her new newly acquired visionary powers, as was the case with the shaman.

"That is not so easily answered."

"You don't know where you're going?" She didn't want to look a gift horse in the mouth, but it would be extremely useful to know where they would end up and if they would have the opportunity to arrange transport back to Savannah.

"We go where the money is good, shall we say?"

Hmmm. "That is very mysterious statement."

"The mysteries of life, yes? But for now, take your friends below for food. I have asked the cook to prepare a meal."

In a small and rustic galley, they were treated to a meal of rice, beans and a mug of liquid by a gruff and solemn-looking cook.

"It's rum!" Summer exclaimed, after a trail of burning liquid passed down her throat.

"Aqua?" she asked the cook, one of the very few words of Spanish she remembered from high school.

The cook grunted, bringing a metal pitcher to the table and pouring a small amount of water into the rum.

"Ask and ye shall receive," she whispered under her breath. "Looks like we're having rum and water with our meal."

"Suits me just fine," Buck said, leaning back in the chair pouring a stream of rum down his throat. "Good food and good rum after a hard day at sea."

Summer grinned. "You're a good man, Buck."

"¡Caramba!" The cook's expletive broke the happy moment. *"¡La mirada lo que usted hizo! ¡Qué lío![11]"* He grabbed a rag and knelt beside Cherry, who was now bent over, her head between her knees. Summer and Buck jumped to their feet.

"What's wrong, Cherry-girl?" Buck asked.

"I'se sick!" she moaned.

---

[11] "Damn! Look what a mess you made!"

Jocelyn Miller

Sure enough, when Summer peeked at the cook's mission at her feet, he was wiping up a mess of rice and beans swimming in rum.

"Oops, guess that didn't agree with you." Summer helped Cherry to her feet. "Buck, go find the Captain, quick!"

Buck looked relieved to exit the scene, nearly galloping past the women and returning shortly with the captain in tow.

"She's sick," Summer said. "Where can she lie down?" Cherry leaned heavily on her arm as they followed the captain to a room aft side. Summer recognized it immediately as the Captain's quarters, and again the vision of her and the captain naked in the bed, popped into her head. *Stop it!*

Later, as she sat by Cherry, the ship rising and falling with the sea, she thought on the vision. It didn't make sense; this was not *her* story. She was an observer, a visitor to this time, so how, then, could she possibly become entwined with the handsome Captain? Why was she having this vision? She loved Guy and *only* Guy. Of this she was certain. She was, therefore, resolute; she would *not*, under any circumstance, become naked with the captain in his bed!

* * *

"Are you feeling better, Cherry?" Night approached and Cherry was now awakening. She had slept for hours, and Summer was envious, as she, too, desperately needed sleep. How long had she been awake? Thinking back on the previous day, she could hardly believe all that had occurred.

"I'se still sick, but I gots to tell you…"

"Tell me what?"

"I—I'se gonna have a baby, Miz Summah. I knows it. Two times I ain't had a monthly and now I'se sick. I hurt here," she touched her breasts and cried into the sorry pillow where Captain Ruiz rested his handsome head.

"Oh, my God," Summer moaned, resting her head in her hands. "Not now!"

"Don' be mad!" Cherry cried. "I can't help it! It was dat bad Mr. Quinn, he don' stop havin' me!"

"Oh, Cherry, I'm not mad. I know you couldn't make him stop. Don't cry, I'm not mad—just worried."

Jocelyn Miller

"I don' want dat man's baby. He a bad man, like Massah Ascot, but he meaner den Massah Ascot. I ain't even home. I want my Mama…I want Evaline!" Cherry's sobs grew deeper, and all Summer could do to comfort her was to hold her hand, wipe her brow, and pray that she could return Cherry to Magnolia before the big event, but she knew that it was not written that way.

* * *

Buck's fists clenched when he heard the news. "I'd kill him all over again," he said. White man always doin' what he want—takin' the women, making white baby nobody wants. The mama don't want him because a mean man take her whenever he want and make her with child. White man don't want him because he black. Black man don't want him because he white."

"I'm sorry, Buck. It's not like that anymore."

"What?"

"I mean it *won't* be like that anymore. Slavery is dead—no more."

"Ain't happening fast as that, missy. Long time before the black man free."

As the sky darkened into night. Buck was easily placed with the work crew in a room of hammocks below, while Captain Ruiz scratched his head over where to put the women for the night; he was obviously not going to give up his cabin.

"Aha!" he said after a time and gave instructions in Spanish to a nearby crew member who disappeared out of view. The women followed as the captain led them below to a large area outside of the crew quarters, lined with rows of barrels which were secured to the sides of the vessel.

"What's in those?" Summer asked.

"Not for the pretty *Señorita* to worry about. They are secure and will not harm you."

"You are a man of mystery," she replied, secretly pleased that he had called her 'pretty'.

The fellow who had followed the captain's instructions returned with two blankets and a bucket. Upon directions from the captain, he laid the blankets on the floor in a far corner, setting the bucket a distance away.

Jocelyn Miller

"I think that's our toilet," Summer whispered to Cherry.

"May you have a restful night," the captain said before bowing at the waist and leaving them to their privacy.

"What a gentleman," Summer said, totally perplexed at their good fortune, and especially after their run in with the hooligans at Fort Dallas and their horrid day afloat at sea.

The morning brought fair weather. The land was no longer visible, and it appeared to Summer as if they were heading into the rising sun—eastward!

"Where are we going, Captain?" she asked again, at the first opportunity.

"To Nassau," he replied. "We are to deliver goods."

"Nassau? In the Bahamas?"

"Ah, yes. Have you been?"

"No. I always wanted to go, but never expected to go in this fashion."

"It is a fine place in whatever fashion you arrive."

"We need to return to Savannah immediately."

"But we go east to the Bahamas, not west, *Señorita*. This is our business. We have no time to take passengers where they wish. We are not a passenger ship, and there is a war going on."

"I don't want to seem ungrateful, but Cherry is pregnant and I must get her home!"

"Ah, but she is thin; she will be pregnant for a long time. I do not see where there is a hurry. And is she not your servant? She must go where you go, no?"

"No, she is *not* my servant, she is my friend and I must get her home. You have a boat and you can take us there."

"*Señorita Verano*, I am a man of business. I go to Nassau. You and your friends go with me." He stopped to look her up and down, pausing at her breasts. She had long tossed her bra in the sweltering heat of the swamplands after developing a severe rash beneath her breasts. Against her will, her nipples tightened and perked at his stare.

"Ah, you need clothes, *Verano*. I will buy you a pretty dress in Nassau so that you are not enticing the men with your, uh, *pequeño pechos[12]*, no? *Pequeño pero encantador[13], yes?*" He raised his eyebrows, his dark eyes twinkling in humor.

Jocelyn Miller

"What?"

"Your breasts, they are small but enchanting."

Damn. Her nipples hardened even more, and she was sure her face was scarlet on top of the scarlet of her sunburn. She crossed her arms over her chest.

"Do not be ashamed," he said. "You are very attractive in a strange way—for an American."

She felt dizzy. Somehow Cherry's plight had turned to the topic of her breasts! "Why do you call me *Verano?*" she asked, in hopes of steering him away from her attributes—or lack, thereof.

"Because your name, 'Summer', is *'Verano'* in my language. It is quite beautiful. I have not heard of a woman with that name before.

"¡Capitán! ¡Capitán!"

Even Summer understood the alarm in the sudden shout for the captain.

"¡Mire! ¡Un barco detrás de nosotros!14 " All hell erupted as the crew dashed madly about the deck.

"A ship! Go below!" he yelled to Summer, and she obeyed quickly, not understanding at all the dilemma. Buck remained on deck following the captain's orders along with the rest of the men, while she climbed through hatch to the hold with the barrels, where Cherry still lay on the blanket on the floor.

"What's happening?" she asked, rising onto her elbows.

"I don't know. There's another ship coming, and everyone went nuts."

The Diablo Volante picked up speed, felt in jarring thumps by the two women below. Captain Ruiz shouted orders to the crew in an alarming voice, while the continuous pounding of footsteps played havoc on the deck above.

"Something's going on," Summer said and made her way to the hatch.

---

12 Small breasts

13 Small but enchanting

14"Look! A ship behind us!"

Jocelyn Miller

"Don' go up der!"

"I'm just going to peek," she replied, but at eye-level with the deck she could see nothing of the cause of action. She advanced the steps until she was standing on deck trying to maintain her foothold on the racing sloop. She spotted the back of Captain Ruiz as he stood on the forecastle delivering his orders. Running to the sidewall she caught sight of the ship that was apparently chasing them. In the short time she had to view it on the downside of a small swell, it was close enough to see the sailors of the other vessel as well as the flag it flew—the Stars and Stripes! This could only mean one thing; Captain Ruiz was a blockade runner!

"Cherry, we are on a ship of the Confederacy!" she informed her friend, once back in the hold. "Those barrels—he's transporting something that the Yankees don't want him to transport."

Both screamed at the sudden and deafening burst of a cannon.

"We gonna die!" Cherry shrieked, holding her ears.

This was a new bit of drama, and Summer wasn't sure she had the stamina for any more disasters. Floating on the cold sea the day before had zapped her energy and lowered her fear threshold. She was scared—darn scared—and being shot out of the sea by a cannonball was *not* in the plan.

The cannon blessedly only boomed two more times while the women huddled together in the hold, terrified. Eventually, the sloop returned to its slower pace, and they were happy to see Buck approach.

"What was that about?" Summer asked.

"It was a Yankee ship. The captain don't like that. We shot three cannonballs but not at the ship. The Yankee ship never shot nothin'. I asked the Capitan why, and he say that the Yankee ship don't want to kill them, just capture and put them in prison and steal their goods.

"And just what *are* these goods, Buck? Do you know?"

"Cigars."

"Cigars? We thought we were going to die over…cigars?"

"Captain say there's big money in cigars. That's what he do in Nassau, sell the cigars."

"I wants to go home!" Cherry cried.

Summer looked at her old friend and distant cousin, sitting on the rumpled blanket on the floor; a counterfeit Seminole in the tattered costume, far from home, pregnant by a man she hated… *saved from the*

Jocelyn Miller

sea by a blockade running Confederate ship, pursued by Yankees and headed to the Bahamas....who would have thought Cherry's life would be such an adventure? Life was certainly full of surprises

Jocelyn Miller

25

S ummer stood on the deck of the Diablo Volante shaking her head. She would never in a million years forget the vision before her—Nassau![15] Who would believe that she was visiting Nassau in the Bahamas in 1864? The port was decked out by countless ships of all sizes, masts tall into the evening sky. Blacks, whites, horses, carriages, it was a moving mass of activity. A new ship arrival signified a clamoring group of dark-skinned men bartering work. Captain Ruiz enlisted a few, who set off below deck and were soon hefting barrels from the hold and delivering them to waiting wagons.

"Come, *Verano*, we buy a dress for you."

"My friends come, too. I won't leave them here."

"*Bien,*" the captain said and signaled Cherry and Buck to follow across the gangplank to solid ground.

"We buy two dresses, no? Your servant cannot wear *la ropa de los indios, aquí*[16]."

"Yes, she needs a dress, too, if that's what you mean."

[15] Nassau, during the Civil War, was sympathetic to the confederate states and became a clearing house for trade goods delivered by the Confederate blockade runners.

[16] "…the clothes of the Indians, here."

Jocelyn Miller

Summer had not expected a civilized Bahamas, but here it played before her: houses, streets, buildings, the port, the busy harbor. It all added up to a world within itself, a community, a city that held its own despite the gruesome war back in the States. In the women's shop—which the Captain knew exactly where to find— Summer and Cherry were inundated with dresses of the most modern fashion for the time period.

"Look at deez clothes, Miz Summah! I ain't seen none like dis for a long time—not since da war start. My mistress's goin' in dirty dresses no matter how much I wash dem. Now *I* gets to wear da dresses!"

Cherry was obviously delighted. Her dream had come true; she would wear a hooped skirt and a bonnet at last. "Dis be a dream!" she said, twirling to make her new hoop sway. Her dress was a lovely red taffeta with back buttons and trim.

Summer, on the other hand, could barely breathe and wished she had been more adamant about not wearing the corset. She was thin enough as it was after the long stint in the swamplands without ample food. She could hear Captain Ruiz say something to the shopkeeper about her *'pequeños pechos'* and turned fire red.

"This corset is too tight, Captain!" she yelled from the tiny dressing area.

"We are going to the Royal Victoria," he yelled in return. "You must look like a woman!"

Cinched and breathless in her new pale blue, hooped and binding attire, Summer followed the group out of the shop. Cherry sashayed ahead, obviously delighted, for the first time in her life to look like the lady she so dreamed to be. Buck, too, was treated to a new pair of pants and shirt. Though difficult to find a shirt to cover his powerful build, the mission was finally achieved with a high-colored cotton shirt that wouldn't quite button around his thick neck. A vest and jacket was out of the question as the tailor would have had to create a suit of clothing from scratch to fit his frame.

Regardless, he and Cherry strutted ahead proudly in the narrow street while Summer, stiff as a board, constrained by the corset, walked arm in arm with Captain Ruiz toward the Royal Victorian hotel, her flowered bonnet hiding her sun-bleached, dried-out blond and shaggy crop of hair. She had to smile; Cherry looked so very happy for once,

Jocelyn Miller

and she had to admit that she felt quite pretty prancing along arm in arm with the handsome captain and into another adventure in 1864.

Jocelyn Miller

26

"**L**ook, Miz Summah!"

There it stood, the Royal Victoria, four stories high, surrounded by royal palms, tropical vegetation and an abundance of colorful flowers. It stood magnificently against a backdrop of blue sky and billowing clouds. Buck and Cherry hesitated at the arched entrance.

"Move ahead, my friends," the captain said.

Cherry's eyes grew large. "Dey let niggahs in heah?"

"You are with me; they will let you in," the captain assured them.

They paused again, once inside. "Oh!" Cherry exclaimed, her jaw literally dropping to her chest. "I ain't never seen nothin' like dis!"

Summer, too, was stunned at the opulence; carved mahogany settees leaned against flower- papered walls. Countless scrolled, brass oil lamps jutted from the papered walls in an orderly line about the huge reception lobby. A wide marbled staircase led to the upper floors while brass and crystal chandeliers hung strategically throughout the lobby ceiling, the largest one over a circular red velvet sofa upon which a highly fashionable couple sat. The woman's gloved hands rested on a closed parasol. Her hat set forward on her head atop a pile of pinned-up

Jocelyn Miller

curls. A large white plume streamed backward on the hat as if a bird in flight were caught in the grasp of its artificial flowers and bows. The woman's dress was a shiny fabric in indigo blue with white lace trim and flowers and bows which matched her hat. Summer and Cherry both absorbed the woman's finery in awe.

"Ain't like da clothes Miz Susannah wear!" Cherry whispered. The man was equally dressed in his three-piece suit, high necked shirt collar, cravat and top hat. The pair of strangers complemented one another not only in their attire, but in their body language, the self-important way in which they sat and viewed the tide of patrons.

"Move on, move on!" the captain instructed. "I have business to attend to!"

The lobby was a busy hub of activity. Not all were as finely dressed as the couple on the red-velvet sofa, but the crowds sauntered about importantly just the same. Under the captain's guidance, they approached the reservation desk where a short and neatly dressed man smiled upon seeing them approach..

"Ah, *Capitan Ruiz!*" he said. "And you have brought..." The man eyed Buck and Cherry suspiciously "...friends?"

"I am a friend to the world, *amigo!*" Captain Ruiz bowed and pulled a cigar from a pocket inside his jacket. "For you, *Señor Duncan.* Only the best for my friend."

Mr. Duncan ran the cigar beneath his nostrils and smiled approvingly.

"I would like my usual room for myself and my servant, Buck."

Buck shuffled at the mention of his name, at which time Summer gave a small tap to his thigh. "Shhh," she said, under her breath.

Mr. Duncan raised his eyebrows. "This is new; you come with a servant now?"

"And," the captain interjected. "I would like a large room for *Señorita Verano* and her servant—close to my room, of course."

Mr. Duncan was silent, scrutinizing both Buck and Cherry. His eyes rested on Summer, and she supposed he thought she was a trollop come for a seedy romp with the captain. Seconds passed.

"And for your trouble," the captain reached again into a secret pocket. "...a little something extra." Two gold coins clinked onto the marble counter of the reception desk.

Jocelyn Miller

"As yes, here we are," Mr. Duncan said, the gold coins disappearing quickly into his own pocket while he viewed the pages of the registration book.

Maneuvering the grand stairway proved challenging for both women. The hoops were wide and the fabric of the skirts heavy. Grace on the staircase was difficult to come by for those unaccustomed to managing such a large entourage of oneself.

"We have no luggage, captain," Summer said, stopping to rest from battling her skirt. The captain seemed engrossed in his thoughts and didn't reply, but continued up the staircase.

Well, why should I worry about luggage now? After all, she had so far survived this journey without personal effects: no toothbrush, no tampons, no hair brush, no makeup. *We're like wild animals, we need nothing but food and water.* That was an earth-shattering thought; how quickly they had reverted to only the basic necessities of life; how little all else meant when it came to life or death.

"Wha'd dat say?" Cherry asked as they stood in the hall.

"15. It's the number of our room," Summer replied, turning the large key in the lock.

"Captain and Buck down in dat room." Cherry nodded as the door to number 17 closed. It was next to their room, as the captain requested. "I ain't never done nothin' like dis," She looked up and down the long hallway, its floor covered in a dark green and flowered runner. "If my mama and Evaline could see me now, dey wouldn't believe it. Dey'd think I was tellin' dem a story!"

Evaline! She doesn't know Evaline is dead; and so horribly killed! Summer shook away the unhappy thoughts of Evaline and her gruesome death and swung the hotel door open to reveal their quarters. They gasped.

"No! Dey never believe dis!"

The room was surprisingly large. A settee and two stuffed chairs sat facing each other across a dark mahogany table set off with a vase of fresh flowers. The walls were papered in a floral design, from which jutted the same scrolled brass oil lamps they had viewed in the lobby. They proceeded to the large open-shuttered window framed in beautiful billowing lace curtains. The window overlooked the front of the hotel where they viewed the uphill road they had walked upon to reach the hotel entrance. The view skimmed the tops of houses and buildings and

Jocelyn Miller

down to the harbor where the Flying Devil was moored, dwarfed amidst larger ships with taller masts. For the first time, they noticed the beautiful blue shade of the sea.

A carved four-poster bed sat against a far wall in the large room, and next to it, a dressing table complete with mirror. Cherry twirled her body to watch her hoop sway in the mirror. "Maybe dis ain't real," she said. "Maybe dis only a dream."

It's a dream for me, Summer thought and removed her hoop and skirt, dropping it to a circle on the floor. She sat on the bed in her pantaloons. They were quite pretty, as she never had a chance to wear them in her previous time-travel visit to Tanglewood Plantation. She set her hat on the nightstand beside the bed and laid her head backward onto the pillow. "A real bed!"

Cherry followed suit leaving her skirt and hoop in a circle next to Summer's, and soon they were fast asleep, side by side, lulled by the sounds of the town below, the breeze that gently brushed their prone bodies, birds calling and faint voices from the activity at the port. When they awoke, it was to the captain knocking on their door and the lace curtains billowing against the darkness of night.

"Wake up! The party begins!" he called.

The party? What party? It took Summer a moment to recover her senses...*Nassau, Bahamas, 1864...Captain Ruiz....* She jumped from the bed startling Cherry who jolted to an upright position.

"What's da matter, Miz Summah?"

"The captain wants us to get up."

The room was dark except for the dim light of the gas lamps at the front of the hotel fading in through the window.

"It's dark in here, captain, we can't see."

"Open the door, Verano, and I will light the lamps for you."

Summer desperately needed to pee, but having no clue as to the whereabouts of a bathroom and toilet, she proceeded to the door in her pantaloons.

Cherry pulled the covers up to her neck. "You's got yo' underwear on, Miz Summah!"

"What's the difference? I wear more clothes now than I did before. At least my *'pequeños pechos'* are covered."

The captain charged right to the bed stand opened its one drawer and pulled out a small box. "Your sulphurs," he said, removing one and

Jocelyn Miller

striking it on the side of the box. He lit a candle on the nightstand, a candle she had not previously observed, then proceeded to an oil lamp on the wall, lighting it as well. She caught a glimpse of herself in the mirror and was horrified; some parts of her hair stuck straight up like porcupine quills; her breath smelled atrociously, and she imagined her teeth were covered in green moss.

"Oh, but you are missing your skirt!" the captain said, and turned to look at Cherry. "Get up! *¡Apresúrese! ¡levántese!* You must get your mistress ready! The party has begun!"

"Where's the bathroom?" Summer asked.

"The bath...oh you mean the toilet?"

"Yes. We have no place to freshen up."

"Wait here," he said, and left.

"Where else would we go?" Summer asked the closed door. "I'm not putting that hoop and skirt back on until we get to the toilet—or whatever it is."

"Here!" Cherry said from the floor behind the bed. "Here's da pot."

"Allelujia!" Summer grabbed the pot and ran to a corner of the room. "Oh for flush toilets and a bathtub!"

"Da what toilet?"

"The flush...oh never mind. No sense teasing you with what's to come."

"Wha'd you talkin' 'bout?"

"Nothing. I guess I'm cranky, that's all."

Cherry used the pot after Summer, but both were forced to drip-dry, as there wasn't a scrap of paper to be found.

Alas, a knock came at the door. When Summer opened it, she was surprised to see three women of color dressed in uniforms of long black skirts, white caps, and with aprons cinched around their waists.

"You's all call for dey watah heah?" one said, and led the others inside and to the tall shaving stand. One maid poured steaming water into the bowl, and the rest into the large pitcher sitting next to it. Another laid towels on the bed, while the other inspected the chamber pot.

"Der's a toilet 'hind dat doah, missy's. Yinna gern use dat one fo sure.[17]

---

[17] Bahamian slang

Jocelyn Miller

Cherry stood bug-eyed, her head cocked. "Wha'd she say, Miz Summah?"

"There's a toilet?" Summer asked. She *did* catch the word 'toilet' if nothing else.

The woman opened a narrow door close to the shaving stand, and sure enough, there sat a toilet! Certainly not the toilet Summer was accustomed to in the 21st century, but what convenience! The room was no bigger than a broom closet and when the maid set a lit candle on a small shelf across from the toilet, they could see a stack of papers waiting for use. The toilet seat was of sanded, stained and varnished wood and sat over an ominous hole in a wooden cabinet that, when peered into, seemed to vanish into a dark cavern. The horrendous odor was overpowering, but beggars could not be choosers and Summer was glad to have a seat over which to place her behind. The fact that the hotel made an effort to make the water closet attractive with flowered wallpaper, and was a comfort in an uncomfortable situation. When the door was closed, the odor did not follow them.

"All the comforts of home," Summer said, and thanked the three maids, who walked single file to the door and left.

"Dems darkner n' me and looks like my peoples, but dey don't talk like my peoples."

"People speak differently all over the world. We didn't understand what the Seminoles said, right? Even though these people here are the same as you, they don't come from Savannah and have a different dialect."

"I didn't know da world was so big. I ain't never gettin' home to see my Percy, my mama, Evaline...all my peoples." Cherry's shoulders slumped, and she sat herself down on the settee.

"Don't start crying now, Cherry. Let's get dressed for this party—or whatever it is the captain keeps jabbering about."

After washing privates and armpits, attempting a shampoo-less hairwash in the bowl of now cooling water, pinching cheeks for color and pinning the stylish hats back over their wet hair, the ladies helped one another tie their hoops back onto their waistlines and replace the heavy skirts.

"What I wouldn't give for a tube of Crest and a toothbrush," Summer muttered. She was positive the fancy woman in the lobby on the round sofa earlier in the day had a whole case of cosmetics, powders, and

Jocelyn Miller

all things necessary to dress for the events of the evening. Summer wished she knew the woman, and therefore could knock on her door and borrow a few things; but of course that was out of the question.

As if the captain had a peephole from which to view the women, he knocked on the door at precisely the moment they were ready. Summer couldn't help but glance around the room looking for any tell-tale signs of peeping holes.

"And just how did you know we were ready?" she asked when she opened the door to find the captain and Buck clean-shaven. Buck at least had the opportunity to borrow the captain's razor.

"Ah, I know much of women, *Verano.*"

"No doubt," she replied, straightening her hat, still wondering if he had a peephole.

The captain offered his arm and the group set off for the grand stairway, Buck and Cherry following behind.

"You look mighty pretty in that dress, Cherry gal." Summer heard Cherry giggle a reply to Buck's compliment, and smiled.

"And you, *Señorita Verano,*" the Captain said. You are a vision of loveliness—and you smell somewhat better, also."

Jocelyn Miller

27

S ummer watched nervously as Cherry and Buck were escorted away from the entrance to the ballroom by a tall Negro dressed in a white jacket dotted with brass buttons, black pants and white gloves covering his large hands.

"It's okay, Verano. They are well taken care of. They will dine with the other servants of guests. They cannot come with us. It is not permitted."

The ballroom was a glorious affair with a continuation of the crystal chandeliers from the lobby, which lit the room in a soft and flattering light. There did not appear to be a woman for every man amongst the group of partygoers, and the sight of a woman walking through the ballroom doorway on the arms of the captain caused a stir with many of the men.

Perusing the room, she was surprised at the number of people milling about. The men were loud, even rowdy in some instances. A few fancy-dressed women danced with partners to music played by a trio of black musicians set up on a small stage. The music seemed upper scale, though the tunes were unrecognizable to her ears. She couldn't help but wonder where the trio had learned to play the instruments, which consisted of a piano, a violin, and a wind instrument of which Summer was not sure. With the stares of the men, she felt good in her hooped

Jocelyn Miller

attire and not like the tattered and torn character she was prior to this visit to Nassau, thanks to the captain's generosity.

The captain guided her across the floor to a table set with a punch bowl sparkling with champagne, and plates of delicate and fancy cookies. With a small sampling of cookies and glass of champagne punch, he led her to a velvet chair set against the wall.

"Please sit a while, Verano. I must conclude some business and will return shortly."

This she didn't like, being alone in a strange place. Every moment was shaky ground; just the realization that she was able to transport herself from the future to the past was curious and frightening enough, without being left on her own with strangers in a strange land. At least with Cherry around she felt comfort. Even Buck was a comfort, but here she sat sipping the champagne punch, *alone*, an observer in a different time zone.

"Pardon me, miss, would you care to dance?"

"Oh, my!" she exclaimed, hearing the unmistakable British accent. She looked up to see a finely dressed young man with light brown hair, neatly combed, and a trimmed beard and mustache. She glanced at the few couples gliding smoothly across the ballroom floor, flawlessly in step with one another, and then at her new suitor.

"I don't know how to say this without sounding like an idiot, but I've never learned to waltz."

"American?" he asked.

"Yes."

"Well, that explains it! Come, I will show you. It's very simple."

She was very grateful that it *was* simple to learn and in no time she was gliding across the floor in the arms of the young stranger. *One, two three; one two three...* so simple! While turning and gliding, her hoop swaying magically with every step, she managed to catch sight of the captain and another man. They were deep in conversation, standing close to a wall that led to a terrace through large, opened doors.

One, two, three; One, two, three.... On her second pass around the dance floor the captain appeared agitated. He gesticulated wildly, and though she couldn't actually hear his voice, she *felt* that she could hear it, as he was very animated and did not look happy. She craned her neck to

Jocelyn Miller

catch another glimpse of him as they waltzed past his station, but the movement of the dance was too rapid for her to observe.

*One, two, three; One, two, three....*on this pass the captain and the man were *gone*. This she absolutely could not stand for! She was a stranger in a strange land, in a strange era, on a strange island with no means of returning to the States without the captain! She excused herself from her partner with the lame excuse of feeling dizzy, and set off onto the terrace.

Calm down! she told herself, but her heart beat wildly in her chest. She had no idea where Cherry and Buck were taken to, and now the captain had deserted her! The terrace was lit with lanterns and a few people milled about, but she did not see the captain or the man he had been arguing with. Leaving the safety of the terrace she ventured down a path lined with royal palms until the captain's voice filled her ears. She stopped to listen.

"....oh but you will, *Señor Giles*. You will bring the money tonight, to my room. I have traveled far through dangerous waters. I have brought Carlos top quality cigars, and you *will* bring me full payment. *Tonight, Señor.* Do not make me send my men."

Trouble! Why did everything have to have a problem connected to it? The captain was a god-send. '*Send my men'...*did me mean the crew on the boat? What was this all about? *Is the handsome and generous captain a thug?*

The man the captain had spoken with suddenly rushed by, breathing heavily. She waited until he was out of earshot before speaking.

"What was that about, Captain?"

"Oh, *Verano!* What are you doing out here alone?"

"Looking for you. You *left* me alone."

"I left you with many people."

"You wouldn't understand my fear, Captain." What was that about, anyway? You threatened that man!"

"It is *my* business, *Verano*, not yours," he said brusquely.

"I'm depending on you to take us back to the States. I'm in a strange land. I got scared."

"Oh, *probrecita!*" he put his arm around her shoulder. "Do not be afraid, *Verano*. I will not let anything happen to you."

"I'm worried about something happening to *you*, Captain."

Jocelyn Miller

"Ah, I see. I have been in this business for a while *Verano,* and nothing has happened to me. I am here; you are here. We are safe, and we are together. Come, let us go and enjoy the party."

"What is this party for?"

"It is what we do when we bring our goods to Nassau. We celebrate our good fortune. There is much money here— much money to be made in the trades."

"It appears there may be danger, too."

"There is danger in every rising sun, but we live on, no?"

"I would like to see where Cherry and Buck went."

"If you wish, we will go, then."

Summer followed the captain on the path leading to the rear of the hotel. Soon, another form of music was heard. Not the sophisticated music of the trio in the ballroom, but the hollow, rhythmic sound of drums. Summer was taken aback as they rounded the corner of the hotel. Torches were lit in the area behind the hotel where a crowd of blacks, men and women, stomped their feet to the beat.

What a contrast! she thought, remembering the few women in the ballroom, their hooped skirts ballooning and swaying to the waltz, while here, in the glow of the firelight, hips gyrated suggestively beneath the colorfully turbaned heads of the women. No hoops and frills in this group, aside from Cherry. The women's skirts hung straight, their lungs unbound by restrictive corsets as blouses hung loose and off the shoulder at times. The women did not have the pinched and reserved look of the woman on the red velvet sofa that morning, or the women waltzing so seriously in the ballroom. These women of color laughed heartily as they moved their hips suggestively to the rhythm. As chaotic as the dancing looked, it did have a pattern and a rhythm that was hypnotic in its effect.

Cherry and Buck stood off in the sidelines watching in awe, smiling. How could one not smile at the joy of the faces in the torchlight?

"Miz Summah!" Cherry called over the beat of drums. She waved, her teeth white in a grin that stretched from cheek to cheek.

"I think I will stay here with Cherry and Buck, Captain Ruiz."

"No, no, *no, Señorita Verano!* You see that Cherry is fine. You must go with the other white women; the party is just beginning!"

"So far, this party looks a lot more fun."

Jocelyn Miller

"Come with me, *Verano.*" He took her arm and guided her back around the hotel and into the ballroom. The voices of men had reached a newer pitch, as well as the music, which had stepped down a notch from the sophisticated plane it had played on when she left, and now played a livelier beat. The man the captain had argued with earlier was nowhere to be seen.

* * *

Something woke her. It was not the music, for that had ended at 1:00 a.m., after which they had retrieved Cherry and Buck, and all went to their respective bedrooms. She lay a moment in the quiet of night and then…it came again. She rose off the bed and stood still, listening. It was garbled, she couldn't make out the words, but she was fairly certain it was the voice of Captain Ruiz. She moved between the water closet and shaving stand, putting her ear to the wall.

"…all I said!" *Thump.* She jumped, for the 'thump' felt as if it had hit her ear. They were closer to her now, just on the other side of the wall.

"Pay up or you will not live to see the sunrise. I do not put in danger my crew or myself for him to cheat me." *Thump.*

What in the world? What is Buck doing through this? He must be awake.

"Cut it out, Ruiz," the other man said. "I'm just the messenger."

"We go to Carlos, *now*!"

"He ain't gonna like it."

"Buck, you come with me!" Ruiz yelled.

Summer continued to listen, but heard only the door shut and footsteps in the hall.

Poor Buck! It was difficult to sleep, wondering what had happened to him now that he was involved in the captain's business—and surely against his will!

* * *

Jocelyn Miller

Summer opened a sleepy eyeball on Cherry who was retching in the chamber pot. The poor girl was hunched over on the floor, the pot beneath her.

"You okay, Cherry?"

"Does I look okay?"

"Sorry. It's the morning sickness. I hope it passes soon so you won't be so miserable."

Cherry's retching was a miserable sight, made more miserable by the circumstance of the mystery of last night's episode on the other side of the wall.

Last night.... Buck! "Oh, my God! Cherry, you slept right through a huge argument last night! Captain Ruiz was fighting with someone in his room. It woke me up. Last I heard, they were going to see someone named 'Carlos,' and the captain made Buck go with him!"

Summer wanted to run next door to see if the men had returned, but since she had nothing on but her underwear, she put that idea on hold. She knocked against the wall, the same area as she had put her ear the previous night to listen. Nothing. She knocked again. Nothing.

"Help me get dressed—that is if you're through being sick—and I'll see if they've returned. I don't like the feel of this."

"I hope nothin' done happen to Buck!"

"I hope nothing happened to either of them. Without the captain, we're stuck here." Once dressed, she ran her fingers through her cropped, sun-bleached hair, and departed their room for the captain's door.

"Ruiz...Buck!" She knocked. No sounds came from within. She knocked again. "Captain! Open the door!" Nothing. She turned and leaned against the door. "What now?" *What if they never return? Where did they go?*

She gathered her wits and took the grand staircase to the reception desk. The stocky man, Duncan, was again behind the counter. She ran her fingers through her hair once more, knowing full well that her cropped hair was very unusual for this time period and the man had already eyed her suspiciously.

"Excuse me," she said.

"Yes, Madame?"

"Uh, do you happen to know a Mr. Carlos?"

"I know many Carlos's, Madamn. Is there one in particular you would like to know?" He raised his eyebrows, his eyes traveling her body.

Smart ass. "I'm looking for a Mr. Carlos whom perhaps Captain Ruiz would be acquainted with."

"I do not scrutinize the friends of our guests, and have no idea which Mr. Carlos is acquainted with Captain Ruiz...*Madame.*"

"Have you seen Captain Ruiz or his servant this morning?"

"No, I have not," he replied curtly.

The man was rude. Without comment, she left him at the desk.

"Where you bin?" Cherry asked upon her arrival back into their room.

"I checked the lobby and asked at reception," but nobody knows where Captain Ruiz is."

"Or Buck?"

"Or Buck." She plunked herself down on the settee and sighed. "All we want is to get back to Savannah."

"Why you goin' to Savannah anyways?"

"Well....I'm helping to take you home, remember?"

"How come is dat? You don' know me. Why you all fired up to help me?"

"Because...*should I tell her? Should I tell her that I know all her people...that I'm one of her people? Should I tell her about Evaline and the horrible death she experienced? Should I tell her that I come from another time, and I am only here to take her home to Magnolia?*

"Oh, someone at da door!" Cherry said and ran to open it. A bellhop gave Cherry a sealed envelope.

"Now wha'd's dis, do you s'pose?"

Summer ran to grab the envelope from her hand. "It must be from the captain!"

She read aloud: *Come to ship. Hurry!*

"Is dat all?"

"That's enough, Cherry. Let's go!"

Within minutes the women were traveling down the hill toward the port, their hooped skirts swaying with each step. Summer had stood at the window of their room getting her bearings on exactly where the

Jocelyn Miller

ship was docked, but everything looked different away from the hotel window.

"Let's just keep going straight down until we reach the water. Then we'll be able to find the ship." she said

"I don' know why the cap'n can't come and get us—or Buck can't come."

"I think it had something to do with where they went last night. We'll find out when we get there, but let's hurry."

They walked for several blocks, unhindered by luggage of any sort. At last they came to the port and stood searching up and down the row of ships moored and docked. The port was its usual hustle and bustle. New ships were arriving, as they could be spotted in the distance, and two ships were sailing out of port..

"Dat Devil ship's so tiny next to the biggun's dat we can't see it!"

"Let's walk this way," Summer said, heading off to the left through the swarm of people, horses, wagons and vendor stalls. Passing the fish vendors was a smelly affair, so they held their noses and practically ran until they were far enough away for the odor to not be offensive.

"Wouldn't want to eat dat fish for supper!" Cherry exclaimed, then stopped to admire the goods of a fabric vendor.

"We can't stop, Cherry. Something is wrong or the captain wouldn't have written us to 'hurry'.

Cherry reluctantly left the stall, and hurried along the cobbled street, avoiding the horse droppings and garbage.

"There it is!" Summer pointed ahead to the Diablo Volante nestled between two three-masted ships. "Hurry up!"

As they made their way further down the road, their haste was cut short when two horses pulling an enclosed carriage cut off their path, their driver purposely blocking the women's passage.

"Wha'd dat idiot doin'?"

"I beg your pardon!" Summer said to the driver. "Look where you're going."

At that moment, a man stepped out of the carriage and onto the street. "You will get in the carriage, ladies."

"Thank you, no. We are meeting someone."

"Get in the carriage, ladies," the man repeated.

It's him! The man Ruiz was talking to at the dance!

"No!" Cherry said. "We's busy."

The man reached inside his jacket and pulled out a small pistol. "Get in," he said.

Cherry squealed, grabbing onto Summer's arm.

"What's this about?" Summer asked, feeling her insides quiver. This wasn't her first encounter with guns, but each time it was different and she sensed imminent danger.

"Get in," he repeated.

They were close enough to the ship for the captain to see them. She glanced in that direction hoping that Buck or Captain Ruiz were on deck and watching for the women, but she did not see them.

"I'm not asking politely again," the man warned. I'd just as soon shoot you here."

Does this mean he's going to shoot us somewhere else? Why?

"Oh, Miz Summah!" Cherry cried, still attached to Summer's arm.

"All right," she said. "Get in, Cherry." *How will we get out of this one?* She needed to think—and fast!

As soon as they sat in the carriage, the man tapped the driver's side and the horses took off. Knowing it was their last chance for rescue, Summer jumped off her seat and leaned out the opened window on the waterside.

"Captain Ruiz!" she screamed. "Buck Buck!" She managed to yell their names twice, screaming at the top of her lungs before the man grabbed the behind of her skirt and pulled her down onto the carriage floor. All she heard were Cherry's screams before she felt a blow to the head, and then blackness.

Jocelyn Miller

28

"**O**h, my head." Summer painstakingly opened her eyes to find herself seated in a thick leather chair opposite another thick leather chair in which sat a distinguished looking gentleman wearing a three-piece suit in the style of the day. Behind him, opened shutters exposed the turquoise sea beyond.

"Where am I?" she asked, rubbing her temples. "Who are you and...and...." Panic set in and she tried to stand, but plopped back into the cushiony leather. "Where is Cherry? What have you done with her?"

"Your servant?"

Definitely British. "Yes, my servant."

"She is fine, Miss Verano."

"You know my name. Who are you?"

"I am Charles Winthrop. You may know of me by the name 'Carlos'."

"You're Carlos? You're Captain Ruiz's Carlos?"

"If we must put it that way, but I prefer that I am my own Carlos, and certainly not belonging to Captain Ruiz."

"Why are we here?"

"I need you for a while. You see, your— our—Captain Ruiz has stolen my gold, and I am holding you for ransom."

Jocelyn Miller

"Ransom? Wait. How has the captain stolen your gold? He brought you cigars, and you were supposed to pay him."

"It was an unfortunate incident, but I found a cheaper seller, and our Captain Ruiz is not happy about this turn of events. I refused to purchase his cigars and so he has stolen my gold."

All this over a bunch of cigars? "Where I come from, nobody gives a hoot about cigars. Why are they so special...so important?"

"Well, where do you come from, my dear? You certainly do not carry the accent of the Southerner."

"I come from Chicago, but I live in Savannah, Georgia, now."

"To my knowledge, cigars are quite special in Chicago *and* Savannah, as well."

"Not in my time."

"Your time?"

"You see, Mr.....Mr. Carlos, I am not really here. I am a time traveler from the year 2013. In that year, nobody gives a hoot about your friggin' cigars. You are all dead, and I am only here in this time warp to bring Cherry home to Savannah." Her head pounded, and she was sick of all the diversions and dangers. She just wanted to get on the damn boat and be off to Georgia.

"That's quite a tale, Miss Verano."

"And," she continued, "I doubt Captain Ruiz is going to pay any ransom for a time traveler and two freed slaves whom he fished out of the water on his way to Nassau to deliver his cigars."

Mr. Winthrop lit a pipe and observed Summer as she slumped in the leather chair, holding her pounding head. He jingled the small brass bell next to his chair, and within seconds a maid appeared.

"Please bring Miss Verano some powders for her headache. "

"Yes sah," the maid said and disappeared, returning shortly with a glass of water and a tin. She spooned powder from the tin into the glass and stirred.

"This should help your head, Miss Verano. I'm sorry, but my man got a little carried away with your shrieking. Perhaps his action has caused some confusion on your part."

"How do I know you're not poisoning me?"

"You are no good to me dead, unless the captain does not return the gold. But, we will worry about that when the time comes."

Jocelyn Miller

I'll worry about it right now, thank you. "I would like to see Cherry," she said, after drinking the bitter mixture.

"Your servant is waiting for you. Alice will take you to her."

Summer followed the maid down a long hallway from which several rooms connected, each room quite nicely furnished. "Mr. Carlos must make lots of money, right Alice?"

"Dunno Missy. Just do me job, dats it. Do me job, go home."

"Perhaps you could tell me how to get out of here?"

"No ma'am. Ain't me job."

So much for Alice.

The maid unlocked a door with a key she kept in her apron pocket.

"Miz Summah! Oh lordy, I was so scared!" Cherry jumped for joy upon seeing her friend, and raced to hug her

It was another nicely furnished room: a heavily carved headboard for the bed, matching high chests, ornate dressing table and mirror—but the one window was heavily barred, certainly raising alarm with the women.

"A pretty room with a prison window. To what sinister purpose has this room been used for, I wonder?" "Oh, what to do now, Cherry?" Their hopes were dashed for escape.

They sat down together on a settee against a wall, beneath a painting of Spanish galleons.

"Where was you? I was scared. I thought you was dead when dat bad man hit you on da head. Thought I was dead from my heart stoppin'!"

"It appears that our Captain Ruiz got mad because the man, Mr. Carlos, whose house this is, bought cigars from another seller and not Captain Ruiz as promised. So, somehow, the captain stole gold from Mr. Carlos last night, and we have been kidnapped for ransom. If the captain doesn't give the gold back to Mr. Carlos, then I don't know what will happen to us."

"Wha'd's dis 'ransom thing?'"

"We stay here until Captain Ruiz returns the gold; the gold is the ransom payment."

"I don' like dis."

"I don't either. Obviously, we can't get out through the window."

Jocelyn Miller

"Maybe da captain know somethin' ain't right since we's not at da boat now."

"I'm counting on that. In fact, I'm hoping that they saw us when the carriage took us away. Let's hope that's the way it was."

* * *

"My belly growin', Miz Summah, and I gots to pee mos' da time."

It seemed like forever and a day had passed. Was it nighttime, now? They had no way of knowing the hour, but were at least able to find a chamber pot beneath the bed to relieve their bladders.

"I'se hungry and thirsty, too. When da captain gonna pay dat ransom?"

Never. He owes us nothing.

"Buck gonna be lookin' for us."

Buck, of course! Buck would never sail off without them!

Soon, they heard the key in the lock, and there stood Alice. "Massah Charles wants y'all for da suppah. Come wid me."

Summer heard her stomach growl as they followed Alice down the hall and out onto a veranda where a beautifully set table was prepared for the evening meal. The sun was setting, which they could see from the hilltop upon which Mr. Carlos's house sat. The sea teased with its shimmering turquoise waters, and Summer couldn't help but think of the irony…a beautiful Island paradise and here they were, captives facing possible death, in the year 1864. Could it happen? She shuddered.

"I gather the ransom has not been paid? Is this our last supper?"

"You have a strange humor, Miss Verano."

"Well?"

"No, your ransom has not been paid. Perhaps you were right in that Captain Ruiz has no interest in saving you."

"Dat not true," Cherry interjected. Buck ain't gonna let us stay here. He gonna come for us."

Summer nudged her beneath the table.

"Is your servant always so outspoken?"

"She's not really my servant, Mr. Carlos. She's actually a cousin of mine." She smiled.

Jocelyn Miller

Cherry looked at her cockeyed, and received another nudge beneath the table.

"How is your headache, Miss Verano? You still seem to be confused. "

"Actually, it's quite gone. Whatever that powder was, it worked a miracle."

Alice brought dishes out to the veranda: soup, fish, plantains, rice, and a mango relish. It was a very attractive assortment in which Summer and Cherry did not hesitate to partake. Summer was actually surprised that she even had an appetite considering the situation. It all seemed rosy; the beautiful house, the scenery, the food, and even Mr. Carlos's educated conversation, but she had to remember that this was a very dangerous situation. If the captain didn't pay, would they die?

"So, tell me about the future, Miss Verano, since you seem to be an expert."

"All right," she answered, laying down her fork. and giving Cherry a warning glance.

"I can tell you right now, that the North wins the war. There is no longer a division between the North and the South. Slavery in the States has ended, as you well know; and in the year 2013, the blacks are no longer called 'negroes' and the word 'nigger' is highly discouraged. Blacks, or, African Americans, as they are also referred to, can go anywhere they want, restaurants, hotels, shops. They can live wherever they want. They attend the same schools as white children and learn to read and write and go to college. The plantations of the South are gone, and what remains of them are mostly museums of the past." She paused.

"Nobody say 'niggah' no more? I didn't know it a bad word," Cherry said, and received another nudge beneath the table.

Mr. Winthrop told her to continue.

"To travel, we fly in airplanes and jets which are like ships of the sky, only they resemble birds more than ships. We drive cars with four wheels— not horses. People ride horses for fun and sport. We have excellent medicines in the 21st century, but, unfortunately, we have excellent weapons as well. We still fight wars with other countries, but we do not fight wars within our United States of America, at least not as what's happening now in your time."

"Very interesting," Mr. Carlos replied.

"Why don't you tell me why cigars are so important?"

Jocelyn Miller

"Certainly. You grow the tobacco in your America. The cigars are very popular in Europe and bring top dollar. However, new tax laws in your country have made it difficult to export without great expense. So we do it this way; we buy cigars from the blockade runners who acquire the cigars from their sources in America. It is a very lucrative business, but Captain Ruiz has grown too expensive. We also transported cotton to Europe in the past, but without the slaves...." He shrugged his shoulders."

"What do we do now, Mr. Carlos?"

"We give Ruiz a little more time."

* * *

"Wha'd was all dat you talkin' 'bout?" Cherry asked, once they were locked in their room. "How do you know 'bout dem things? Who win dis war...ships dat fly... niggah bein' a bad word. How you know these things?"

"I don't know how to explain this, Cherry. I barely understand what has happened—why I'm able to travel back and forth in time."

"Where's yo' flyin' ship?"

"I don't need one; it just happens."

"What else you know? You know me?"

"I know you, Cherry. I know Percy, Ruth, Lucy—I know all of them. I know about the Yankees burning the furniture in the magnolia fountain. I know the bad things the soldiers did to you; I know that Arthur Ascot is Percy's father. I know everyone from Magnolia."

"And Evaline? You know Evaline?"

Silence.

"...and Evaline?"

Summer took Cherry's hand in hers. "Evaline is dead, Cherry."

"No! You's lyin'!"

"I'm not. Evaline was trying to save you from the Yankees. They chased her. She ran into the river and that big alligator —the one who killed Juba—he killed Evaline, too."

"No!" Cherry screamed She screamed so loudly that Mr. Winthrop and Alice both came running.

"What's wrong in here?" Mr. Winthrop asked.

Jocelyn Miller

"Nothing," Summer replied, holding the sobbing Cherry in her arms. "She's scared."

"Good lord, I thought there was murder going on."

"No…not yet, anyway." Summer replied icily.

"No…" Cherry whimpered after Alice locked the door behind her. "You's lyin'. Evaline can't be dead!"

"I'm so sorry, Cherry. I know how you and Evaline were friends."

"If you know all dat, den what about my Percy? What about baby James? My Mama?"

"I wish I knew more about Percy and your mama, but the last I saw of them, they were fine."

"Baby James?"

"Miss Susannah takes care of baby James. He grows up and marries a white woman. Baby James is my great-great-great-grandfather; this how you and I are related. Arthur Ascot was the father of Percy, *and* the father of baby James.

"You crazy, Miz Summah?"

"No. You don't have to believe me, Cherry, but it's the truth. I've come to help you get home to Magnolia."

"Well, we ain't movin' very fast."

Summer laughed. "I agree. I think we're moving at a snail's pace!"

"Wha'd about dis baby here in my belly. Where's dis one goin'?"

"I think I know the answer to that, Cherry, but I'm not quite sure. Give me time."

"I think you's one o' dem voodoo peoples dat comes from Africa where da niggahs comes from. Don't matter, we gots to stay together 'cause I'd be mighty scared if you wasn't here with me."

"Don't worry; we will be together. And do me a favor, stop saying 'nigger.' It's not a pretty word."

"Wha'd I call myself den, and all de other niggahs?"

"Call yourselves 'black', or 'people of color', or African Americans. Be proud."

"Will I get home to Magnolia?"

"That's why I'm here, Cherry, I'm going to get you home somehow, someday. I promise I will get you home."

29

Bam! Bam! Bam! Covers flew. Summer and Cherry both jumped off the bed. The room was pitch black, their having turned off the lantern hours before. Cherry shrieked when she saw the figure shadowed in the doorway, but Summer quickly realized it was Buck. Who else could have that physique?

"Buck!" she called. "You've come!"

"Buck? Heaven be praised! We's saved!" Cherry yelled.

"Where's Mr. Carlos?"

"Tied up. Now hurry. The captain waitin' on you! He's ready to sail!"

The women grabbed their skirts and hoops, bunching the yards of fabric in their arms as they raced after Buck. There was only a slight glimmer of light which came from the room with the leather chairs as they passed. Summer glanced to see Mr. Winthrop in his night shirt, tied and knotted into the leather chair. Across from him was the man from the carriage, also tied and knotted in the chair.

"You tell Ruiz I'll get him for this, young lady!" Winthrop yelled. "He won't get away with my gold!"

Summer felt a certain remorse for Mr. Winthrop's temporary position, as he had treated them kindly; but again, she had to remember

Jocelyn Miller

that he may have murdered both she and Cherry if Ruiz hadn't paid—which he obviously hadn't.

They literally flew on their legs; Buck far ahead with his wide strides, while she and Cherry raced behind holding on for dear life to their skirts and hoops, which continued to drape and slip out of their arms, the fabric being of the slippery sort. The hooped petticoats alone were difficult to control as they continuously sprang and lifted in front of their faces, blocking their vision. At one point Cherry tripped over the skirt fabric, was blinded by the hooped petticoat and crashed onto the cobblestone street. She squealed in pain, which brought Buck immediately to her rescue. He grabbed the skirt and petticoat out of her hands and into his own.

"Come on, Cherry-gal," he said, lifting her off the ground. "Cap'n sailing soon!"

"You're a good man, Buck," Summer said, gasping between words; the run was killing her! She wondered if there was anyone left at Winthrop's house to chase them.

Again they took off, following Buck through the empty streets—empty for the wee hour of the morning it was—until finally, they came to the port and the Diablo Volante.

"Apúrate! Apúrate![18]" the captain yelled as Summer, the last person to board the ship from the gangplank, heaved herself onto the deck, flat out, spread-eagled, the skirt and petticoat squished beneath her.

"Oh, my God," she said, finally catching her breath. She had remained lying on the deck catching her breath as the crew made haste around her, fixing the sails, jumping to the captain's commands.

"Ah, so nice to see you again Señorita Vernano."

"Likewise," she said, rising up to a sitting position, then realized she was in her underwear in front of the captain and crew. Then, again, acknowledging that she was wearing more clothes than an Eskimo considering she would have thought nothing of prancing around deck in a bikini in the 21st century! Time travel was very confusing.

She looked at the captain in the ship's lantern light. He appeared even more handsome than she remembered, as he knelt beside her, offering his arm.

---

[18] "Hurry! Hurry!"

Jocelyn Miller

"I could slug you, Captain. You stole from Mr. Winthrop and got us kidnapped! How can you live with yourself?" She reached for his arm, which he dramatically retracted.

"What? *Que paso?* Carlos made business with me; sent me to Charleston through Yankee ships and soldiers to retrieve his shipment. *¡Caramba, Verano!* You take the side of Carlos and not me, who has saved you from the sharks!"

He would have to put it that way.

"Not only that, but I have also saved you from a sure death! Mr. Winthrop is not a...a...angel like you have in your head, Verano. He is a killer. He would not think to kill you and your servant. It would make no difference to him."

She could see that she was losing this battle. The captain was becoming quite animated and she didn't know whom to believe, and it was silly to feud with her rescuer in the first place.

"Okay, okay. Let's forget it. Thank you, Captain Ruiz, for saving our lives....*twice*. We certainly owe you."

"There now, that is better," the captain said, offering his arm again.

It never occurred to Summer that she would be content to collapse onto a blanket in the hold of a ship, but she *was* content, as was Cherry. They lay next to each other, quietly drifting with the rolling flow of the sea beneath them; lulled, satisfied to be safe, and that much closer to home.

Jocelyn Miller

30

S ummer woke, stretched, peed in the bucket, ruffled her hair, and climbed the ladder to the deck in her bloomers and shimmy; modesty was ridiculous at this point, her having only one outfit to wear. The hoop was a hindrance onboard.

The captain stood on the at the ship's wheel. Once in a while he turned to look behind and then forward again. It was a lovely day, wherever they were. White billowing clouds punctuated a sharp blue sky—the kind of clouds she remembered making pictures out of when a child. The breeze was comforting, as the ship sailed at a good clip.

"Ah, Vernano," the captain said, seeing her approach. "Did you sleep well?"

"Sure did, captain. Cherry is still sleeping, but I expect she will be up vomiting soon with the morning sickness. We need to get home to Savannah!"

"Her sickness will pass soon, I know much about this."

"How is that?"

"*Mi madre*, I am the oldest of seven children. I saw many times her sickness. I know much of women."

I'll bet you do.

"Where are we going?" she asked.

"New Orleans. It is my home."

Jocelyn Miller

"Can we get to Savannah from there?"

"Oh yes, I will arrange for you."

"Oh, that's wonderful, Captain!" Alas, a good sign!

"But first we must get through the blockades and the small islands. Sometimes it is difficult."

"How long will this take?"

"Perhaps six days. It depends on the weather, the blockades, all these things."

What was six days? She thought. *Will they pass as days had been passing in this time travel venture? Would years pass in these 'six days?' Would Cherry get home?* She gave herself a headache when she tried to figure out the perplexing time-passing question. And, did Guy know she was gone? What would he think of her standing here in her underwear with the handsome captain, a handsome captain who rang her chimes every time she looked at him?

"You are troubled, *Verano?*"

"No...no," she said, returning to the present situation. "I was just thinking of home."

"Do you have a man?"

"Yes!" She said this so loudly and adamantly that the captain jerked his head backwards.

"Sorry. I didn't mean to yell."

"How can he let you go on such a perilous journey?"'

"Well...he doesn't know." *Or does he?*

"You have run away? Perhaps you no longer love this man."

"I do—I do love that man!" His brown eyes twinkled with humor when he spoke with her. "I see the devil dancing in your eyes, Captain."

"Ah, but I see a beautiful and strange woman in her pantaloons!"

A thrill ran through her at his words. *Shame on me, I'm lusting for him—a ghost! He* is *dead.* Could she then lust for him without guilt? Did a dead man count in the book of lust? Was it cheating?

At that moment, Cherry's head appeared at the hatch. "Der you are, Miz Summah. Help me wid this!" Promptly the pee bucket appeared and summer ran to grab it before it—God forbid—tipped over onto the deck.

"Ewww!" Summer exclaimed, tossing the contents over the rail. "You were sick again, you poor thing," she said to Cherry who was now

Jocelyn Miller

standing beside her looking quite worn out. "But I have good news! The captain is sailing to New Orleans and from there he will arrange for us to get you home to Magnolia!"

Cherry sighed. "I hope so. I'se sick. My belly's growin'. Don' feel so good."

"You'll feel better soon. The captain says so."

* * *

"*Un barco!*[19]" a sailor yelled later in the day when the sun hung low in the westward sky.

The captain was quick to grab his spyglass and quicker yet to yell orders to the crew. In his long spiel in Spanish, Summer caught the word 'Carlos.' She ran to the rail and spotted another ship on the horizon, similar to the one on which they sailed.

"What is it?" she demanded upon reaching the captain.

"It is our friend, Carlos. We will outrun him. You and your servant go below."

"Does he have cannons?"

" The captain raised an eyebrow and looked at her cockeyed. "Yes."

"Are we going to use *our* cannons?"

"We will try to outrun them, first. Now, *Verano,* I am a busy man. Please go below until it is safe to come up."

An hour passed, and in the dark hold with only the light from the portholes filming through, Summer paced. The speed of the Diablo Volante had increased dramatically, and the beautiful sailing day had now become a dangerous one.

Cherry sat on the floor, her arms wrapped around her knees. "Wha'd if dey shoot us with dem cannons and sink da boat? I can't swim! I just want to be home with my mama— with Percy!"

Summer peeked through a porthole, but couldn't spot Carlos's ship. "Darn," she said and approached the ladder to top deck. "I'm just going for a quick look."

---

[19] "A ship!"

Jocelyn Miller

'A quick look' required standing full on deck while the crew scurried about like hornets. The captain was at his station, spyglass in hand.

"Where are they?" Summer yelled from the hatch, her anxiety increasing by approaching nightfall.

"Why are you up here, *Vernano?* My sailors will see that you do not obey orders and will expect me to whip you," he yelled. He did not look calm.

"You wouldn't dare, Captain!" she yelled. W*ould he?*

"No? Do not question my autho…" He didn't finish. At that precise moment a deafening explosion erupted onboard. Summer shrieked, and ducked instinctively back into the hatch. Debris flew, splintering the air; wood, rope, metal, some falling into the hatch opening, striking her face and arms.

"You's bleedin'!" Cherry screamed as Summer stepped onto the hold floor. "Don' go up der no more!" Cherry grabbed a blanket to clean Summer's face. "You gots two cuts, here and here, she said touching near the wounds on the cheek and forehead. "Oh, Buck! Poor Buck! Where is he?"

"He's okay. I think I saw him with the other men," Summer said, but now terrified; this was all so real! Another blast of cannon from Carlos's ship again rocked the Diablo Volante, sending the women onto their behinds. They screamed, and having no idea of what was happening on deck, huddled together, shaking, praying it would come to an end.

It didn't. A 'boom' generated from overhead—from the Diablo. *We're in battle!* Gunfire was now heard with the captain yelling orders over the shouts of the men. *At least he's still alive…* What on earth would happen if the captain were killed?

Later a 'thump' hit against the ship, as if something had bumped it. Summer crept up the hatch ladder and stuck her head through the opening and screamed to Cherry, who came running, and squeezed next to Summer at the top of the ladder. Carolos's ship was close enough to touch!

"Dey's comin'!" Cherry screamed, and hurried back down the ladder. Summer followed, after a futile attempt to close the hatch, but it was far too heavy.

Shortly, yells, grunts, gunfire, and heavy footsteps thumped rapidly overhead.

Jocelyn Miller

"Dey's on da boat!" Cherry grabbed onto Summer and held for dear life. They now cringed in a dark corner of the hold hoping they would not be seen should anyone decide to hunt for sailors below. What would Carlos do with them now?

After many terrifying minutes, a roar of victory reached their ears, but the women remained in the dark corner without any means of knowing who the victor was. They waited their fate, trembling.

"*Verano!*" the captain called, much to their relief. "It is finished. We clean up first, before you come."

The dragging and splashing sounds overhead lead Summer to believe that perhaps the captain and crew were throwing bodies into the sea but she wouldn't know for sure if she didn't look for herself. But then, would she want to look at the carnage? As if in response to her thoughts, Buck appeared.

"You's safe!" Cherry exclaimed.

"Miz Summer, Cap'n say you and Cherry come up now."

"What happened up there?"

"Men from da other boat jump on us and we fought them off. They wasn't tough as this crew. We killed some o'them and they sailed off. Cap'n happy. That man who took you gals, was on da other ship and he don't look too happy when they's sailin' away."

"I hope this is the end of it."

"Amen, Miz Summer. I don't want no more fighting. I'm free now and I wants to live."

* * *

A rum barrel was brought on deck in celebration of the day's victory. The sun was long set, and yet the party continued, all relieved to be alive and sailing toward New Orleans. Cherry sat close with Buck, and Summer was happy to see *her* so happy. She had endured so much on her forced journey from Magnolia, and it appeared to Summer that Buck was to become a permanent figure in Cherry's life; he was here for a reason.

"Here, *Verano*, have another cup of rum."

It was incredulous that only a few hours ago men had lost their lives on this very deck, and here she was, drinking rum with the captain on a sloop beneath the beautiful stars of a clear night. *Drinking with a*

Jocelyn Miller

thief, she reminded herself, lest she forget. However, with the buzz from the rum, his crime of theft did not seem as important as it had earlier, and the captain looked ever more handsome as he rambled on about....*about what?* She didn't really know, as she was mesmerized by the astounding day and the charming man beside her. The vision of her in the captain's bed resurfaced, but she didn't shake it off this time. She let it play in her head and knew instinctively that she couldn't change it—*it was going to happen.*

31

"Oh, my God," Summer groaned. Her stomach rolled along with the sea; her head was a ball of lead upon the pillow. She opened an eyeball to see the other side of the bed ruffled, and empty. *You will pay for this, Summer Woodfield.* She rolled over onto her back, the lead in her head thumping to the back of her skull. *Never again. No more rum!*

She stared at the wooden ceiling above, darkened with age and dampness in the creaking ship, and felt herself blush with the memory— or was it the horror of what she had done? Oh yes, she could remember parts of last night; the laughing, the singing...*the rum*. The captain...*his bed*. "Oh, my God!" she said again, remembering his muscular chest, her nakedness, his hardness, his entry...*my ecstasy*.

"Vernano, you are awake!"

She quickly pulled the cover over her head. *I cheated! I cheated on Guy!* How could she live with herself?

The captain pulled the cover off of her, exposing her naked body. She lay still, in total embarrassment.

He handed her a cup. "A bit of rum for your head. It will help you to feel better."

Jocelyn Miller

She gagged. "Take it away!" Just the thought of the sweet, dark rum brought her stomach to her throat. She reached for the cover and pulled it to her chin.

"I will drink it myself." He downed the rum with one swallow and sat next to her prone body on the bed.

"Oh, Captain, what have we done?"

"We do what men and women do, enjoy one another. There is no shame in this. Did you not enjoy our union?"

She wanted to cry; between the sour stomach, severe headache and the knowledge that she had cheated on the man she loved, she wondered if she could ever forgive herself.

She looked at him, dressed, his hair combed, his eyes bright, his demeanor nonchalant as if he had not touched a drop of rum the night before or partook in carnal abandon.

"I have cheated on the man I love. I have cheated with *you*, a man I don't even know....and to answer your question, yes...what I remember, I enjoyed very much. Oh, I'm so confused!" she said, hiding her face in her hands.

"It is our secret, *Verano*. Don't cry." He slipped a hand beneath the covers, cupped a small breast and whispered in her ear. "I enjoyed myself very much. You are beautiful and special...so unusual!"

She couldn't help but turn her face to his—to his lips. This world—*his world*—had consumed her, body and soul. *He is a ghost, it doesn't count..."* and again, with her foul breath, healing wounds from the explosion, pounding head, and cheating heart, he took her again, while the Diablo Volante sailed on.

* * *

Wha'd you doin' with dat man? I was scared to death down here by myself," Cherry scolded when Summer appeared in the hold dressed in her attire of pantaloons and shimmy, now blood splattered from her minor wounds of the explosion.

"I have a terrible headache, Cherry, too much rum. I lost my head; I slept in the captain's bed! Oh, what would Guy say if he knew? He would leave me, for sure!"

"Who's dis Guy? Yo' man?"

Jocelyn Miller

"Yes, my man. He loves me, and I love him, and here I've slept with the captain!"

Cherry was silent a while. "What time is Mr. Guy in? Maybe since you says you ain't from dis time it don't matter."

"If only I could believe that!"

"Buck say last night dat he love me. He a good man, dat Buck. I loved my Juba more den anyone. I cry when I think of Juba killed by dat gator. I cry when I think of the mens who hurt me, so I try to not think of dem: Massah Ascot, dem soldiers, dat bad Tom Quinn to steal me away. He on me mor'n he off me, I swears, and now I gots his baby. But Buck? He don' touch me. He know I hurtin'. He respect me. He say it my body, not no mens body. He don't touch me lessen' I wants him to. I can love dat man."

"He's a good man," Summer agreed, lying on her thin blanket, the boat rocking gently beneath her. "He's a smart man, too."

She drifted off into a dreamless sleep and when she woke, the sun was high in the blue sky. The captain was at his station, and she joined him.

"Where are we?" she asked, hoping she didn't carry the telltale blush of lustful shame on her face.

"Ah, my *Verano*. Is your head better now?"

"Yes, thankfully. No more rum for me, Captain."

"I hope that is all there is no more of, my love. You are in my head, and I stand here thinking of our next union."

Union. She had to laugh; it was such a funny way of putting it.

The captain laughed too. "Come over here, my little American. He circled her in his arms, the ship's wheel in front. "You steer the ship…steer us to our next union!"

She laughed, again. "You make me forget my shame, Captain."

"There is no shame, *Verano*," he said, kissing her neck, sending shock waves through her body. She leaned into him and felt his hardness growing through her thin shift and pantaloons.

"Captain, you are such a bad boy."

"And you, *Vernano*, you are making me *loco*." He released her from his grip. "You must step aside or my men will think their Capitán has been bewitched by a woman." He then straightened himself and yelled an order in Spanish.

Jocelyn Miller

"You didn't answer my question," she said, shielding her eyes from the bright sun. "Where are we?"

"We are passing Key Largo. We will be in the Gulf of Mexico and then New Orleans."

New Orleans! I can get Cherry home! Oh, but that thought was now bittersweet. She loved Guy desperately but, like the captain, she, too, anxiously awaited their next 'union'. She was trapped in his web. He held her captive—*a willing captive*—and she could do nothing but give in to her desire. Soon the journey would end, Cherry would be home to Magnolia and she…where would she be?

She headed to the hatch, her dilemma heavy in her thoughts as she passed two crewmen. *The crew,* they smirked and whispered when she passed. She was feeling quite the wanton woman now and decided that in the future, she should steer clear of the captain when alone in view of the crew.

Jocelyn Miller

32

The sky darkened after leaving Key Largo behind and sailing into the Gulf. The winds accelerated from the southeast behind them, and soon it was obvious a storm was imminent. To make matters worse, another ship showed itself in the eastern sky, and the captain was obviously disturbed over this turn of events. Though they had seen other ships, this one was of particular interest to the captain.

"It is the Nassau Queen," the captain informed Summer. "It is the ship of *Señor* Winthrop—Carlos. He has returned."

Summer's heart fell and Cherry grabbed onto her arm at the news. "No! We's gonna die, Miz Summah!"

"Cherry, I know for a fact that we will be okay, so trust in me." She tried to reassure her cousin, but she didn't like this news, either. The blasting cannons were a terrifying experience. The damage to the Diablo Volante from the previous battle, was minor and quickly repaired, but what about this time? She looked out at the water, which now showed whitecaps and small swells, which they felt beneath them in the quickening winds.

"They're not going to attack in the storm, are they, Captain?"

Jocelyn Miller

Captain Ruiz lowered his telescope. "One never guesses what Carlos has planned. But, they will not catch us for a time, if they catch us at all."

The women went aft, holding onto the rail as the sea lifted and lowered with the swells. The Nassau Queen was still in the distance, which brought a temporary release of stress, but the sky was darkening rapidly.

The captain yelled orders in Spanish, and their course changed; they were heading inland. Summer knew the captain didn't like to approach land unless necessary because of the threat of Yankee ships guarding the ports, but perhaps with the storm approaching, the Yankees were a lesser evil than the storm, or Carlos; she didn't know.

As night fell, they sailed onward up the Gulf, closer to the land. Their proposed lustful 'union' did not occur as the captain was quite busy with the approaching storm, and the Nassau Queen on their tail.

Cherry moaned in the hold with the rise and fall of the ship, and indeed it was creating a difficult balance factor for the women. They could not walk without holding onto whatever was nailed down and available. Cherry was nauseous and uninterested in eating, and Summer headed to the galley alone for a bite of bread or biscuit, or whatever the cook had managed to concoct in the rolling wrath of the sea.

"*Hola Señorita Verano,*" the cook greeted. The galley was very small, holding only a rugged table for six, a stove and a closet to hold the supplies. It was midship between the hold where Summer and Cherry slept, separating them from the captain's and crew's quarters.

"Is there anything to eat?" she asked, pointing to her mouth knowing he would understand by now, her obvious and ridiculous sign language.

"Ah, *si, Señorita,*" he said, signaling her to sit.

She did as he bid, and watched him balance himself against the stove and ladle a mess of something into a bowl, placing it in before her, along with a spoon.

"*¡Coma![20],*" he said.

"*Gracias.*" She was relearning bits and pieces of the language.

The soup—or stew—was fairly palatable but a bit of a mystery in the dim lantern light. She hoped it did not become a lump in her

---

[20] "Eat!"

Jocelyn Miller

stomach which she had to throw up later. So far, sea sickness had not been an issue for her.

Finishing the last drop in the bottom of the bowl, she thanked the cook and indicated that she would like to borrow one of his lanterns. She couldn't resist the temptation to visit the captain's quarters. All hands were on deck, and the thought of returning to her blanket on the floor in the hold was not at all appealing. Holding the wall for balance, she passed the crew's quarters, their hammocks swinging ghostly and empty, and into the captain's room. Just looking at the bed alone, its cover rumpled and askew as they had left it, sent chills through her. She ran her fingers over a dusty chest while relishing the smell of the room, the dank, creaking atmosphere as the ship swelled beneath her. The wind whistled through the closed windows, which looked forward, ahead into the darkness of night. She held tight to the lantern, daring not to set it down should it tip and start a fire, and at the same time, tried to pull the chest open, but the lid was deceivingly heavy…or perhaps locked? *None of your business*, she thought. *What am I doing in here, anyway, snooping around in the captains things?*

Her decision to leave the room was thwarted when she heard footsteps approaching, and the captain and cook talking. Frantic, she searched the room for a place to hide. The quarters were small, and the bed boxed in from the floor up. *No place there to hide there, damn!* She then noticed hooks on a wall upon which hung a long and heavy coat. Blowing out the lantern, she set it in a dark corner and hid behind the coat, pressing her body against the wall. *Please, please, please, don't let him find me!* It was just too darned embarrassing to be found loitering in the captain's quarters.

The room lightened with the captain's entrance. He held a lantern before him as he walked across the room. Summer viewed him through a small slit between sleeve and body of the jacket. She barely breathed as she watched him set the lantern on a shelf. He took a key from beneath the mattress and unlocked the trunk. There, he reached in and pulled out a large sack, a heavy sack that clinked as he removed it, and placed it on the bed. Then, he reached into the trunk again removing a small chest, which looked to Summer like it was made of metal. He hefted the heavy sack into the chest, closed the lid of the large and carried the small chest to the other side of the bed. There, he removed a section of wood on the wall exposing a dark hole in which he placed the

Jocelyn Miller

box. After replacing the section of wood, he took the lantern and left, leaving Summer in total darkness.

She felt her way to the lantern in the corner, and then to the door, quietly closing it behind her. In the galley, she placed the lantern on the floor where the cook would see it, as his back was turned, and quickly made her way to her blanket on the floor in the hold.

Was it Carlo's' gold? She had a strong inkling that it was, and figured that her lover, her captain, was hiding the gold coins in case the Nassau Queen should overtake them.

* * *

Day broke, but the winds had not decreased. They seemed to *increase* instead, which obviously caused the captain great concern as he had the crew scurrying about like a disrupted beehive when Summer stuck her head through the hatch.

Ominous sky, she thought, holding on for dear life as she managed her footing on the unsteady deck. The captain was again (or still?) at the sterncastle issuing orders. The wind made it impossible for her to be heard over its constant howl, and she inched her way against its force to speak to Captain Ruiz. "What's happening?" she asked, looking up onto the sterncastle, the wind slapping the words back into her face.

"Verano, you must go below. It is not safe here!" he yelled.

"Where are we?"

"We have rounded Cape Sable," he yelled.

"Where is the Nassau Queen?"

"It is still in view!"

She held tight to the base of the sterncastle and searched southerly for the challenging ship. "I can't see it!" The sky was dark regardless that sunrise had come. Tall, thick, black clouds loomed overhead like hungry beasts.

"It is there; now go below!" he ordered.

She obeyed, as it was impossible to stand on the deck fighting the wind for any length of time. She would leave that to the experienced sailors.

Below, Cherry sat on her blanket.

"I can't believe you're not vomiting."

"Ain't sick today, but I don' like dis rollin' business."

Jocelyn Miller

"It's pretty wicked out there."

"Feel my belly, Miz Summah. It growed overnight. Dat Yankee baby gonna come no matter dat I don't want him."

"Come on, Cherry. How could you not love your own baby?"

"It a Yankee baby, and it Tom Quinn's baby. I don' like neither. Ain't fair all dis bad stuff happens to me."

"No, it isn't fair, but I'm going to get you home to Magnolia and your mama, and you're going to take good care of that baby. Percy will have a brother or sister to love and Auntie Ruth will have another grandchild to fuss over.

"Percy dark. Wha'd if dis baby white? Can it be white? Evaline's James look white to me, but Evaline's daddy was Massah Woodfield, and he white, so she was white too— halfways. And look at you! You's white as cotton fluff and you's tellin' me dat baby James is yo' great-granddaddy. Dis baby gonna be a curse. I knows it."

"Cheer up, Cherry. We're here, we're safe, and we're going home.

"It keep me goin', Miz Summah, thinkin' 'bout goin' home. Dat and Buck. He say he gonna come with me."

* * *

The gloomy morning turned to gloomy afternoon. The sloop sped along, pushed onward by the howling winds behind it. Over the frightening swells, it ballooned to unsafe heights and deflated to the valleys between. Summer tried to check their bearings at one point, but the sight of walls of water coming at her sent her heart into a drumroll, and her crawling back to her blanket, wet with salt spray. She tried to calm her shaking body, but there was a dreadful fear enveloping her. Visions again popped into her head: ships colliding, breaking, sinking; bodies falling into the sea. She pulled the blanket over her head hoping to block the vision, but it wouldn't leave—screams, yells, shrieks, wind, waves...*breaking ships*. She shuddered. *Please don't let this happen!*

33

Summer crawled to the hatch ladder on all fours. It was nearly impossible to walk now, with the angry sea tossing the ship in all directions.

"We's gonna die!" Cherry screamed, to which Summer told her to shush. "We are *not* dying, so stop it!" Her own nerves were shattered to their limit without Cherry having a nervous breakdown. She climbed the ladder, white-knuckling her way to the top only to be tossed to the floor by two serious 'thumps' portside of the ship.

"What was dat?" Cherry shrieked while Summer again attempted to climb the ladder.

Over the roar of the wind they heard men yelling. She peeked through the hatch opening and her heart fell. *Carlos!* The ships were side by side, rolling over the swells, thumping against one another as men shouted in alarm. Gunfire and total chaos surrounded her as she watched, horrified. *The captain...Buck! Where are they?*

A body fell next to the hatch, narrowly missing her. It was one of their crew. He held a long knife, a machete, but his attacker was quicker, bashing him on the side of the head with the butt of a pistol, sending blood splattering in all directions. She screamed as a spray of blood hit

Jocelyn Miller

her face. The attacker pointed the pistol at her, but quickly, Buck jumped him and the men rolled on the deck, grunting, kicking and punching.

"Get below!" Buck yelled after he had stabbed the man several times with his knife. "Get below!" he ordered again.

Summer climbed down the ladder, shaking uncontrollably. She hadn't seen such violence since the night at Magnolia when the Yankee soldiers were killed—murdered—by Mick Mason. This was not good. She crawled to Cherry.

"To the corner!" she yelled over the deafening noise overhead. "Hide!"

"Was dat Buck I heard?"

"Yes, he's okay. Don't worry."

And my captain? Where is he?

The fighting did not abate, but grew louder with the sound of scuffles and the pounding of boots overhead. They pushed themselves into the dark corner as tightly as was humanly possible, molding themselves into one, hoping to be invisible to the enemy.

Approaching footsteps!

"Shhh," Summer whispered into Cherry's ear. She felt the vibration of Cherrry's heart pounding rapidly, as well as her own. Their hearts pounded in unison and she wondered if whoever had come below would find them just by the beating of their hearts.

As the footsteps approached, Summer caught sight of the man, a huge beast of a man, who carried a machete in his hands.

"Come out girls," he growled. "Carlos wants you."

He knows we're here!

The man turned circles, scouring the parameters of the hold. "Ain't no use hiding, cause I'll find ya."

The floor creaked as he walked toward them. He looked behind, and to the sides, flipping each blanket up with the tip of his blade.

I can' smell ya, so ain't no use hiding."

Summer thought she would pass out with fear. The muscles of her legs ached from the force of pushing herself backward against the wall.

"Ha!" he yelled, eyeing them. "I see ya hiding there!"

He approached so quickly there wasn't a moment to run. He first grabbed Cherry by the neck of her frock and pulled her up. "Little black one. Think I should have ya before I toss ya overboard."

Jocelyn Miller

Cherry fainted dead away, and he threw her to the ground.

"Ah, the little white one. Come here little pussy...." She kicked him in the shin as he reached for her.

"You bitch," he said, swinging the machete. She ducked just in time as the sharp blade dug into the wall behind her.

Terror was not the word; it did not cover the trembling of her body, the pounding of her heart. Her mind raced for an escape route, but she couldn't leave Cherry, who was still unconscious on the floor.

The man removed the machete from the wall with one powerful fist, while raising Summer off the floor with the other. He was so tall that she only came up to his chest. "Spunky thing, ain't ya? Well I'll teach ya," he said," and ripped the shimmy clear off her body, exposing her breasts.

She prayed for unconsciousness; this was too much. *Wake up! Take me back to Magnolia!"* she screamed, hoping she would find herself home and safe. Still, she remained in the hold of a ship on the tossing sea, the monster of a man before her, Cherry unconscious at her feet.

The man, in a matter of seconds, dropped his knife belt, dropped his pants, dropped the machete, picked her up and, holding her against the wall with one hand, ripped the pantaloons clean off her!

"Captain!" she screamed. "Buck!" though she knew no one could possibly hear her with the racket overhead. She glanced at his member, which was huge and erect and ready to impale her.

"White bitch" he said, thrusting her downward, toward him. She closed her eyes, waiting for pain, waiting for humiliation, but instead, she fell to the floor onto her naked behind. When she opened her eyes, the giant was on his knees before her, staring blankly into her eyes, the blade of his machete sticking outward through his stomach. He fell to the side and, thankfully, not on poor Cherry who remained comatose on the floor.

Summer looked up to see the captain grinning. "You did not think I would let that beast defile you, did you, my *Verano?"*

She could only sob.

"Hurry!" he said, grabbing her hand. She retrieved her ruined clothing and let him lead her through the galley, through the crew quarte rs,over the bloody body of the cook, and into his own cabin.

"Cherry!" she said. "We can't leave Cherry!"

"I will get her." He left quickly, and returned, holding Cherry up as she stumbled and collapsed on the captain's bed.

"Do not leave here!" he said forcefully, and left, shutting the door behind him.

34

*N*ow *what?* This was by far the most frightening, dangerous and deadly episode in Summer's brief time-travel career. *What can I do?* On deck, a deadly war raged, and the vision of the ships colliding and sinking played over and over again in her head. The sea rolled and heaved, tossing the crafts in excruciatingly perilous angles, while slamming them together with each rise and fall of the swells. It was an ominous sound, the deadening *thump, thump, thump;* the creaking of wood the tearing of planks.

The women shrieked as one bone-chilling deafening collision nearly knocked them off the bed.

"The ship is sinking!" Summer screamed, ripping Cherry from the bed. "We have to leave!"

"No. I ain't goin'. Der's nowheres to go and I can't swim!" Cherry, beat on Summer's arm attempting to release her grip. "Ain't goin'!" she cried.

"Oh, yes you are!" She dragged Cherry to the door, staggering like drunks as they tried to keep their footing. "You either go down with the ship and die, or you take your chances with me. I'm not leaving you behind!"

Jocelyn Miller

Cherry paused a moment, stared at Summer briefly and made her decision. "Let's go!" she yelled.

Summer swung the door open and out they went, bumping against walls, stumbling their way past the crew quarters. The empty hammocks swung wildly in the sway and roll of the ship. They stumbled over the body of the cook, and after making it to the ladder, held onto the rungs for support as the ship was seriously listing now.

"We don't have much time. Follow me!" Up they went, Summer peeking her head above the hatch hole. The body of the crewman who was killed earlier by Buck slid across the deck to starboard in the direction of the list. His body rocked against the side wall, which dipped perilously into the swells. The howl of the wind, the waves, the swells, and the sea spray, and yet *the silence of men's voices* sent ripples of gooseflesh through Summer.

My God, what do we do now? Where is Buck? The Captain? It was obvious that the battle between men was over; the battle now, was survival from the sea.

"We're going in—there's no other way!" The angry storm roiled around them, tossing, heaving. They slid to starboard, holding hands, both screaming in fear, and off they slipped, into the cold and deadly sea.

"Hold on!" Summer screamed, battling to keep them afloat, the weight of Cherry in her panic, pulling her downward. "Don't let go!" It was her worst fear, losing hold of Cherry as she knew she would never find her again. Summer kicked her feet, gasped for air, helplessly dipped below the surface, rose again, and rode the swells, all the time Cherry instinctively trying to climb on her, use her as one would a raft. *A plank! We need something...a plank...anything that floats!*

Her prayers were answered. Within seconds a large object nearly knocked them senseless. Summer wasted no time in grabbing hold. It was large and long. She had no clue how large, but it was large enough for the two to hold on. It had metal bars attached, as if made for this very purpose, grips with which to hold in case of emergency. The women held tight to the bars, and now, between swells, they were able to view the two ships, battered, broken... and sinking. The ships had fought and created their own demise. It was hopeless; they would never sail again.

"Buck..." Cherry whimpered. "Where's Buck?"

The captain? Is he going down with his ship? Is he dead— again?

Jocelyn Miller

"Captain! Buck!" Summer yelled but doubted she could be heard over the chaos of the storm. Then, a miracle. A figure appeared on deck and Summer was positive it was Buck. No other sailor on the ship had his silhouette aside from the evil man who had attempted to rape her, but he was dead—*she hoped*. Who knew, in this crazy time-travel world? After all, Tom Quinn was dead and he had appeared to both she and Cherry.

"Buck!" the women screamed and attempted to wave their arms without losing grip of the metal hand-holds.

They watched, helplessly unheard, as Buck stood on the high portside of the sinking ship. Behind him, the bow of the Nassau Queen rose into the sky, one broken mast splitting from its base. Even over the storm, they heard the mast splintering and creaking;

It's going to snap! "Behind you!" The women screamed; and when Buck leaned over they thought he had heard their warning, but he stood upright again, holding a man.

The captain! Oh please let it be Ruiz...let him be alive! It appeared to Summer that the man was not in good condition, as Buck continuously had to reinforce his hold on him to keep him from falling.

Both ships were sinking, and rapidly now. The Diable Volante suddenly began to roll. Buck stepped quickly backwards like a lumberjack on river logs, dragging the injured man with him, as the ship turned belly up. With a powerful 'crack' the broken mast of the Nassau Queen snapped, breaking in two. Still secured by its rigging, it swung wildly against the black sky.

"Duck!" Summer screamed. "Duck!"

As the top half of the mast swung forward, it hit the injured man square in the head, the impact throwing both of them into the sea.

"My God!" Summer screamed. "No!"

She and Cherry both shrieked, kicking their lifesaving raft toward the sinking ships. It was useless, as the power of the sea controlled all things and they were merely creatures of minor importance, unfortunately locked in its grip.

In silence they watched as the sea swallowed the doomed sloops to their graves. With the battle and the ships gone, they now became aware again of the treacherous situation they were in, afloat in unknown territory in a horrid storm, with nothing to save them but a large rectangular piece of wood, blessedly punctured with hand-grips.

Jocelyn Miller

"We's done for, Miz Summah," Cherry moaned. I don't wants to be like dis—with no hope—but wha'd we gonna do now?"

"We're going to hold on...we'll be saved...you'll see." But the ominous sky, heavy winds, and angry sea did not in any way foretell that ending. She felt hopeless, herself. *I don't belong here—I could be safe, at home with Guy, with Jesse....*

That thought vanished in the blink of an eye when Cherry pointed out a bobbing figure. "Buck! Buck! Buck!"

Summer was suddenly ashamed of her thoughts; Cherry alone in this sea would have perished for sure. She was sent here for a reason; she had to buckle up and take charge of her waning will to bring Cherry home. *No pain, no gain.*

Together, with the sound of their voices, they brought Buck to their floating raft. Things were looking up.

35

The threesome sat on a sandy beach looking out to sea. Unbeknownst at the time, they had not been far off from land when the ships sank, and there sat the Diablo Volante, one mast sticking up out of the grey waters, a marker, a morbid reminder of their perilous journey and the fact that the dashing Captain Ruiz was dead. Summer was especially sad, viewing the wreckage. She wanted it to disappear, to wipe away the memory of the captain and their 'union', to wipe away the laughter in his eyes, that little smirk, the way he teased. She placed her hands over her ears. Would she always hear him calling her '*Verano*'?

They had washed ashore quite quickly after Buck had joined them at the raft, which turned out to be the ship's hatch. Buck pulled the hatch ashore, far up onto the beach before they hightailed it to higher ground to find cover from the dangerous winds. "We can use this!" he shouted over the wind that night.

In the morning, the turbulent seas had subsided, exposing the mast from the Diablo Volante. The sky was blue, the clouds nonexistent, and here they sat, tattered, torn, exhausted, stranded, hungry and thirsty, not to mention the great sadness Summer felt for the departed captain.

"Look at dat!" Cherry said, pointing down the beach.

Jocelyn Miller

Buck surprised them by jumping up from the sand and running to the object, the top part of the Nassau Queen mast. He pulled it further up onto the beach and appeared to be cutting something. He returned with a length of rope which he wound into a lasso-type circle. "We can use this," he said. "Best we look for anything we can use."

The trio scoured the beach for debris from the sunken ships. The women scavenged for clothes, as their attire was nothing now but the remnants of their prior undergarments. Summer's torn garments were tied catawampus around her private body parts. Modesty had no place in this circumstance. Buck was a gentleman, and did not stare at the women and their scanty outfits.

"It was the captain," Buck had told her of the man he tried to save. "He been shot, but the mas' done hit him and he was stone dead then." *Stone dead*...oh how those words hurt!

Several bodies washed up on the beach over the afternoon, and Summer was terrified one would be the captain. She did not want to see him in his horrific death condition. With great relief, Buck told her they were of both crews, but the captain was either lost to the sea, or would appear later. She hoped not, even though a proper burial would have been appropriate considering their relationship.

She and Cherry gathered useful clothing from the wash-a-shores before Buck buried them in shallow graves at the head of the beach. Removing clothing from the corpses was not a cheery task, but necessary, as between them they only sported rags.

The women cheered when Buck speared a large fish with a stick he had sharpened with his knife, and cheered even louder when he started a fire. Long gone was the flint-striker and fish hook, but Buck was a wealth of knowledge at fire starting. Summer had never witnessed in person, the starting of fire from nothing but sticks and pieces of fluff, which Buck gathered from various dried plant fibers.

Afterward, they sat again on the beach, digesting their meal and staring out at the mast of the Diablo Volante, which sprouted up from the calm and sparkling sapphire blue waters, a complete contrast from their harrowing night.

"We need fresh water," Summer said, her tongue sticking to the roof of her mouth with dryness. "Maybe there are some coconuts here somewhere. We don't even know where we are."

Jocelyn Miller

"There's water on that boat," Buck said. There's barrels there, maybe some rum if it ain't floated away."

It was then, Summer remembered the gold.

"Buck! There's gold on that ship, too!" she said. "I saw it—I saw where the captain hid it!" She stood and walked to the water's edge. "Can you dive, Buck? Hold your breath?"

"I been dumped in the water three times now and ain't drowned yet."

"Gold ain't gonna buy us nothin' here," Cherry said.

"You're right. But we can use it later. Maybe we'll need it to barter, who knows. That's what Carlos was after."

"It bad luck, dat gold."

"Nonsense."

"Bad mens, bad boats, bad babies, bad storms, bad gold. It all bad."

"We're alive, aren't we?"

Cherry pouted and rose off the sand. She walked off inland, in the direction of the vegetation. "Dat ship bad luck. I'se gonna look for water in dem trees. I found it one time b'fore, when I was with Mistah Quinn.

"Go with her, Buck. We'll talk about the gold later. Maybe there is a water source in there somewhere."

With Cherry and Buck gone to search for fresh water, Summer stood at the edge of the tide. Small crabs scurried here and there at the interruption of her presence. She wondered if they were edible, and then marveled at how desperate a person becomes when thrown into a wilderness without supplies. She now eyed every living creature as a food source—even the small ugly crabs that scurried at each foot fall.

She walked further into the water, desperate to find out how deep the Diablo Volante lay. Was it teetering on something? Had it lodged on a reef? Was the water really that shallow? The tide seemed to be coming in, though she didn't think it would nearly reach the heights it had during the storm.

She was up to her thighs. Small fish nibbled at her feet, causing her to shudder. The waters frightened her, but at least she could see in this water, so unlike the Savannah River which was dark and murky, and hid horrid creatures, or the stormy waters of the sea in which they had floated the previous night.

Jocelyn Miller

The closer she came to the ship, the deeper the water. She returned to the beach and removed her clothing, checking first to make sure Buck was out of sight. Again, she tread into the sea until she was forced to swim. When she reached the mast she held on, dipping her head beneath the surface. She opened her eyes and was shocked at the clarity. The ship had broken in half, spilling debris across the ocean floor. Plates, cups, lanterns and indistinguishable items nestled in between coral ridges and sea urchins. Fish scouted the new arrivals to their habitat. Her eyes burned, and she raised her head from the water. *The captain's quarters are intact!*

Viewing again beneath the water's surface, and beyond the Diablo Volante, she saw the Nassau Queen, which seemed to have completely dismantled, its debris scattered across the sandy floor further than her eyes could focus.

Judging the depth of the ships, she thought perhaps 15 feet. Could she dive it? Could she hold her breath? *Get sane, stupid,* she told herself, and swam back to the beach to retrieve her clothing and wait for the others to return. Perhaps she and Buck could dive for the box of gold coins together. Besides, she might run into the captain down there, and didn't want to be alone should that happen.

* * *

They hung onto the mast, Buck in his skivvies and Summer stark naked. When it came down to it, there was nothing she could wear to swim in that wouldn't be a hindrance. *Men always have it lucky,* she thought, watching Buck swim off to the mast ahead of her. Cherry giggled, watching her disrobe on the beach, and then thought better of it.

"He my man. Don' you forget dat." She warned.

"Good grief, Cherry. This is embarrassing enough without you harping on me. I'm *not* going to steal your man." Even though he was a ghost, it was downright red-faced embarrassing to have to dive naked with him. Once in the water, which was cool and refreshing, she forgot her nakedness and focused on the business at hand. Buck had promised not to look at her body parts, and she had to trust him.

Hanging onto the mast, they took their deep breaths and headed below, to see how far they could comfortably dive and how long they

Jocelyn Miller

could stay under. She had never been deeper than nine feet and supposed Buck had never made a habit of swimming under water at all.

She was back up in a flash holding onto the mast and gasping. *Damn, what was that?* A large and narrow fish had come close, sharp teeth glimmering in the diffused sunlight. Not only that, the salt water was keeping her buoyant.

What's wrong, Miz Summer? "Buck had returned.

"I saw a fish."

"There's gonna be lots o' fish down there."

"I know…I know…and beside, the salt water is making me float"

"I tells you what. Come down and show me where the box is and I'll get it."

Could she do it? It required swimming into the open cavity of the ship. Would she panic? This project was a lot harder and scarier than she thought it would be. If only the ship had settled a few feet higher.

"I'm making a practice run first, Buck." She took a breath and kicked with all her might to at least get deep enough to touch the ship and return to the surface, her ears threatening to burst. *Do not look for fish!* she reminded herself. She managed to touch the ship at the ragged split, but found her lungs screaming for air by the time she broke through the surface.

"You done good!" Buck said.

"But I run out of breath!"

"Show me where the box is. Let's go together."

She was determined to make it this time, at least to the captain's cabin door. It was hard to tell what the structure would be like inside, hard to tell if it would be intact.

Upon reaching the opening of the split, she did not hesitate but followed Buck into the cavern of the hold, which turned out to be the crew's quarters. She was horrified to discover that the hammocks had shifted and twisted into a grotesque maze before them. At this surprise visual, she turned and kicked her way to the surface, as did Buck, both desperate for air.

"Oh, my God! Did you see that? It's creepy, Buck. How can we get through it?"

Buck was quiet a moment, catching his breath. "What if we look from the outside?" he asked.

Jocelyn Miller

"What do you mean?"

"Maybe we can pull the wood away from the outside."

"With what, our bare hands?" She had to admit, though, that it was a much more appealing approach. The thought of attempting to weave through the mangled hammocks was terrifying, nearly causing her to hyperventilate.

"Let's look," he said, and down they went again, but this time approaching the captain's quarters from the outside.

Summer pointed to the right of the captain's window. The trunk had been below the window and from inside, the bed had been to the left of the window. She had to judge the size of the bed and the distance from the bed to the hidden loose panels.

They rose again to the surface to catch their breath. "Watch where I tap, okay? I think the box will be in that area. It's a start anyway." They filled their lungs and dove.

In order to judge the size of the bed, she had to reflect on her drunken night in it, rolling with the captain. It was larger than a twin, and but perhaps a bit smaller than Elizabeth's bed at Magnolia. With that knowledge, she dove to several feet to the right side of the captain's window and indicated where she judged the hiding place to be.

As the ship was so damaged from its collisions with the Nassau Queen, many of the outer boards were loose. Buck was able to stick his large fingers between some of the boards and pull them apart. This took several tries and several swims to the surface for air. Summer dove with him each time, to watch the progress. She ignored the curious fish, but kept her eyes open for the long one with the teeth as she had inkling it was a barracuda. She had never heard much nice about them, and therefore kept a vigil.

After breaking off and releasing many loose and broken boards, which floated to the surface, Summer spotted an object in the black hole of the ship. She pointed it out to Buck, and they both dove to the top to refresh their air supply.

"That may be it!" she said, excitedly.

"I hope. Sun's goin' down soon."

"Darn! Just when we're getting somewhere." She glanced at the sun, heading low on the horizon. She looked again, squinting. "Oh, oh." She did a double take, for there, not less than thirty feet from the mast, she saw a dorsal fin!

Jocelyn Miller

"Buck!" she pointed. "Shark!"

Buck's eyes nearly popped out of his head. "Two sharks!"

Summer broke out in the shakes; her entire body trembled in fear. *Naked! I'll be eaten naked!* She felt totally vulnerable to the sharks without her clothing. "What do we do?"

"I dunno. I never seen sharks before!"

Not only were two separate dorsal fins heading their way, but another...and another.

"Oh, sweet Jesus, save us," Buck prayed.

The sharks were too close for them to make a swim for shore. Surely any movement or splashing would attract them.

"Hang onto the mast, Buck, and don't move. Don't move an inch."

Summer glanced at Cherry, watching from the beach. She had sat there for hours, but now she stood.

"Wha'd dos things?" she yelled. "Big fish comin'. Maybe you can catch one for us to eat!"

"Don't answer." Summer whispered. She had no clue what to do but stay statue stil,l hoping the sharks would ignore them. She wrapped her legs around the mast and told Buck to do the same.

The sharks swam around them now, sometimes diving, sometimes close enough to feel the whoosh of water as they passed. On one occasion, Buck was 'bumped'. He closed his eyes and prayed..

They counted seven big dorsal fins. The temptation was great to stick their heads in the water and look, but then again, Summer felt for sure they would panic, make waves and perhaps end up shark bait. Instead, they hung tight to the mast, their legs and arms entwined and molded to it, their breaths steady but soft, staring into each other's eyes, yet not seeing.

"Wha'd you two doin'?" Cherry yelled from shore. "Wha'd are dem things?"

Summer figured Cherry was losing patience with their silence.

"You two kissin'?" she yelled. If it hadn't been such a terrifying moment, Summer would have laughed herself silly.

Several minutes passed before the fins moved away. A straggler or two remained for a while, and then headed off up-shore.

"Do you think they're gone, or swimming below?" she asked Buck in a whisper.

Jocelyn Miller

He gently placed his face through the surface of the water. "They's gone," he said, rising up.

"Let's go, but don't splash."

Slowly, they made their way to the beach, where Cherry stood, fists on hips and a scowl on her face. "Wha'd you two doin' out der? I been callin' and callin' and you don' tell me nothin'. Look like you two was kissin'."

Buck had walked onshore, but Summer remained laying on her belly in the shallow water, not wanting to walk naked on land in front of Buck. "We were *not* kissing, Cherry. Those 'fish' you wanted us to bring for dinner were sharks, And if you don't know what a shark is, it's a giant fish that would think nothing of biting your legs off and then ripping the rest of you to pieces. You're lucky we're alive and not leaving you stranded here alone."

"Oh," was her reply. "I'se sorry, Miz Summah. Guess I's all crazy with dis baby in me."

"Buck, could you please turn your back so I can get out of the water before the crabs decide to eat me?"

"Come on, Cherry gal."

They headed back to the makeshift camp, leaving Summer to replace her mismatched-stolen-from-dead-crew-members outfit of a large, food stained, torn shirt, and a pair of stripped cotton pants tied around her waist with a cut of rigging. She looked back at the mast, a noble sentry against an orange and fuchsia sky. The sun hung low and red at the edge of the horizon.

36

"I don't like dem sharks, Miz Summer."

Buck had worked his magic with sticks and fluff again, and the trio sat around the campfire after a tasty meal of grilled fish. Buck was a wonder with his spear, and the fish were plentiful.

"Dat gold is bad luck."

"If we don't get the gold, Cherry, someone else will. This is most likely the easiest sunken treasure find in the entire world; there's the mast, there's the gold. We'd be fools not to get it. This is for you and Buck, for the baby, a nest egg, something for your future."

"Don't need no bad luck eggs."

Summer turned her attention to Buck. "I don't like those sharks either, believe me. I dread the thought of going under again, but we'll have to keep a watch for them. The worst is over. If that is the chest with the gold, then all we need to do is bring it up."

The next morning, after checking the horizon for dorsal fins, Buck swam safely to the mast while Summer undressed on the beach. She scanned the horizon for fins, before setting off to join him. Again, they dove to the hole Buck had created on the side of the ship. Both had become more and more adept at holding their breath for longer periods of time, though the pressure in their ears was a constant reminder that they

Jocelyn Miller

did not belong in the sea. The sharks now preoccupied their thoughts, and she constantly kept a look out while Buck tugged at the stubborn plank that was the last strong-hold to the box.

"I think one more pull, and we gots it," he said, on their air break. They both scanned the surrounding waters for the dreaded fins before returning below to the ship. This time, she helped tear the remaining plank from its position, and though it didn't break off like the others, they were able to pull it far enough away for Buck to reach for the chest.

He tugged, but the chest barely moved. He tugged once more, bringing it a few inches closer to the hole opening, and they again had to surface for air.

"It's too heavy," he said between sharp intakes of breath. Ain't never gonna swim it to the top. We need rope."

After checking the water for sharks and seeing none on the surface, they swam back to shore. Buck beached first and walked straight to the camp, allowing Summer to dress in private.

"Bad luck." Cherry said. "You don' listen to me, but dat gold is bad luck."

Cherry had busied herself making their camp as comfortable as possible. She had gathered palm leaves for bedding, dried sticks for the evening fire, and Spanish moss, *('fluff'* as Summer called it,) for fire-starting. The coconuts they had discovered on an earlier excursion into the thick tropical forest had kept them alive with coconut milk, and created a wonderful treat; for the divers, the sweetness relished after the saltiness of the sea. Fresh water had not been found, so the gathering of coconuts was necessary for their survival.

When Summer caught up with Buck at the campsite, he had gathered the rope he retrieved on their first day from the mast of the Nassau Queen.

"I think I gots it," he said. "We's gonna take the hatch cover with us, hoist the chest up with the rope and float the chest back to shore."

"Brilliant!" *It's nice to have a man around the camp! What if Buck had not survived and she and Cherry were stranded alone?* She then reminded herself that he had appeared with 'Yank' Woodfield in the 1870 census. *He survives, but what happens to Cherry?*

"Wha'd you looking at me like dat fo'?" Cherry asked.

Jocelyn Miller

Summer shook herself loose from her thoughts. Cherry was such an innocent victim of circumstance. She hadn't deserved her treacherous fate, but *what becomes of her?* "I was just thinking how big that baby's getting."

Cherry patted her growing belly, which had suddenly blossomed. She now looked *very* pregnant. "Bad luck baby, dis is."

Is time passing faster? Summer looked from Cherry's suddenly bloomed belly to the surrounding camp. They seemed to have settled in from the time she and Buck had swum to the ship that morning. Cherry definitely looked more pregnant than she had before.

Where did that come from? She stood frozen in place viewing a hut of sorts, which sat at the edge of the jungle forest. A roughly thatched roof covered a structure which appeared to be made with planks from the sunken ships.

"When did..." she caught herself before she finished the question. *They won't know what I'm talking about.* This was not *her* time, it was *theirs.* She had no control but to coexist in it, and, as always, the movement of time remained a mystery. Apparently, they had been there a while.

"Ready to go back?" Buck asked, shaking her from her thoughts and into the task ahead of them.

"Oh...yes...let's go." She looked once more at the hut and wondered if they all slept in there together; it was big enough.

After scanning for sharks, Buck swam to the mast, the ship's hatch secured with the rope. Summer disrobed and followed, always eyeing the horizon for the dorsal fins, but at the same time knowing that the beasts could be beneath her. She couldn't help but peek through the surface of the water to look for them, though the salt of the sea was a constant irritation.

It took two trips, but Buck managed to secure the small chest and pull it out of the hole, letting it sink to the ocean floor where its weight dug an inch or two into the sandy bottom. Summer watch from above, holding onto the rope now looped through a metal block[21] imbedded in the ship's mast. The end of the rope was tied around a hand grip on the hatch, keeping it from floating away.

---

[21] Pulley through which rigging rope runs

Jocelyn Miller

Buck broke through the surface, a big grin spread across his wet face. "It's ready!"

The two of them wrapped their legs around the mast, her legs above his, as they had done during the previous shark episode, and with all the strength they could muster they pulled...and pulled...and pulled on the rope, the chest slowly rising from its grave.

"The captain must have been very strong," she huffed. "When I saw him move the chest, it didn't look this heavy."

At last, it appeared at the surface. "I'll hold," he said, his words obviously strained with the sheer strength the task had taken. "Get the hatch."

Summer obeyed, swimming the hatch to the edge of the chest. Instinctively, she dipped the edge of the hatch into the water, shoving it beneath the chest. Buck gave the chest a hearty push, she released the hatch, and there it sat, on board the hatch cover.

She squealed with delight. "We did it, Buck! We did it!"

Buck released the rope from the metal block and threw it on top of the hatch. They set off, proudly pushing their treasure back to shore— not seeing the dorsal fin that followed.

"Dat fish! Dat fish!" Cherry screamed from the beach.

Something was wrong. Cherry waved her arms frantically from the beach, and pointed. When Summer turned to look behind them, her heart skipped a beat.

"Oh, my God! Shark!" she half whispered, half yelled. "Don't move...."

They stopped kicking and floated with the tide. This one was big. The back fin stood many feet behind the huge dorsal. It cut through the water like a saw, smooth, ominous. It circled them. The tide was coming in and Summer prayed they could get closer to the beach where the water was shallow...too shallow for sharks, *she hoped*.

It dove. They held their breath. Summer peeked in the water. "It's as big as a whale," she whispered, fighting the trembling that overtook her. Buck then put his face in the water and held it there. She wondered if he were drowning himself to avoid a horrific death by shark, as he did not come up for air for what seemed like minutes. When he did, she had never seen such terror in a person's eyes. Words were unnecessary; they were in serious danger.

Jocelyn Miller

Summer spotted Cherry, wringing her hands on the beach. She seemed so close, yet not close enough, as the shark rose again, his dorsal fin much too close for comfort. She could touch it if she reached out. She felt the whoosh of his body as he passed. She could see him, without dipping her head beneath the surface; an endless body of muscle and teeth. It suddenly dove. All was quiet and then a thunderous 'thum' raised the hatch several feet into the air, and they, losing their grip on the hatch, could not help but scream out in alarm.

"Swim!" Cherry shrieked from the beach. "Swim!"

Can we make it? Maybe the shark was only interested in the hatch? Was it possible? After all, he had ample opportunity to take a leg, an arm— a torso.

The chest had shifted, but still sat on the hatch, the rope secured around it. "Let's go...leave it behind...quiet...don't move too much."

Buck quickly removed the rope from the hand grip of the hatch and holding onto it, drifted away toward shore, moving his arms ever so slowly. Summer was a length ahead, hoping Buck was behind her. She didn't dare turn to look. She didn't want to see death speeding toward her.

37

"I don't think I've ever been so scared in my life." Summer lay belly down on the sandy shore, the incoming tide splashing against her bare behind.

"We still got the rope." Buck sat beside her on the beach, catching his breath. "The chest is still on the hatch. I'm pulling it in."

"Put dis on, Miz Summah." Cherry stood above her, arms full of dead-men's clothes. Buck politely looked out to sea while she dressed, the sand scratching her skin; it was impossible to brush it all away.

Later, after carrying the chest to the campsite, Buck pried it open. He pulled the bag out of the chest, opened it, and dumped the contents back into the chest. Dozens upon dozens of golden coins clinked and clanked their way into the cavity.

"What in the world?" Summer reached in and grabbed a handful of the coins. "This is unbelievable. They look like…like something out of a pirate movie."

"Like what?" Cherry asked. "What is dey? Is dat money?"

"I think they're Spanish doubloons. Good grief."

"Gold coins," Buck said matter-of-factly. "Never thought I'd be seein' these."

"They're yours, Buck, yours and Cherry's."

"Don' you want none?"

Jocelyn Miller

"Remember what I told you, Cherry—about me?" It was their secret. Perhaps Cherry thought she was nuts, but she agreed to keep the time-travel business between the two of them. Summer put the coins back into the bag. "These coins are for your future, and for the baby."

"I dunno. Dey's bad-luck. I just knows it."

Ignoring Cherry's negative comments, and after counting the coins—all 472 of them—Summer and Buck put them back into the pouch, returning them to the chest.

"You can't let anyone ever see this chest, Buck."

"Oh, I knows that, Miz Summer. Can't be no nigger man with gold on him."

* * *

While Buck fished for dinner and Cherry foraged the tropical forest for fruit and coconuts, Summer peeked into the new (or so she thought) palm-leaf covered hut. There was just enough room on the sand floor for the three mats they used as bedding. She had no recollection of ever sleeping in the hut, but obviously this was the arrangement and had been for some time.

She returned to the campfire and threw on more dried branches to keep it going. Buck had started it before he left for fishing so that it would be ready when he returned with the catch. It was a beautiful place, lush and green with food aplenty, but cool at night and the fire felt good.

No sooner had she sat when a terrible shriek filled her ears.

"He comin! Miz Summah! He comin'!"

Cherry burst through the brush, her big belly swaying in front. Summer stood to yell at her to stop running or the baby was going to pop right out of her, but something caught her eye and the hairs of her arms stood on end. Tom Quinn! They had forgotten about Tom Quinn, but there he was, face bashed in, eyeball dangling and club in hand!

Cherry gasped for breath as she grabbed onto Summer, her fingers digging into flesh, not realizing the power of her adrenaline-based strength. "Run!" she screamed.

Indeed, Summer wanted to run, but stood fast. It took every ounce of courage she could muster to stand watching the horrid apparition stomp toward them. *It's a ghost...it's a ghost...it can't hurt us....* She hoped that was true.

Tom Quinn raised the bat and shook it. "I found ya, Cherry gal. You ain't getting' away from me!"

"Run!" Cherry shrieked.

"Stay!" Summer yelled. "Stay behind me!"

Tom Quinn approached, but the closer he came, the more translucent the vision, until he stood on the other side of the campfire, a vapor, his horrid face faintly visible. "I'll get ya!" he howled, and disappeared.

Cherry burst into sobs. "He ain't never leavin' me alone! Sweet Jesus protect me!" She collapsed onto the sand and laid prone, her hands on her big belly. "He ain't never leavin' me..." she cried.

"What's wrong?" Buck came panting, having run from his fishing point. "What's the hollerin'?"

"We seen him! We seen Tom Quinn!"

"Tom Quinn is *dead*," Buck said.

"He ain't."

"We *did* see him, Buck. He was here, but he vanished. He's a ghost."

"Ain't no such thing." He helped Cherry up. "You gots to be calm. Look at that belly. You don't want to hurt that baby, do you?"

"Dis is Tom Quinn's baby, and he bad luck."

"You gonna be good to that baby. That baby don't know it's Tom Quinn's baby. Maybe it's a pretty little brown-skinned gal like you."

Cherry managed a smile. "You's too good to me, Buck."

Yes, thank God for Buck Henry.

* * *

At first, Summer wondered if Tom Quinn had returned again. She lay on her mat, having been awakened by rustling sounds from the camp. She glanced to her left and saw Cherry, and then Buck on the far side of the hut, both sound asleep in the early morning light.

"Cherry," she whispered. "Wake up."

"Huh?"

"Shhh. Wake Buck up...something's in camp."

Jocelyn Miller

Cherry woke Buck, telling him to shush. She pointed to the hut door, and he crawled on all fours to peek out of the opening. "Istonko," he said after a few moments.

Istonko? Summer crawled to the opening. *The Seminoles!*

Buck was already up and out of the hut. He said a few more words to the Seminoles standing by the fire pit.

"Come out," Buck said, seeing Summer and Cherry both peeking from the hut door. "It's alright."

Soon, three more Seminole men appeared, and looking out to the beach, Summer noticed two dugout canoes pulled up onto the sand. The Seminole eyed her suspiciously, as they did all white people.

"We can go with them," Buck said.

"Where will they take us?"

"I dunno, but we can get out of this place. I'll get the chest." The chest was all they had.

A lot of jabbering went on between the Seminole men when it came time to enter the canoes. They glanced at Summer many times during their heated discussion, and she surmised that neither canoe wanted her because of her color. Finally, it was decided that Buck would ride in one canoe, and Cherry and Summer together in the other. It was odd being the one discriminated against. The Seminole had commented on Cherry's big belly, and smiled often at her. Her beauty was apparently quite to their liking, as it had been in their first encounter with the Seminole. Buck was very much accepted, but Summer—she was an outcast and very obviously made to feel that way.

The men paddled the canoes swiftly, staying close to shore. After several hours, and a very sore back from sitting so long, Summer spotted islands. She had lost all concept of where they were on the map of Florida, but she hoped they were stopping at one of the islands, or at least that the Seminole camp was close by. Poor Cherry was feeling the effects of sitting on a hard plank the entire day, her big belly a cumbersome appendage. Her bladder had leaked because of the pressure, but the Seminole had not stopped ashore for potty-breaks. If one of the men had to relieve himself, he stood in the canoe and did so.

"Oh, no!" Cherry screamed all of a sudden, causing all on board to jump. The Seminole men turned and said something in their language but Summer couldn't understand a word of it.

"The baby's comin'! My water broke!"

Jocelyn Miller

"Well, holy crap," Summer said. *Why does everything have to happen at the worst possible moment?*

Summer tapped Cherry's belly and did a baby-rocking motion with her arms, hoping the natives would get the idea.

"It's gonna come!" Cherry's screamed.

"Buck! The baby!" Summer yelled at the top of her lungs, hoping that he, in the canoe ahead, could hear. "The baby's coming!"

Buck apparently said something to the Seminoles in his canoe, as the natives yelled back and forth from canoe to canoe and pointed ahead. They blessedly rowed faster, as Cherry's pains were coming quicker.

"Dis baby comin' fast!"

"Hold on! Don't push...don't push!"

"Can't help it—it comin'!"

Even the Seminole men were rowing faster having gauged by Cherry's moans that birth was imminent. They seemed to know their islands very well, as they were able to tie the canoes up to a landing on an island that was not so thick with mangrove.

Buck quickly carried Cherry from the boat to a spot of land patchy with a growth of grasses and shaded by trees. He removed his shirt, placing it beneath her bottom. The Seminole men stood by their canoes, softly talking amongst one another, while Cherry grunted with involuntary contractions. Summer held her hand, which tightened like a vise with each push.

"It's okay, Cherry. Let the baby come. You're safe." *Oh, God, please let this go smoothly!*

Her pains were very close together, barely stopping long enough for a decent rest. "Pull me up!" she suddenly screamed, and Summer did, lifting her to a sitting position. There was no turning back now.

"Come on, Cherry gal. I see the head," Buck said, ready to catch at the proper moment.

A final push, and the baby came into the world with a sharp and hearty squeal.

"You done it, Cherry! It's a fine boy!"

"What do I do?" Summer asked, suddenly panicked. I don't know what to do now!"

"I does." Buck said. "I birthed babies before. I had a wife once...." His voice trailed off as he cut the cord with his knife, and waited for the placenta.

Jocelyn Miller

A wife?

He handed Summer the baby and massaged Cherry's belly until the rest of the matter expelled itself.

The baby screamed in her arms, his face scrunched, delivering a mighty yell. His little legs kicked while his tiny hands jerked in the air. She held him close, securely, hoping to calm him, and herself. *He's so white*...and she remembered when little James was born; he was white too, *but not this white*.

The new baby's hair was wet and matted against his skull. *It looks light, too.* When he calmed down, and his face relaxed, she swore she saw the startling blue of his eyes.

Jocelyn Miller

38

"**D**at can't be my baby." Cherry sat with her back against a palm, the baby glaringly white against her dark skin. "He too white to be my baby."

"He's the only baby on the island, Cherry, and he's yours. Buck caught him, and I held him soon as he was born. He's yours, and he's beautiful. Just look at him!"

With the infant now washed and wrapped in Buck's shirt, it was plain to see that he was a fine looking boy.

"You and Ruth told me that all black babies are white at first. Remember how white James was when he was born? Well he got a little darker."

Cherry looked confused for a moment. Summer knew it was difficult for her to comprehend the fact that the white woman she and Buck had fished out of the St. Johns River knew the happenings at Magnolia Plantation, and all the people on it.

"I'm sorry. I forget how hard it is for you to understand how I know all this stuff. But, aside from that, your little baby here might get darker; give him a chance."

"He a Quinn baby. I don't want no babies from dat man."

Jocelyn Miller

"Cherry, he's just a helpless baby. You *have* to take care of him. *You* have the milk, *I* don't."

"I take care of him alright, and den I give him to one of dem Indians to take home."

"The Indians don't like white folks, remember?"

"See. Even you knows he white and he gonna stay white."

She was so right. Quinn's offspring was as white as Summer. After several hours, he seemed to get even whiter. The fuzz on his head was nearly platinum, and his eyes were a startling blue even now as a newborn.

While she tended to Cherry and the baby, Buck had gone off with the Seminoles. When they returned they had several fish and even fresh water, carried in inflatable bags tied to the Indian's belts. *Water!* It was so good after drinking nothing but coconut milk for however long they had been at the other camp.

Buck brought the chest of gold coins from the canoe to the new camp, not chancing the canoe floating away, or the natives vanishing with it. As it turned out, he had made the right choice; the following morning, the canoes and the Seminoles were gone.

"I knew they was gonna do that." Buck said, as he and Summer stood on the bank where the canoes had been tied. "They got jittery. A white baby from a nigger-gal scared them."

"I'm so sorry, Buck. Now we're stuck here…wherever *here* is."

"We gots food and water. I'll build another shanty."

Regardless of Cherry's disdain for the baby, she nursed him. He quickly latched on to a breast and fed until he passed out. When he woke, the entire scenario was repeated. Cherry held him as she would a chicken she was plucking, with total detachment. Summer's heart ached for the baby and his lack of love from Cherry, but she hoped Buck could show him the love he deserved and perhaps, with time, Cherry's heart would be won over by the infant.

* * *

The baby was healthy and robust, and as he depleted the milk from Cherry's breasts, more was produced. Despite the constant physical closeness with the infant, Cherry remained cool. "Dem eyes—just like Tom Quinn. Ain't natural, dat color."

Jocelyn Miller

Tom Quinn. Where is he now? Will he return? So much had happened since his last horrific appearance at the shipwreck camp, that she rarely thought of him unless Cherry mentioned him. At times, she mentioned him enough to conjure him up.

"Why don't you forget about Tom Quinn? Put him out of your mind?"

"Every time I see dis chile' I see Tom Quinn. He comin' to haunt me and ain't never gonna be out o' my mind."

She has a point. "You have to give the baby a name."

"I gots one picked out. He a Yankee baby, so I'se gonna call him Yank."

Yank? It all made sense now, the old man in the nursing home, Jesse's cousin, *Taylor Yank Woodfield.*

Buck built them a fine shanty a distance inland from the water's edge, thinking ahead to when Yank could crawl and walk. The shanty was made of shell and *muck. Muck* is how Summer thought of the mixture he created from oyster shell and sand. 'Tabby'[22], he called it and said that where he came from, that was how the slave cabins were built.

How long had Buck worked on the structure? This was one of the reasons why she couldn't judge the passing of time, because it passed in sporadic jumps. How long had they been here? The baby looked to be several months old, now. His color stayed true—white—his hair platinum and his eyes a brilliant shade of blue. Obviously they had been there for months but not in *her* time; in her time it felt like hours.

Buck's concern for the welfare of the child was heartwarming. As Summer had hoped, Buck made up for Cherry's lack of love. He built a cradle for the boy, even rocked him at times when Cherry needed a break. The baby took to him, the low masculine sound of Bucks lullabies nodding him off to sleep, and sometimes Summer too!

"You have a wonderful voice, Buck." She said one day while Cherry was in the forest getting water. They sat on their stump chairs, little Yank sound asleep in Buck's muscled arms, the baby so white against his blackness. Even she was amazed that genetics could work in such a fashion. But then, look at her own self; she was as white as Yank, and she hailed from black slaves stolen from Africa.

[22] A mortar made from oyster shells and sand, sometimes used to build slave housing in the old South.

"You mentioned you were married once, Buck. Where's your wife?"

"She gone—sold," he said sadly, looking out across the water.

"And you had children?"

"I had a boy, but he was sold with his mama. I don't like to think on it."

"I'm sorry Buck. You're so good with the baby, and Cherry, too. It breaks my heart that you lost your family."

"I pray every day that they's alive somewhere, and together."

He was silent, and Summer felt badly for prying into his past, bringing to light events that were painful.

"I don't know what we would have done without you when little Yank was born."

He rose, the baby still asleep in his arms. "I gonna put him in his cradle and go fish," he said, leaving her.

* * *

"Buck, the sky is getting black," Summer said, one day after sitting on a tree stump looking out at the water and other islands she could see from their settlement. She had been reminiscing about Captain Ruiz and how strange it had been to have the brief torrid romance, and how quickly he disappeared. *I'm not ashamed*, she told herself, not quite sure if she had cheated or not; not knowing if ghost sex counted in the book of cheating. She missed Guy desperately and wondered what was happening in her time. Was he worried? Was he looking for her? A swift breeze shook her from her thoughts, and she noticed the darkening sky.

"I think we have a thunderstorm coming. Better bring the loose stuff in." They had worked hard to create dishes from coconut shells, chairs from tree stumps, a shade lean-to from palms; but all were loose items that could be lost in a windy storm. Buck was working on a storage shack so that the main shanty was not so cluttered when things had to be secured indoors. He was also working on a dugout from a cedar tree that had fallen. They wanted to investigate the other islands and perhaps find the mainland or the Seminole village. They had not seen the Seminoles since Yank was born.

As the day went on, the dark clouds opened up in torrential rains. The winds also picked up with increasing gusts that bent the trees and

Jocelyn Miller

sent smaller objects that hadn't been secured, flying into the tropical forest, or banging into the shanty.

"I wonder if we're having a hurricane?" Summer said as the wind rattled and shook the world outside.

The threesome huddled in the shack, Cherry holding onto Yank whom, despite her animosity, had an instinctive attachment to his mother. At times, he screamed if she left him during his waking hours, which pushed her nerves to the breaking point. "Don' surprise me if we's havin' a hur'cain wid all da bad luck goin' 'round."

Summer tried to overlook Cherry's negativity even though she understood where it came from. The poor girl had had nothing but misery; raped by Author Ascot at thirteen, a baby by fourteen; the loss of her love, Juba, the Yankee soldiers, the kidnapping, and now stranded on an island far from home with a white baby by a man she hated—and one who haunted her! Summer so wanted her to find some happiness, and truly felt Buck was the one to deliver it. It gnawed at her that Cherry wasn't on the 1870 census...*just Buck and Yank.*

As night fell, the severity of the storm and intensity of the winds increased until even the tabby shanty seemed to rock with the wind. Larger objects now hit the shanty, slamming the oyster shell outer walls with tremendous blasts and thumps that brought shrieks from the women, and cries from Yank. The door, which Buck had labored intensely on, tying a row of thinner bodied trees together with salvaged rope and vines from the forest, blew open with a howling forceful gust of wind. The women screamed as it flew inward, held precariously onto the frame by vine and rope at the top corner. They flattened their bodies against the wall so as not to be hit by the wildly flapping door only a few short feet from their faces. Buck crawled toward it, against the force of the wind which now overtook their space, sending objects ricocheting dangerously around the inside, banging against the walls and creating greater panic and fear. The women instinctively lowered their heads lest they be hit; Yank screamed hysterically on Cherry's lap.

No sooner had Buck reached the fiercely flapping door, when its remaining connection—the bit of vine and rope tied at the top corner— broke loose, jamming the door square into his forehead. He collapsed backward, the door flying over him toward the back of the shanty, missing the women by inches.

Jocelyn Miller

"No!" Summer screamed. With Buck injured or worse, dead, they had lost their protector! The wind was incredibly strong. Crawling on all fours, Summer felt as if she were being forced backward, not forward as she crawled, inch by inch, toward Buck. The wind whipped the moisture from her eyes and causing the flesh of her face to press backward against her ears. When she at last reached Buck's prone body, she placed a hand on his chest; he was breathing! She ran her hand over his eyes, his nose; *intact*. She put her hand on his forehead, and there, she realized his injury: an indented wound that oozed a sticky liquid. Blood. She tried to view it in the darkening night, but it was impossible.

"Buck is hurt!" She yelled, the words ripped from her mouth by the wind, fading into the howl of the storm. He was far too heavy for her to move alone. She wanted to cry; she had no training on how to handle this emergency; no flashlight, no strong arms to help move his body, no 911—nothing! There was *nothing* with which to secure the door back onto its frame to block the deadly winds...*nothing* with which to treat Bucks wound. She was desperate, *they* were desperate, and she didn't have a clue as to how they would survive the night.

Summer crawled back to Cherry. "You have to help me move Buck," she yelled. "We have to get him out of the doorway!"

Cherry laid the screaming baby down on his back. They crawled back to Buck, both grabbing an arm, the force of the wind rippling the flesh on their faces.

"Pull!" Summer screamed, and they each tugged, moving Buck a few inches toward the back of the shanty. After several attempts they were able to move him out of the direct path of the wind, which screamed like a banshee through the opened doorway.

Summer cried in pure helplessness at the situation as they crawled back to Yank, the tears torn from her eyes and lost in the wind. They were cold, wet, terrified, and Buck was still unconscious. And just what could he do should he come to? He was hurt, and she wasn't sure how badly.

Somehow, she, Cherry and Yank managed move out of the direct force of the wind and eventually huddled together and dozed off. Perhaps it was the pure exhaustion and hopelessness of the situation, that they were able to block out the tirade of Mother Nature who furiously banged, bashed, and blew around them, and through the shanty with the threat of blowing it to shreds.

Jocelyn Miller

Jocelyn Miller

39

She woke with a start. The fog lifted from her mind and she realized she was in the shanty. It was dark outside and the wind still howled through the door opening, though much diminished. *Something* woke her....Cherry! Cherry was screaming!

"He here!" Cherry shrieked, along with Yank, who surely was jarred awake by his mother's screams.

"He here!"

Summer shot up to a sitting position and focused on a glow in the far corner. It was *Tom Quinn!* She herself shrieked and then steadied herself. Cherry had crawled away, leaving the baby screaming on the shanty floor. Yank was between her and the apparition, so she reached in the dark for him and hugged him to her breast. Quinn glowed in the dark of the shanty, as if he'd been doused in radioactive material.

"Cherry!" Summer yelled. *Where is she?* "Come back!" There was no reply, and all Summer could do was hug the baby and watch as Quinn passed her by—*floated by*—the club gripped in a fist. His mouth moved, but she couldn't hear his words.

"Buck, wake up!" She needed him desperately at this moment. Was he still out cold? Was he dead? "Wake up, Buck!"

He groaned; a good sign.

Jocelyn Miller

"Buck, Cherry has run out into the storm!"

He groaned again, and she realized he would be of no help. She laid the crying baby down as far out of the wind as possible, and crawled to the shanty doorway.

"Cherry!" she screamed, using her hand as a visor against the wind and rain. Blessedly, the wind was not as strong as it had been earlier. There was a faint sign of sunrise, a break, a thin streak of red through the black clouds. "Cherry!" she screamed again, but there was no answer; she was gone, as well as was Quinn. He was nowhere in sight. She slumped to the ground and cried. Her quest was to save Cherry, to bring her home, but where had she gone? The baby cried behind her. She couldn't leave him alone and Buck was as helpless as he was.

Dawn came, and with it the promised clearing. The sun rose but revealed nothing of Cherry. The water swelled and splashed against the bank, still reeling from the torment of the storm. Buck had woken, and Summer was able to wash his wound and wrap it with a strip of fabric from the dead sailor's shirt that she wore. The baby was hungry, and in this she felt totally helpless and desperate. What could she give him? Where was Cherry? They waited and waited for her to return, but when the sun shone straight up in the sky, she had not come back. Yank howled with hunger, and Summer left to forage for coconut. He would have to drink from that, as there was nothing else she could think of that would have any nutritional value.

"Cherry!" she called as she walked their beaten path through the tropical forest. Trees had fallen everywhere; some split in half, still held together by sinew and bark, leaning over, dusting the forest floor as if resting their weary tops after the stormy night. She found two brown coconuts on the ground and also spotted ripening bananas on a tree, making a mental note to return for those. Perhaps the baby could eat mashed banana if it were ripe enough.

"You're up!" she said, returning to camp with a coconut in each hand.

Buck sat on a tree-stump chair, the whimpering Yank in his lap. "Oh, I gots a headache like no other."

"You have quite a gash on your head. Take it easy, because we don't know if you have a concussion."

Jocelyn Miller

He rose to retrieve the coconuts, but immediately sat down on the stump. "Don't think I can open them for you."

"I know how to open them, thanks to you," she said. "I've certainly watched you do this enough times."

"What about Cherry gal? Why'd she run off like that?"

"It was the ghost of Quinn. He came last night. I know you don't believe us, but I saw him too."

"Hope she ain't hurt, and can find the camp."

"Me, too, Buck. Me, too. I'm scared for her."

It wasn't easy, but Summer bashed the coconut with their coconut-cracking-rock, retrieved by Buck in the beginning of their stay for just this purpose. It was a heavy stone, and she had to lift it high above her shoulders and force it down upon the coconut with all the strength she could muster. It took four tries before the coconut cracked and split revealing the brown hairy husk inside. Her strength was not a good match for pulling away the husk, a difficult task at best, but the sound of Yank in the background screaming for food encouraged her to work quickly. Once the husk was removed she was able to get to the milk by taking Buck's knife and forcing a hole through its narrow end.

"Okay, Buck, hold Yank upright and let's give this a try." She poured some of the coconut milk into one of their drinking shells and brought it to the baby's lips. He had never drunk from anything but Cherry's breast, and at first was not at all cooperative. He gagged, coughed, and turned his head away, flailing at the coconut shell with his small fists. It certainly wasn't as comforting as his mother's breast, but Summer dipped her finger into the coconut cup and stuck it into his mouth and he sucked greedily. Once he got a taste of the milk, his hunger took over and he wanted more. Between her finger and the cup, Summer was able to feed him ever so slowly.

When the sun was halfway to setting, Cherry had not returned. Summer took off again into the forest to search for her. Surely a ghost could cause no harm! Even a horrid looking, nasty beast like Tom Quinn could do no harm with his ghostly hatchet!

Buck remained at the camp with Yank, who was fast asleep in his hand-hewn cradle in the shanty. The third feeding of coconut milk had satisfied his hunger and he drifted off sucking his thumb. Buck was still feeling the effects of the bash to the forehead, and Summer insisted he stay put and watch the baby. Even though he was desperate to find Cherry, he was in no condition to disagree.

Following the beaten path again, she came to the fresh water spring, but there was no sign of Cherry. Beyond the spring lay a thicker forest. It was first time she would pass the spring and go beyond, into the forest. Perhaps Cherry had gotten lost on the other side of the island? Had she run that far? It was worth checking. There was no trail, so she tore more strips from the dead sailor's shirt and tied them to branches as she fought her way through the thick growth. The brush scratched her arms and legs through the fabric of the shirt and pants. *Perhaps this isn't a good idea. Cherry couldn't have come this way— she wouldn't have come this way in the dark.* The mosquitos buzzed relentlessly about her head, up her nose, into her ears, and she dare not open her mouth. Just when she thought she was hopelessly caught in the twisted growth of the island, she spotted water. *The other side!*

"Cherry!" she called, hoping against hope. A nagging vision had entered her mind as she fought her way through the trees and brush, a vision of the red bandana floating in the water, and it was making her quite nervous. Her stomach fluttered with dread as she walked along the water's edge looking for the bandana, or any clue that Cherry had been in the area. A stretch of mangrove caused her to head inland again, battling the brush and vines. *I should have gone back to my trail,* she thought, remembering how she had tied the strips of fabric to branches as she walked. The sky seemed darker to her, indicating that the sun was further down toward the horizon.

She returned to the water and then to the spot where she had come out of the brush. It was a race, now, to return to the camp before the sun fell below the horizon. She thanked herself for marking the trail with the strips of fabric. *Stay calm, stay calm,* she thought, racing the setting sun and watching for snakes as she went. All three of them had lost their shoes during the shipwreck, and though the soles of their feet had toughened, the threat of a puncture wound or snake bite was always of great concern.

* * *

Motherhood was a difficult task to take over. After arriving back at camp preparations had to be made for the overnight care of Yank,

Jocelyn Miller

whose hunger was nearly insatiable. The task temporarily took their minds off of Cherry, but Summer was heavyhearted once Buck and Yank were asleep in the tabby shanty. The door frame was still empty of a door, so she lay looking through its rectangular frame into the tropical night. *She's dead. She has to be dead. And, if not, why hasn't she come back?* Remembering how terrified Cherry was of Quinn, it broke her heart wondering what transpired after Cherry crawled out of the shanty. Where did she go? Could Quinn's ghost have done something to her?

Neither she nor Buck had a good night's sleep, as Yank woke several times demanding more coconut milk. At dawn Yank was finally in a heavy slee,p and she crawled from her bed to the door, trying not to wake either. Thoughts and worry for Cherry hit like the hurricane, and the vision of the red bandana floating on water nagged like a toothache. She needed coffee and wished there were some. She needed to think. She needed more sleep.

Dawn was beautiful, as were most on the island. She walked to the water and let the incoming tide splash around her ankles. She would look for oysters, or crab, or anything for breakfast. Coming up with food every day was a time-stealing chore, but it had to be done or they would starve. Hopefully Buck could fish today.

She turned right, and walked along the shoreline, her head heavy from lack of sleep and worry. Maybe there was conch, or clams, or perhaps a fish would....

"Buck!" she screamed. "Buck!" Her heart fell. Her stomach fell. She dropped to her knees. There is was—the red bandana—floating in with the tide. Silently, it dipped fluttered and swayed on gentle swells that lapped and foamed when they reached their final destiny on the sandy beach. It was a deceivingly peaceful sight, so unlike its owner, whose life had been nothing but torment.

Buck had not heard her. He had not come to her screams. She reached for the bandana, holding it up by a corner as the sea water dripped rapidly from its opposite end. Her eyes followed the shoreline further beyond the bandana, soaked and wet against the morning sky, and there lie the answer: Cherry, beautiful Cherry, lying face down at the water's edge; she had finally returned—with the tide.

40

Their grief was unbearable. Neither she nor Buck could keep the tears and sobs away for long; Summer grieved because her intent had been to save Cherry, her friend—her beloved cousin—and return her home to Magnolia, to her family. Buck, because he had loved her. He had lost one woman and child to slavery, and now he had lost another woman. Then, there was the baby, Yank; a motherless child.

There was nothing to wrap Cherry's body in for burial, so they had gathered palm leaves to place over her; neither could bear the thought of pouring dirt onto her pretty face.

"This is a nightmare!" Summer sobbed, kneeling by the open grave, little Yank gurgling happily beside her in the grass, unaware of the tragedy. "I promised to take her home!"

Buck had chosen a beautiful, shaded spot beneath a large cypress near the fresh water spring, for her final resting place.

"She's home now," Buck said, pulling Summer to her feet. He had dug the grave with hand-hewn tools: a shovel from tree bark, coconut shells, his own hands. It had not been an easy task, but he had dug it deep.

"I'm going to miss her," Summer said, peering into the pit, the palm leaves completely covering the body. "I failed my mission."

"That thing won't scare her no more."

Oh yes it will. Tom Quinn is chasing her through eternity at this very moment. She couldn't tell Buck that, but she knew it to be true. *Somehow* she would have to complete this mission—she would have to make it right for Cherry.

"Let's cover her up," she said, unable to bear the pain any longer.

"One more thing," he said, reaching into his pocket. He pulled out three of the gold coins and tossed them onto the palms. "She ain't goin' to heaven poor. She ain't goin' a poor colored gal with no gold."

"She said the coins were bad luck. Maybe she was right."

"No. She was wrong. The coins are *good* luck, because now we ain't poor. Now we can have a life, Yank, you and me. We gotta make it good for Cherry. Her baby ain't goin' to be poor."

Summer wiped the tears from her eyes. *It's for you and Yank, Buck. I gotta get home somehow.*

"Here," Buck said, handing her the red bandana. Wipe your tears here, for Cherry."

"Oh!" Summer exclaimed. "This should go with her!"

"No, this should be with *us*, so we remember our gal."

* * *

That night, she woke to screams. She knew where they came from—*the living nightmare*—the nightmare that replayed itself over and over again, and would, until it was finally resolved. Only, she didn't know how to resolve it, and she didn't know how to get home.

She scrawled to the doorway and stuck her head outside into the night.

"Evaline!" Cherry screamed, breaking through the brush, luminous, opaque and *terrified.*

Summer knew what came next—Tom Quinn. He barreled through the brush after her, the same grotesque face, the same club in hand, the same evil intent glowing from the one eyeball that had remained intact.

Without thought, she sprang from the doorway and ran after the luminous figures. She followed them down the beach and when they turned into the thick of the forest, she followed.

Jocelyn Miller

She was surprised that the path they had taken had brought her to the fresh spring but, once there, the luminous figures were gone...*vanished*. It was dark except for a bit of moonlight filtering through the trees. The night sounds made her shiver. It was one thing to be at the spring in daylight, but another to be there in the dark of night, alone. Or was she? Her hackles spiked, causing her to turn, to look behind. Tom Quinn was coming toward her—*glaring at her!*

He sees me! It was all out terror as she frantically tried to find the pathway to the beach—and couldn't. He came at her, seeming to float, not walk. She wondered how fast he could float—could she outrun him? What if he caught her? Should she just stand still? *No! I can't!* All reserve was lost as she crashed through the brush ignoring the biting stems and thorns that slashed at her arms, her legs, her face. The forest thickened, seeming to hold her—capture her—yet on she ran, stumbling, screaming, knowing now, firsthand, how terrified Cherry must have felt when Tom Quinn pursued her. Then, all of a sudden, she was trapped. She couldn't move forward; the thickness of the forest caught and held her like a bug in a spider's web. One final scream shattered the night and the world went black.

* * *

"Thank God you're safe!"

"Wha...?"

"Summer Woodfield, don't you ever do this to me again. I'm never letting you out of my sight!"

It was a comfortable place. She wanted to sleep, a long, dreamless sleep. It felt good to have arms around her, to be safe. She opened her eyes.

"Guy! Oh, thank God! Guy, is it really you? Am I dreaming?"

Guy helped her to a sitting position and handed her a bottle of water. "It's me, and I'm never letting you go again."

She drank the water down in loud gulps, until it was empty. "We're still here," she said looking at her surroundings.

"We're here, and you're lucky we found you—*alive*. If you hadn't left me the message when you went out with Captain Jack, I never would have known something was wrong until it was too late."

"Captain Jack... oh, my God! Captain Jack is dead!"

Jocelyn Miller

"We know. The park rangers found his body floating out there somewhere. That's how we knew to look for you.

"He was murdered, Guy."

"We know."

"I know who murdered him, too."

"The rangers will be glad to hear that." He helped her up. "You're a mess."

"I'm sure I am," she said, brushing the dirt from her behind. "I'm cut to shreds. Some wicked brush in this place." She suddenly wavered, and he reached to keep her from falling.

"I...I just remembered!"

"What?"

"What happened. Not to Captain Jack, but what happened with Cherry." She wavered again, her head feeling light and dizzy. It had been such a time, a long journey from the St. Johns River to the Everglades, to this moment. "It's going to take a long time to get through this."

"Through what?"

"What's happened."

"Here." A park ranger appeared with a first aid kit. Let's see if we can clean you up a bit."

Summer sat on a log while the two rangers worked at the wounds on her arms and legs. Guy stood before her, shaking his head once in a while.

"I guess I had you pretty scared, huh?" she asked.

"*Scared* doesn't quite cover it. You've got to stop this craziness."

"It isn't craziness. I'll tell you about it later." She turned to the rangers. "I know who killed Captain Jack."

"You do?" one ranger asked.

"I certainly do. I saw the whole thing."

"Get to the radio, Jeff. Tell them we have a witness and we're coming in." He turned to Summer. "Okay, let's get you out of here."

"Wait. We can't go yet."

"Why not?"

"Uh, I'm not finished yet."

"We really need to get you to some real medical help," the ranger said.

"I'm not leaving yet!" she said, quite adamantly.

Jocelyn Miller

"Look," Guy came to her defense. "Could you give us a little private time?"

"Alright. We'll wait at the boat, but don't be long. The police will be waiting—and an ambulance."

"I don't need an ambulance."

"It's just a precaution," he said, and left.

"Cherry is buried here," Summer said, after the ranger was out of sight. "I won't leave her here."

"Cherry is bur....Summer!"

"I know, I know, you hate this stuff, but it's true, Guy. She's here. I helped bury her. I know you believe me and I'm going to prove it to you, too. We have to dig her up."

"How the hell can we tell those rangers that we have to stay here a while to dig up a body that's been dead for God only knows how long? And just what are we going to dig her up with?"

"Well...I know what. We'll go back with them and return tomorrow—with shovels. We'll hire a boat, you can drive it."

Guy was silent. She loved him. She loved him dearly. He looked so handsome standing there, even with the grumpy look on his face. Captain Ruiz suddenly raced across her memory and she felt her face turn red. Had she cheated? Never in a million years would she intentionally hurt Guy, but she had slept with another man! *Was* he a man? A ghost? Was it cheating? She hid her face in her hands overcome by the memory of her union with Captain Ruiz.

"All right. I have to listen to you, Summer, because you found Mick Mason...the Union soldiers....the hoop. I know you're telling the truth—I just don't want to believe it's possible. Let's go back with the rangers and discuss this later. They have lots of questions for you, as do the police."

"Let's go," she said, anxious to make plans for the morning. "We have to find out the name of this island so we can find it again."

As they motored away in the ranger's outboard, she and Guy both looked long and hard at the island they were to return to, she trying to remember where it fit in amongst the other islands in the chain.

"What's the name of that place?" Summer yelled over the roar of the motor.

"Buck Key," was the reply.

I should have known!

Jocelyn Miller

* * *

"I feel so good knowing I've been instrumental in resolving Jack's murder." Summer yelled over the sound of the motor the next morning as she and Guy zipped along in their rented boat. With a chart of the islands, GPS, insect repellent, two shovels, a case of water, a bag lunch, and a large and sturdy burlap bag, they headed back to Buck Key.

The night before, she had relived the entire scenario of the events leading up to Jack's death, for the police. They knew exactly who the men were that she had described and, by now, Summer hoped they were sitting in jail. Despite his shady side, Jack seemed like a nice fellow and didn't deserve to die the way he did.

"This is it; this where we stayed," she said, once on the island, standing on the spot she remembered as the place the tabby shanty stood. They had driven the boat around the island until Summer recognized the spot that had been their temporary home.

They cut a new path through the old route to the spring, as it was totally obliterated by decades of overgrowth. When they came to the spring, she was amazed that it still existed. Cherry's burial was still fresh in her mind, and she knew the approximate area where Buck had dug the grave; but some things had changed. The large cypress tree that marked Cherry's gravesite was gone. Luckily, there remained a stump of the tree, which she had nearly tripped over in her search.

"Here!" she said assuming the tree stump was the remnant of the old tree. "I'm pretty sure this is it." *I hope.* For her own credibility in Guy's mind, she prayed this was the spot.

They both dug. At first, the ground was unrelenting. They had made a wide circle of sticks, encompassing a large enough area for margin of error. Starting on opposite sides of the circle, they dug inward, resting often, she more than he, as she simply did not have the upper body strength to equal his.

"I hope you're right about this," Guy said, the sweat dripping like hot candlewax from his face.

Me, too. She studied the surrounding terrain. "I'm pretty sure this is it, Guy. Maybe it happened 150 years ago, but for me it was practically yesterday."

Jocelyn Miller

The afternoon wore on. The pit became wider and deeper. The mosquitos buzzed relentlessly. Sweat poured and emptied bottles of water piled up. They had stopped for lunch at one point, and then wished for a nap instead of more digging; but they dug on.

"What's this?" Guy asked, reaching over to retrieve something from the pit.

"Let me see…."

It was unmistakable; encased in dirt, but there it lay in Guy's palm like a beacon of light shining to Summer's heart.

"It's a gold coin! The ones I told you about!"

Guy wiped it on a pant leg to clean off the dirt and held it up to the light. "You're right!"

"There are two more down there. Let's be careful. We're getting close."

After the second coin was found, a flash of dull white caused Summer to drop the shovel and move backward against the dirt wall. She was up to her neck in the pit, and knew they would have to dig no further. "It's her," she said morosely. "It's Cherry." Her heart skipped a beat as the vision of Cherry lying face down on the beach came to mind. Falling to her knees, she gently brushed the dirt away with her hands. Guy did the same, and soon the bones revealed themselves, dirty and dull.

A feeling of dread gripped like a vise. "Help me out, Guy. I can't do this! I'll get the bag, but *please,* you gather the bones." Tears formed in the corners of her eyes and she fought to keep herself together— to not breakdown at this important moment. This is what she came for, ultimately; to bring Cherry home.

41

"End of story," Summer whispered.

The headstone was set at the head of Cherry's grave in the family cemetery at Magnolia.

It read:

'Here lies Cherry Woodfield, beloved daughter of Ruth, mother of Percy and Yank Woodfield and cherished friend and cousin of Summer Woodfield.'

"You don't think that's a little strange, huh? Having your name on the headstone?" Guy asked for the hundredth time.

"No, I don't."

"It might confuse people."

"I don't care. She led such a sorrowful life, that I want her headstone to show that she lived, and she was loved. I'm not afraid of what people might say. And besides, who the heck will be visiting this little cemetery besides us?"

"Good point."

"I have one more thing to do," Summer said as they walked back to the house.

"Oh, no…and what might that be, I'm afraid to ask?"

"I need to pay a visit to Mr. Taylor Yank Woodfield."

Jocelyn Miller

* * *

The very next day, Summer parked her car in the nursing home parking lot. She looked at the beautiful building and grounds where Mr. Woodfield would spend his remaining days.

"I'd like to see Mr. Taylor Woodfield," she told the receptionist, who checked her watch and looked up and down the hall until his whereabouts registered. "Oh, yes, he is probably in the library at this time."

Sure enough, Taylor Woodfield sat in his wheelchair leafing through a book. Next to him, from floor to ceiling, was a grand bookcase, polished to a shine.

Quite the place, she thought, wondering how much it cost to spend your last days at River Crest Nursing Home.

"Hello, Mr. Woodfield."

"Oh, it's you, again." He set the book back into its slot in the case. "What do you want this time?"

"I want to show you something." She removed a photograph she had taken of the headstone. "Look at this."

Taylor Woodfield took the photograph, adjusted his glasses and looked. A few moments later, he handed her the photo. "You found your Cherry, I gather?"

"Yes, I found Cherry. You told me I would find information on Cherry if I went to the Everglades."

"So what? What's it to me?"

"Cherry was a freed slave who was kidnapped by a deserting Yankee soldier named Tom Quinn. He was a nasty beast. He dragged her all the way from Magnolia Plantation to the Everglades. He was killed by the Seminoles, leaving Cherry pregnant. She had a baby— a white baby— by Tom Quinn.

"So what? I don't want to hear all this. It has nothing to do with me."

"It has *everything* to do with you! Cherry named her baby Yank, Yank *Woodfield, your* ancestor!"

"Bullshit!"

Jocelyn Miller

"Yank was raised by a nice black man named Buck Henry," she continued. "And do you know why you can spend the rest of your days in this nice place?"

Taylor moved to turn the wheels of his chair in order to escape Summer's tirade.

"...because Buck Henry dove for lost treasure, and found it! He brought lost treasure up from the ocean floor for Yank Woodfield, child of Cherry Woodfield, black woman of Magnolia Plantation. He made sure Cherry's descendants were taken care of, and just *look* at you...a bitter, nasty old man alone in a fancy nursing home!"

"Nurse!" Taylor yelled, amazingly loud for the old guy he was; but Summer had him blocked between the bookcase and a leather chair.

"Here!" She flung the photo at him. This is yours. And that woman who was here with me that day, the one you insulted? She *is* your cousin. Cherry would be so ashamed of you. I'm glad she never knew how her baby fared and produced the likes of you. She died before he was a year old."

"What is it, Mr. Taylor?" asked a young woman racing into the library. "Are you not well?"

He stared at Summer—*glared* at her.

"Is this woman bothering you?"

"No...not anymore. Take me to my room. Goodbye, Miss Woodfield."

As the nurse pushed him through the doorway, he picked the photo up from where it had landed on his lap, and studied it. "Thanks, Miss Woodfield," she heard him say softly as he disappeared down the hall.

Exhausted, she left the building and sat in her car to cry.

* * *

Often, she found herself in Evaline's old bedroom, the one with the doorway to the attic. She had waited months for an indication from Cherry that she was now at peace. Cherry had not visited her again, here at the balcony doors, frantic with fear and with Quinn on her heels— not since before her adventure in the Everglades. Perhaps this was a good sign, but she needed *more*, she needed to know for sure.

Just one little sign, Cherry, so I know all is well....

Jocelyn Miller

It was on one of those days when, again, she found herself standing in Evaline's room staring at the door and chiding herself for doing so, when she heard a rustle in the attic. Her heart leapt! *Cherry!*

She raced to the door, anxious to see Cherry at the top of the stairs; Cherry, smiling, no longer sad, no longer frightened. With her hand on the latch, she swung the door wide open, stuck her head into the stairwell and shifted her eyes upward to the top of the stairs. Just as quickly, she slammed the door shut and stood back, eyes wide.

"My God! It can't be!"

With trepidation, her hands now shaking violently, her heart beating in rapid '*thump, thump thumps*', she opened the door again, and gingerly stuck her head around the corner; there was no denying it.

"Verano! Where have you been? I have been waiting for you!"

THE END

About Jocelyn Miller

Jocelyn writes from Chesapeake Bay, MD and from Sanibel, Florida. Historical fiction, spiced with ghosts, time travel and adventure, are her favorite writing topics; and especially when a young woman with attitude is involved. Be it from street urchin to high society, self-centered to giving; a life-lesson must be learned by her heroine.

Visit:

www.jocelynmiller.blogspot.com

Jocelyn Miller

40237172R00129

Made in the USA
Lexington, KY
29 March 2015